THE PROMISE

The Promise

DAMON GALGUT

Chatto & Windus
LONDON

9 10 8

Chatto & Windus, an imprint of Vintage,
is part of the Penguin Random House
group of companies whose addresses can be found at
global.penguinrandomhouse.com.

Penguin
Random House
UK

First published by Chatto & Windus in 2021

penguin.co.uk/vintage

A CIP catalogue record for this book is available from
the British Library

HB ISBN 9781784744069
TPB ISBN 9781784744076

Federico Fellini is quoted with the kind permission of the Fellini estate.

Typeset in 12.5/15 pt Bembo
by Integra Software Services Pvt. Ltd, Pondicherry

Printed and bound in Great Britain by Clays Ltd, Elcograf S.p.A.

The authorised representative in the EEA is Penguin Random House
Ireland, Morrison Chambers, 32 Nassau Street, Dublin D02 YH68

Penguin Random House is committed to a sustainable future for
our business, our readers and our planet. This book is made from
Forest Stewardship Council® certified paper.

MIX
Paper from
responsible sources
FSC
www.fsc.org   FSC® C018179

This morning I met a woman with a golden nose. She was riding in a Cadillac with a monkey in her arms. Her driver stopped and she asked me, 'Are you Fellini?' With this metallic voice she continued, 'Why is it that in your movies, there is not even one normal person?'

– Federico Fellini

to Antonio and Petruchio
for all the agentry, cookery and travelry

MA

THE MOMENT THE METAL BOX speaks her name, Amor knows it's happened. She's been in a tense, headachy mood all day, almost like she had a warning in a dream but can't remember what it is. Some sign or image, just under the surface. Trouble down below. Fire underground.

But when the words are said to her aloud, she doesn't believe them. She closes her eyes and shakes her head. No, no. It can't be true, what her aunt has just told her. Nobody is dead. It's a word, that's all. She looks at the word, lying there on the desk like an insect on its back, with no explanation.

This is in Miss Starkey's office, where the voice over the Tannoy told her to go. Amor has been waiting and waiting for this moment for so long, has imagined it so many times, that it already seems like a fact. But now that the moment has really come, it feels far away and dreamy. It hasn't happened, not actually. And especially not to Ma, who will always, always be alive.

I'm sorry, Miss Starkey says again, covering her big teeth behind thin, pressed-together lips. Some of the other girls say Miss Starkey is a lesbian, but it's hard to imagine her doing anything sexy with anyone. Or maybe she did once and has been permanently disgusted ever since. It's a sorrow we all have to bear, she adds in a serious voice, while Tannie Marina trembles and dabs at her eyes with a tissue, though she has always looked

3

down on Ma and doesn't care at all that she's dead, even if she isn't.

Her aunt goes downstairs with her and waits outside while Amor has to go back to the hostel to pack her suitcase. She's been living here for the past seven months, waiting for what hasn't happened to happen, and every second of that time she's hated these long, cold rooms with their linoleum floors, but now that she has to leave, she doesn't want to go. All she wants to do is lie down on her bed and fall asleep and never, never wake up. Like Ma? No, not like Ma, because Ma is not asleep.

Slowly, she puts her clothes into the suitcase and then carries it down to the front of the main school building, where her aunt is standing, looking into the fishpond. That's a big fat one, she says, pointing into the depths, have you ever seen such a big goldfish? And Amor says that she hasn't, even though she can't see which fish her aunt is pointing at and none of it is real anyway.

When she gets into the Cressida, that isn't real either, and as they float down the winding school drive the view from the window is a dream. The jacarandas are all in bloom and the bright purple blossoms are gaudy and strange. Her own voice sounds echoey, as if somebody else is speaking, when they get to the main gate and turn right instead of left, and she hears herself ask where they are going.

To my house, her aunt says. To get Uncle Ockie. I had to rush out last night when it, you know, when it happened.

(It did not happen.)

Tannie Marina glances sideways with little mascara-rimmed eyes, but still no reaction from the girl. The older

4

woman's disappointment is almost palpable, like a secret fart. She could have sent Lexington to fetch Amor from school, but instead she has come personally, because she likes to be helpful in a crisis, everyone knows that. Behind her round face with its kabuki make-up, she is hungry for drama and gossip and cheap spectacle. Bloodshed and treachery on the TV is one thing, but here real life has served up an actual, thrilling opportunity. The terrible news, delivered in public, in front of the headmistress! But her niece, the useless plump lump, has hardly said a word. Really, there is something wrong with the child, Marina has noticed it before. She blames it on the lightning. Ag, shame, she was never the same after that.

Have a rusk, her aunt tells her crossly. They're on the back seat.

But Amor doesn't want a rusk. She has no appetite. Tannie Marina is always baking things and trying to feed them to people. Her sister Astrid says it's so she doesn't have to be fat alone, and it's true their aunt has published two cookbooks of teatime treats, popular with a particular kind of older white woman, much in evidence these days.

Well, Tannie Marina reflects, at least the child is easy to speak to. She doesn't interrupt or argue and gives the impression she's paying attention, all that's required. It's not a long drive from the school to where the Laubschers live in Menlo Park, but time feels stretched today and Tannie Marina talks in emotive Afrikaans the whole way, her voice low and confiding, full of diminutives, even though her motives are not benign. It's the usual topic, about how Ma has betrayed the whole family by changing her religion. Correction, by going back to her

5

old religion. To being a Jew! Her aunt has been extremely vocal on this subject for the past half a year, ever since Ma fell ill, but what is Amor supposed to do about it? She's just a child, she has no power, and anyway what's so wrong about going back to your own religion if you want to?

She tries not to listen, by focusing on something else. Her aunt wears little white golfing gloves when she drives, an affectation from who knows where, or maybe just a fear of germs, and Amor fixates on the pale shapes of her hands, moving on the steering wheel. If she can keep focused on the hands, the shape of them, with their short, blunt fingers, she will not have to listen to what the mouth above the hands is saying, and then it will not be true. The only thing that is true is the hands, and me looking at the hands.

... The truth is that your mother gave up Dutch Reformed and went back to the Jewish thing just to spite my little brother ... It's so she won't be buried on the farm, next to her husband, that's the actual reason ... There's a right way and a wrong way and I'm sorry to say your mother chose the wrong way ... Well, anyhow, Tannie Marina sighs as they arrive at the house, let's just hope God forgives her and she is at peace now.

They park in the driveway under the awning, with its beautiful green and purple and orange stripes. Beyond it, a diorama of white South Africa, the tin-roofed suburban bungalow made of reddish face brick, surrounded by a moat of bleached garden. Jungle gym looking lonely on a big brown lawn. Concrete birdbath, a Wendy house and a swing made from half a truck tyre. Where you, perhaps, also grew up. Where all of it began.

6

Amor follows her aunt, not quite on the ground, a few centimetres above it, a giddy little gap between her and things, as she heads for the kitchen door. Inside, Oom Ockie is mixing himself a brandy-and-Coke, his second of the morning. He has recently retired from his government job as a draughtsman in Water Affairs and his days are listless. He jumps to guilty attention when he's bust by his wife, sucking on his nicotine-stained moustache. He's had hours to dress himself properly, but is still wearing tracksuit pants and a golfing shirt and slipslops. A blockish man with thinning hair Brylcreemed sideways across his scalp. He gives Amor a clammy hug, very awkward for both of them.

Sorry about your mother, he says.

Oh, that's okay, Amor says, and immediately starts to cry. Will people be sorry for her all day because her mother has become that word? She feels ugly when she cries, like a tomato breaking open, and thinks that she must get away, away from this horrible little room with its parquet floor and barking Maltese poodle and the eyes of her aunt and uncle sticking into her like nails.

She hastens past Oom Ockie's gloomy fish tank, up the passage, its walls marked with a dimpled-plaster effect popular in these parts at this time, to the bathroom. No need to dwell on how she washes away her tears, except to mention that, even as she continues to snivel, Amor opens the door of the medicine cabinet to look inside, something she does in every home she visits. Sometimes what you find is interesting, but these shelves are full of depressing items like denture cream and Anusol. Then she feels guilty for having looked and to absolve herself has to count the objects on each shelf

7

and rearrange them into a more pleasing order. Then she thinks that her aunt will notice and disarranges them again.

On her way back down the passage Amor pauses at the open bedroom door of her cousin Wessel, youngest and largest of Tannie Marina's brood, and the only one still living at home. He's already twenty-four but ever since finishing the army he's done nothing except sit around at home, attending to his stamp collection. Apparently he has some problem with going out into the world. He's depressed, according to his father, and his mother says that he's finding his way. But Pa has voiced the opinion that his nephew is just lazy and spoiled and should be forced to do some work.

Amor doesn't like her cousin, and especially not at this moment, with those big, blobby hands and his pudding-bowl haircut, and the suspect way he says the letter S. He would never make eye contact anyway, but he hardly notices her right now, because his stamp album is open on his lap, and he's peering through a magnifying glass at one of the favourites of his collection, the set of three commemorating Dr Verwoerd, issued a few months after the great man's murder.

What are you doing here?

Your mother picked me up from school. Then she came to get your father and some groceries.

Oh. And now you're going home?

Yes.

Sorry about your mother, he says, and glances at her at last. She can't help it, she starts crying again and has to dry her eyes on her sleeve. But his attention is back on the stamps.

Are you very sad? he asks absently, still not looking at her.

She shakes her head. At this moment it's true, she doesn't feel anything, just vacant.

Did you love her?

Of course, she says. But even in response to this question, nothing stirs inside. Makes her wonder if she's telling the truth.

Half an hour later, she sits on the back seat of Ockie's old Valiant. Her uncle, who has dressed in his church outfit, brown trousers and yellow shirt and shiny shoes, sits jug-eared in the driver's seat in front of her, smoke from his cigarette scribbling across the windscreen. Next to him his wife, who has freshened up and sprayed herself with Je T'aime and brought along a bag of baking supplies from her kitchen. At this moment they are driving past the cemetery on the western edge of the city, where a small crowd stands around a hole in the ground, and nearby is the Jewish cemetery where very soon, but no, don't think about that, and don't look at the graves, though you can't help seeing the sign for Heroes' Acre, but who are the heroes, nobody ever explained, is Ma a hero now, don't think about that either, and then you are sinking into that horrible zone of cement and car washes and dirty-looking blocks of flats on the other side. If you stick with the usual road you will soon leave the city behind, but you can't take the usual road today because it goes past Atteridgeville and there is trouble in the township. Trouble in all the townships, it's being muttered about everywhere, even with the State of Emergency hanging over the land like a dark cloud and the news under censorship and the mood all over a bit electrified, a bit alarmed, there is no silencing the voices that talk away under everything, like the thin crackle of static. But whose are they, the voices, why can't we hear them now? Shhh, you'll hear them, if you pay attention, if you will only listen.

... We are the last outpost on this continent ... If South Africa falls, Moscow will be drinking champagne ... Let's be clear about it, majority rule means communism ...

Ockie switches off the radio. He's not in the mood for political speeches, much nicer to look at the view. He imagines himself one of his Voortrekker ancestors, rolling slowly into the interior in an ox-wagon. Yes, there are those who dream in predictable ways. Ockie the brave pioneer, floating over the plain. A brown-and-yellow countryside passes outside, dry except for where a river cuts through it, under a huge Highveld sky. The farm, which is what they call it, though it is in no meaningful way a real farm, one horse and a few cows and some chickens and sheep, is out there among the low hills and valleys, halfway to the Hartbeespoort Dam.

Off to one side, over a fence, he can see a group of men with a metal detector, watching some native boys dig holes in the ground. This whole valley once belonged to Paul Kruger and there are persistent rumours that two million pounds in Boer War gold have been buried somewhere under these stones. So, dig here, dig there, hunting the wealth of the past. It's greedy, but even this gives him a nostalgic glow. My people are a valiant, durable bunch, they outlasted the British and they will outlast the kaffirs too. Afrikaners are a nation apart, he really believes that. He doesn't understand why Manie had to marry Rachel. Oil and water don't mix. You can see it in their children, fuckups, the lot of them.

In this perception, at least, he and his wife are in harmony. Marina never liked her sister-in-law. Everything about the arrangement was wrong. Why couldn't her brother just marry into his own tribe? I made a mistake, he said, and you pay for your mistakes. Manie was always stupid-stubborn. To go against the wishes of his own family for somebody like that, vain and proud, who of course dropped him in the end. Because of sex. Because he just couldn't keep his hands off. An activity Marina herself has never much cared for, except that one time in Sun City with the mechanic, but aieee, be quiet, don't bring that up now. Always my brother's downfall, ever since he started shaving he turned into a little goat, having fun and causing trouble, till he made his mistake and then everything changed. The mistake is somewhere out there now, doing his military service. They sent a message to him this morning, he'll only get home tomorrow.

Anton will only be home tomorrow, she tells Amor, then falls to adjusting her lipstick in the visor mirror.

They arrive at the turn-off from the wrong side and Amor has to get out to open the gate and close it again behind the car. Then they are bumping along a rough gravel track, rocks sticking up in places, scraping metallically at the undercarriage. The noise seems heightened to Amor, biting into her. Her headache is worse. While they were on the open road she could almost pretend she was nowhere, drifting along. But now all her senses are telling her they're about to arrive. She doesn't want to get to the house, because when she does it will obviously be true that something has happened, that something has changed in her life and will never change back again. She doesn't want the track to do what it does, go under the pylons and head towards the koppie, she doesn't want it to go up the rise, she doesn't want to see the house in the dip on the other side. But there it is, and she sees it.

Never liked it much. A weird little place to start with, even when her grandfather first bought it, who would build in that style out here in the bush? But then when Oupa drowned in the dam and Pa inherited it he started adding rooms and outbuildings that had no style at all, though he called them vernacular. No logic to his plans, but according to Ma it was because he wanted to cover up the original art deco, which he thought looked effeminate. Oh, what rubbish, said Pa, my approach is practical. Supposed to be a farm, not a fantasy. But just look at how it ended up. A big mishmash of a place, twenty-four doors on the outside that have to be locked at night, one style stuck on another. Sitting out here in the middle of the veld, like a drunk wearing odd bits of clothing.

Still, thinks Tannie Marina, it's ours. Don't look at the house, think about the land. Useless ground, full of stones, you can do nothing with it. But it belongs to our family, nobody else, and there's power in that.

And at least, she says aloud to Ockie, the wife is out of the picture at last.

Then, oh God, remembers the child in the back seat. Have to watch what you say, Marina, especially for the next couple of days, till the funeral is over. Speak in English, it will keep you in check.

Don't understand me wrong, she says to Amor. I respected your mother.

(No, you didn't.) But Amor doesn't say it aloud. She has become very rigid in the back of the car, which is finally coasting to a stop. Ockie has to park a little way down the drive, because there are too many other cars in front of the house, unfamiliar cars mostly, what are they doing here? Already there is an inward pull of people and events, drawn towards the Ma-shaped hole at the heart. As she gets out, closing the door with a thunk, Amor sees one car in particular, a long dark one, and the heaviness of the world gets worse. Who is the driver of that car, why is he parked outside my house?

I told the Jewish people not to take her yet, Tannie Marina announces. So that you can say goodbye to your mother.

At first Amor doesn't understand. Crunch crunch crunch goes the gravel. Through the front windows she can see a crowd of people in the lounge, a dense fog of them, and at the centre is her father, bowed over in a chair. He's crying, she thinks, then it comes to her instead, No, he's praying. Crying or praying, it's hard to tell the difference with Pa these days.

Then she does understand and thinks, I cannot go in. The driver of that dark car is waiting inside so that I can say goodbye to my mother and I can't go through the door. If I go through the door it will be true and my life will never be the same. So she delays outside, while Marina clip-clops importantly ahead with her bags of ingredients, Ockie shuffling in behind her, and then she drops her suitcase on the steps and shoots around the side of the house, past the lightning conductor and the gas canisters in their concrete alcove in the wall and over the back patio where Tojo the Alsatian lies sleeping in

13

the sun, purple balls showing between his legs, over the lawn, past the birdbath and the kapok tree, past the stable buildings and the labourers' cottages behind, running towards the koppie.

Where is she? She was right behind us.

Marina can't believe what that damn fool girl has done.

Ja, Ockie confirms and then, eager to contribute, repeats it. Ja!

Ag, she'll come back. Marina is in no mood for indulgence. Let these people take the poor woman away now. The chance is wasted on the child.

The driver of the long car, Mervyn Glass, has been sitting for the past two hours in the kitchen, wearing his yarmulke, waiting on the instruction of the bossy woman, the sister of the bereaved, who is now telling him to get moving. This is a very difficult family, he can't work out what's going on, but doesn't appear to mind. Waiting in respectful silence is an essential part of the job and he has developed the capacity to simulate deep calm while experiencing none of it. In his core, Mervyn Glass is a frantic man.

Now he springs to his feet. He and his helper proceed to remove the mortal remains of the deceased from the upstairs bedroom. This involves a stretcher and a body bag and a final display of anguish from the spouse, who clutches at his dead wife and implores her not to go, as if she is leaving of her own volition and can be persuaded to change her mind. Nor is this uncommon, as Mervyn will tell you if you ask him. He has seen all of it before many times, including the curious pull that a corpse exerts, drawing people towards it. By tomorrow already this will have changed, the body will be long gone and its permanent absence covered over with plans, arrangements, reminiscences and time. Yes, already. The disappearance begins immediately and in a certain sense never ends.

But in the meantime there is the body, the horrible meaty fact of it, the thing that reminds everyone, even people who didn't care for the dead woman, and there are always a few of those, that one day they shall lie there too, just like her, emptied out of everything, merely a form, unable even to look at itself. And the mind recoils from its absence, cannot think of itself not thinking, the coldest of voids.

Fortunately she isn't heavy, the sickness hollowed her out, and it's easy to get her down the stairs and around the challenging angle at the bottom and along the passage to the kitchen. Out the back, the bossy sister orders them, down the side of the house, don't carry it past the guests. If the visitors are aware of this final departure, it's only in the sound of the long car starting up outside, the note of the engine a fading vibration on the air.

Then Rachel is gone, truly gone. She came here as a pregnant bride twenty years ago and hasn't left since, but she will never walk back in through the front door again.

In the hearse, I mean the house, a certain unspoken fear has ebbed, even if people aren't sure why and it's barely been said in words. Most of the time, in fact, it's words that deflect fear, Can I get you another cup of tea? Would you like to try one of my rusks?

Marina speaking, of course, she's adept at pouring oily phrases onto turbulent depths that threaten to spill over. While she twists her necklace.

No, I'm not hungry.

And that's Manie, her much-younger brother, who looks to her eyes like an owl, a baby owl she'd picked up and kept once as a child.

Come now, have some tea at least. You're dehydrated from all that crying.

Oh please please please, he says with a vehemence that sounds like anger, though he may not be speaking to her.

What happened to that owl? Something bad, she seems to remember, though she can't quite pin it down.

I'll never drink tea again, he says.

Ag no, she says irritably, don't talk nonsense.

She doesn't understand why he's taking his wife's death so badly, the woman has been dying for half a year now, he's had ages to prepare for today. But Manie is unravelling, like the bottom of his jersey, she's noticed him jerking at the thread.

Stop that, she tells him. Take it off and give it to me to fix.

Dumbly, he obeys. She carries it away and goes in search of a needle and thread. If Rachel keeps such things. Kept. The mental correction is satisfying, like a stiff joint clicking into place. Rachel will always be in the past tense now.

Manie shivers without his jersey, although the spring day is warm. Will he ever thaw out again? Never while she was alive did he need Rachel as fiercely as he does right now and her absence is like a steely coldness deep inside. She knew how to get to that innermost part of me, sticking her little knives in there. Couldn't tell the difference between hate and love, that's how close we were. Two trees twisted together, roots locked like fate. Who wouldn't want to escape? But only God can judge me, only He knows! Forgive me, God, I mean to say, Rachel, my flesh is weaker than most.

Crying again. Marina sees him from across the room. She has after all discovered a sewing kit in a drawer and settled herself into a corner, from where she can observe the traffic in the house while being publicly helpful. Stitching and baking, she has practical hands. But is nevertheless so distracted by the sight of her husband passing, holding a fresh drink, that she stabs herself on one finger.

And just then, out of nowhere, remembers what happened to the owl. Ag, shame. Those white feathers clotted with blood.

Eh, I'm watching you, she calls to Ockie.

But he's drifted on, moustache tasting of brandy, thinking inside, Shutup, who are you? He has, for the moment, forgotten why he's here and says to a man in the lounge, You having a good time?

What? the man says.

But Ockie has recollected himself and jiggles back and forth on his feet. You know, under the circumstances, he says.

The man he's talking to is a trainee minister in the Dutch Reformed Church. Tall and nervous, with a pronounced Adam's apple, this trainee minister, over the past year, unbeknownst to anybody, has almost completely lost his faith. He feels himself stumbling in a thorny wilderness and consequently smiles a great deal. At the moment that Ockie addresses him, he is smiling to himself while he ponders this very question, of not believing in anything any more, and jumps guiltily when he's spoken to.

Amor can see the two of them, her uncle and the doubting dominee, through the sliding glass doors of the

17

lounge. From the top of the koppie she can see the whole front of the house, all the windows on display, which is why she likes to sit here, although she's not supposed to do it alone. It's never been so busy down there on the ground floor, multiple human figures moving around like toy people in a toy building. But her attention is not on them. She is looking at only one window, upstairs, third from the left, thinking, She's in there. If I just go down the hill and up the stairs, she'll be in her room, waiting for me. Like always.

And she can see somebody moving around in there. A female figure, bustling about. If she half closes her eyes, Amor can imagine that it really is her mother, her body strong and healthy again, cleaning up the medicine from next to her bed. Not needed any more. Ma is better again, time has been turned back, the world is restored. Easy as that.

But she knows she's just pretending and the person in the room isn't Ma. It's Salome, of course, who has been here on the farm for ever, or that's how it feels. My grandfather always talked about her like that, Oh, Salome, I got her along with the land.

Pause a moment to observe, as she takes the sheets off the bed. A stout, solid woman, wearing a second-hand dress, given to her by Ma years ago. A headscarf tied over her hair. She is barefoot, and the soles of her feet are cracked and dirty. Her hands have marks on them too, the scuffs and scars of innumerable collisions. Same age as Ma supposedly, forty, though she looks older. Hard to put an exact number on her. Not much shows in her face, she wears her life like a mask, like a graven image.

But some things you do know, because you saw them yourself. In the same impassive way that Salome sweeps and cleans the house and washes the clothes of the people who live in it, she looked after Ma through her last illness, dressing and undressing her, helping her to bathe with a bucket of hot water and a lappie, helping her to go to the toilet, yes, even wiping her arse for her after she used the bedpan, mopping up blood and shit and pus and piss, all the jobs that people in her own family didn't want to do, too dirty or too intimate, Let Salome do it, that's what she's paid for, isn't it? She was with Ma when she died, right there next to the bed, though nobody seems to see her, she is apparently invisible. And whatever Salome feels is invisible too. She has been told, Clean up here, wash the sheets, and she obeys, she cleans up, she washes the sheets.

But Amor can see her through the window, so she's not invisible after all. Thinking about a memory, not understood till now, of an afternoon just two weeks ago, in that same room, with Ma and Pa. They forgot I was there, in the corner. They didn't see me, I was like a black woman to them.

(Do you promise me, Manie?

Holding on to him, skeleton hands grabbing, like in a horror film.

Ja, I'll do it.

Because I really want her to have something. After everything she's done.

I understand, he says.

Promise me you'll do it. Say the words.

I promise, Pa says, choked-sounding.)

She sees the picture still, her parents tangled together like Jesus and His mother, a terrible sad knot of clutching and crying. The sound somewhere else, higher up and apart, the words not reaching her till now. But finally she understands who they were talking about. Of course. Obviously. Duh.

She's sitting in the spot she likes, between the rocks, at the bottom of the burnt tree. Where I was when the lightning struck, where I nearly died. Pow, white fire dropping out of the sky. As if God pointed at you, Pa says, but how would he know, he wasn't here when it happened. The wrath of the Lord is like an avenging flame. But I didn't burn, not like the tree. Except for my feet.

In hospital two months, recovering. There is still tenderness in the soles, and one small toe is missing. She touches it now, fingering the scar. One day, she says aloud. One day I'll. But the thought breaks off midway and what she'll do one day hangs there, suspended.

What's happening now is that somebody else is climbing the hill from the other side. A human figure approaching, filling itself in slowly, putting on age and sex and race, like items of clothing, till she's looking at a black boy, also thirteen years old, wearing ragged shorts and T-shirt, broken takkies on his feet.

Sweat sticks cloth on skin. Pull it loose with your fingers.

Hello, Lukas, she says.

Howzit, Amor.

First it is necessary to beat the earth with a stick. Then he settles himself on a rock. Easy to speak to each other. Not the first time they've met up here. Children still, on the verge of not being children any more.

I'm sorry about your mommy, he says.

She nearly cries again, but doesn't. It's all right when he says it, because Lukas's father died too, on a gold mine near Johannesburg, when he was only little. Something joins them together. What she just remembered spills over, she wants to tell him about it.

It's yours now, the house, she says.

He looks at her, not understanding.

My mother told my father to give it to your mother. A Christian never goes back on his word.

He looks down the hill to the other side, where he lives, in the crooked little house. The Lombard place. That's what everyone calls it, even though old Mrs Lombard died years ago, before Amor's grandfather bought it to stop that Indian family moving in and let Salome live there instead. Some names stick, some don't.

Our house?

It'll be yours now.

He blinks, still confused. It's always been his house. He was born there, he sleeps there, what is the white girl talking about? Growing bored, he spits and stands up. She notices how long and strong his legs have become, the wiry hairs growing on his thighs. She can smell him too, the stink of sweat. All this is new, or maybe the noticing is new, and she's embarrassed already, even before she's aware he's looking at her.

What? she says, huddling over, arms on her knees.

Nothing.

He jumps over to her rock, crouches down next to her. His bare leg is close to hers, she can feel the warmth and prickle, she jerks her knee away.

Urgh, she says. You need to wash.

He gets up quickly and leaps back to the other rock. Now she feels sorry for chasing him away, but doesn't know what to say. He picks up his stick and hits with it again.

Oraait, he says.

Okay.

He walks back down the hill the same way he came up, slashing with the stick at the white tops of the grass, pushing it into termite hills. Letting the world know he's there.

She watches him till he disappears, feeling lighter now because the big black car has gone and a big blackness that was sitting on her has gone too. Then she wanders down the other side of the koppie, pausing here and there to look at a rock or a leaf, to her own house, or the house she thinks of as her own. By the time she comes in through the back door, a hundred and thirty-three minutes and twenty-two seconds have passed since she ran away. Four cars, including the long dark one, have departed, a single new one has arrived. The telephone has rung eighteen times, the doorbell twice, on one occasion because somebody has sent flowers that improbably turn up all the way out here. Twenty-two cups of tea, six mugs of coffee, three glasses of cool drink and six brandy-and-Cokes have been consumed. The three toilets downstairs, unused to such traffic, have between them flushed twenty-seven times, carrying away nine point eight litres of urine, five point two litres of shit, one stomachful of regurgitated food and five millilitres of sperm. Numbers go on and on, but what does mathematics help? In any human life there is really only one of everything.

As she creeps into the kitchen she can hear distant voices, though this part of the house is quiet. She climbs the stairs to the second floor. Starts up the passage to her room. On the way she has to pass the door to Ma's room, empty now, Salome gone to wash the bedding, and even though she knows what didn't happen didn't happen here, she must, she has to, go inside.

Small girl looking at her mother's things. She knows all of it by heart, how many steps from the door to the bed, where the light switch is for the lamp, the swirly orange pattern in the carpet like the onset of a headache, etc., etc. Out the corner of her eye she thinks she sees Ma's face appear in the mirror, but when she looks directly it's gone. Instead she can smell her mother, or a mix of smells she thinks of as her mother, but are actually the traces of recent events, involving puke, incense, blood, medicine, perfume and an underlying dark note, perhaps the smell of the sickness itself. Exhaled by the walls, hovering in the air.

She's not here.

Her sister Astrid speaking, who has somehow spotted her and followed.

They took her away.

I know that. I saw.

The bed has been stripped and the bare mattress stained with something indefinable. Both of them look at that intense dark outline as if it's the map of a new continent, fascinating and fearful.

I was with her when she died, Astrid says at last, her voice vibrating because she's telling an untruth. She wasn't with her mother when she died. She was behind the stables, talking with Dean de Wet, the boy from

Rustenburg who comes to help on the farm sometimes, cleaning out the stables. Dean's father passed away a few years ago, and he's been counselling Astrid through her mother's dying. He's a plain, sincere boy, and she likes his attention, part of a larger male awareness she's become receptive to lately. So the only people who were with Rachel Swart when her time came were her husband, aka Pa or Manie, and the black girl, what's her name again, Salome, who obviously doesn't count.

I should have been there. So Astrid thinks. That she was flirting with Dean instead only adds to her guilt. She believes, wrongly, that her younger sister knows the truth about her. Not only this truth, others too. For example, that she vomited up her lunch half an hour ago, as she regularly does, in order to stay slim. She is prone to paranoid fears like these, suspecting sometimes that her mind can be secretly read by people around her, or that life is an elaborate performance in which everybody else is acting and she alone is not. Astrid is a fearful person. Among other things, she's afraid of the dark, poverty, thunderstorms, getting fat, earthquakes, tidal waves, crocodiles, the blacks, the future, the orderly structures of society coming undone. Of being unloved. Of always having been that way.

But now Amor is crying again, because Astrid said that word as if it is a fact and it isn't, it isn't, even though the house is full of people who shouldn't be there, aren't normally there, or not at the same time.

We should be getting ready, Astrid says impatiently. You need to change out of that uniform.

Getting ready for what?

Astrid has no answer, which irritates her.

Where did you go? We were all looking for you.

I climbed up the koppie.

You know you're not allowed up there alone. And what are you doing in here? In her bedroom?

I was just looking.

Looking at what?

I don't know.

This is the truth, she doesn't know, she is just looking, that's all.

Go and get changed, Astrid orders her, trying out an adult voice, now that a position has become vacant.

You can't boss me around, Amor says, but she does go, just to escape Astrid, who, the moment she's left alone in the room, picks up a bracelet she's spotted lying on the bedside table, a pretty little circlet of blue and white beads. She has seen her mother wearing it, she has tried it on before. Now she slips it onto her wrist again, feels it snugly taking her pulse. She decides that it has always belonged to her.

I am not beautiful. So thinks Amor, not for the first time, as she regards herself in the mirror behind her cupboard door. She's in her underwear, which includes a small, recently acquired bra, the sensation of budding flesh still new and unsettling. Her hips have widened, and the thickening seems heavy to her, exaggerated, obscene. She dislikes her stomach and her thighs and the way that her shoulders hang down. She dislikes her whole body, as many of you do, but with special adolescent intensity, and it seems even more present than usual today, more thickly, heatedly present.

At such moments of internal gathering, the air around her becomes charged with clairvoyance. It's happened a few times recently that she's known in advance, just a millisecond ahead of time, that a picture will drop off the wall, a window will fly open, a pencil will roll across the desk. Today she looks past her reflection in the mirror, feeling certain that a fire-blackened tortoise shell, which sits on the bedside table, will lift into the air. She watches it lift. As if she's carrying it with her eyes, she observes it move calmly into the middle of the room. Then she lets it drop, or throws it perhaps, for it smashes quite forcefully onto the floor and breaks.

The tortoise shell is, or rather was, one of very few objects she's collected, all of them picked up in the veld out there. A weirdly shaped stone, a tiny mongoose skull, a long white feather. Otherwise the room is empty of the usual signs and clues, it contains just the single bed with its blanket, the bedside table and lamp, the cupboard and chest of drawers, the wooden floor with no carpet or covering. The walls are also bare. When the girl herself is absent, the room is like a blank page, almost no marks or clues to say anything about her, which perhaps does say something about her.

She's holding a piece of the tortoise shell when she descends the stairs a little later. There are still people drifting about, and she keeps her eyes straight ahead and moves towards the figure of her father, still slumped over in the chair.

Where were you? Pa says. We were very worried.

I was on the koppie.

Amor. You know you're not supposed to be there by yourself. Why do you always go back?

I didn't want to see her. I ran away.

What're you holding?

She hands over the shard of gnarled shell, not quite able to remember, in her dazed state, what it is or where it comes from. It looks like a giant old toenail, how disgusting, sis. Something she's picked up out there. Always bringing in scurvy bits and pieces from the natural world. He almost throws it away but the impetus fades and he holds it like she did, limply.

Come here.

Now he's filled with a great tenderness for her, both profound and sentimental. So defenceless, a simple soul. My child, my little child. Gathers her to him and suddenly both of them melt back to a similar moment seven years ago, in the whiteness just after the lightning strike, the dreamy half-awake aftermath of the accident. Carrying Amor down the koppie. Save her. Save her, Lord, and I'll be Yours for ever. For Manie, it was like Moses descending the mountain, it was the afternoon the Holy Spirit touched him and his life changed. Amor remembers it differently, as the reek of burnt meat on the air, like a braaivleis, the stink of sacrifice at the centre of the world.

The koppie. Lukas. The conversation. It's what she came downstairs to say and she pushes back from where she's been squashed into his shirt and the smell of sweat and grief and Brut deodorant.

You will keep your promise, she says. Not clear to either of them whether it's a statement or a question.

What promise is that?

You know. What Ma asked you to do.

Pa is weary, almost granular, all the sand might run out of him soon. Ja, he says vaguely, if I promised then I'll do it.

You will do it?

I said I will. He takes a hanky out of his jacket pocket and blows his nose into it, then looks into the hanky to see what he's produced. Puts it away again. What are we actually talking about? he says.

(Salome's house.) But Amor also runs out of power and collapses back against his chest. When she speaks he can't hear her.

What did you say?

I don't want to go back to the hostel. I hate it there.

He thinks about it. You don't have to go back, he says. It was just temporary, while Ma ... while Ma was sick.

So I'm not going back?

No.

Not ever?

Never. I promise.

Now she feels sunken and removed, as if she's in a hot, silent, underground cavern. Fickle is the heart. The afternoon is tapering towards its long yellow end. My mother died this morning. Soon it will be tomorrow.

Manie tires of her clinging, and has to quell an unseemly urge to push her away. He has always worried, based on nothing tangible, about whether Amor is actually his child. The last-born, not planned, she was conceived in the most troubled period of his marriage, the middle bit when he and his wife started keeping separate bedrooms. Not a lot of loving going on, yet that was when Amor arrived.

But wherever she comes from, she's no doubt part of the Heavenly plan. For sure, she was the instrument of his conversion, when the Lord nearly took her from them and Manie at last opened himself to the Holy Spirit.

It was soon after that, in a moment of deep prayer, that he'd understood what he had to do to cleanse himself. He, Herman Albertus Swart, must confess his failings to his wife and ask her forgiveness, and so he had told Rachel everything, including about the gambling and the prostitutes, he had bared and pared himself, but instead of turning clear his marriage had gone dark, instead of forgiving him she'd judged him and found him greatly wanting, instead of following him into the vale of light she'd turned in the other direction, back towards her own people. The ways of the Lord are forever mysterious to us!

He twists around in the chair and takes Amor's face in his hands, turns it up towards him, looking at her features, searching for some sign that could only come from his body, his cells. Not the first time he's done it. She stares back at him out of her dark constellations, frightened.

He might be about to say something to her, but is prevented, fortunately, by the arrival of Dominee Simmers. The good minister has been here for much of the day, providing prayer and counsel to an important member of his congregation. In the years of questing and searching since Manie was brushed by God's fire and turned at last to the truth, Alwyn Simmers has been his guide and his shepherd. The rigours of his Church are the joists and stays that keep me upright.

I'm afraid I have to go, the minister says. But I'll come again tomorrow.

He perceives Manie as a complicated blur, for the dominee is losing his sight, his eyes are hidden behind thick, dark lenses, and he needs somebody to lean on wherever he goes. Literally so, Jesus is only a metaphor under these circumstances. Hence the presence of the trainee minister, the one who has mislaid his faith, who is now attempting to angle the dominee so that the conversation lines up correctly.

Manie at last has a reason to put his daughter to one side, carefully, like a piece of fragile furniture, and forgets her in an instant. I'll walk you out to your car, he says. As he leads the two men slowly towards the front door, he passes a framed photograph of himself on the sideboard, taken twenty years ago at Scaly City, his reptile park, soon after it opened. Coining it from the first day, and you can see it in the broad grin of the young man in the picture. Manie at twenty-seven. Considered a catch in his time. A lot of fun, always playing the fool, and with good looks too, check out the pic if you don't believe it. Long, limp forelock, a toothy, insolent grin. Bit of a bad boy. Holding a furious, deadly snake in each hand, black mamba in the left, green mamba in the right, beaming his youth and health and certainty out of the frame. Dark glasses, of course, with big shiny frames, coppery side-burns profuse, same colour as the hair bursting out of his bare chest. Fertile, free-ranging, everyone wanted a piece of him, no wonder Rachel gave it all up on his account. Then changed her mind when he changed too.

Outside, the dominee fumbles Manie in for an embrace, hard-breathing but manly. Take strength in Christ, he says into his ear. A meaningless statement, if you think about it, but Manie says that he will, he will take strength in Christ. He's been doing it for a long time already. You'll come back tomorrow? he says anxiously, not sure if Christ alone will suffice, and the minister promises he will.

Then they are driving away from the farmhouse, or rather the apprentice minister is at the wheel, the older man next to him. They don't speak at all on the bumpy ride to the front gate, though the Adam's apple of the driver bobs up and down, like a float on a fishing line, as if he has something to say.

Only after they are through the gate and have turned onto the tar road does Alwyn Simmers stir.

Wonderful family, he remarks. And that man will not break.

The driver listens, smiling enviously to himself. Not to break! Is such certainty possible? Not for me. Not tonight. Even to believe he can stay on this road, with his hands so slippery, is too much faith.

The old minister is a large, soft man, with a sideways wave of crinkly brown hair. Much about him has a crumpled look, for his sister Laetitia, who tends to him at home, is not a dab hand with an iron. And the skin on his hands and neck and face, all that's visible of him, is loose and lined, and you really wouldn't want to see the rest, under his clothes.

He has a natural heaviness, but he's especially ponderous this afternoon, because the death of Rachel, a woman whose hand was raised against him from the very first, yea, a stubborn, proud woman who kept her face turned away from the Lord, has brought him close to something he very much wants. Not for himself, no, of course not! For the Church only, and the furtherance of Heaven's work. I am merely the instrument. But the instrument can sense that the way ahead is clear at last, and he may soon acquire a desirable piece of land.

Pick me up at four tomorrow afternoon, he decides.

Are we going back to ... to those people?

Ja, we are returning to the Swart family. My work there is not yet done.

By the time the sun goes down, especially vividly out here, all the visitors have gone and only the family is left. Oom Ockie is by now listing a little to the right, weighted perhaps by his uneven smile, hitched up only at one end. He and Pa sit in the lounge, watching the news on the TV, which bears bad tidings from all over the country. A limpet mine in Johannesburg, troops in the townships. Every now and then Pa breaks down and sobs for a while, as if he's moved by the state of South Africa. Ockie just sips and smiles.

In the kitchen, Marina supervises the black girl, who has a pile of plates and cups to wash. The way she drags herself around, so heavy and slow, you'd think she's the one who's lost a family member. Unforgivable to be lazy on a big day like this, she has to be pushed along like a boulder, it's exhausting giving orders all the time. Crossly, Marina does a last march through the house, looking for leftovers. In the dining room she encounters Amor, whom she hasn't had a chance to chastise yet. Where did you run off to? she demands, more angry than she knew, and finds herself pinching her niece on the upper arm, a flash of genuine cruelty in her fingernails.

Ow, Amor says, but doesn't otherwise answer, and Marina stomps on with disgruntled satisfaction up to the second floor. She goes into Rachel's room and hesitates

32

for a moment before closing the windows and curtains. It seems to her there is a faint tincture, an odour, on the air. Outside, it is night.

It is night, the same night, but later, the stars have moved on. Only a cuticle of moon, casting the faintest metallic glow onto this landscape of rocks and hills, making it look almost liquid, a mercurial sea. The line of the main road is stitched out now and then in slow motion by the headlamps of a car, carrying its cargo of human lives, going from somewhere to somewhere.

The house is dark, except for floodlights fore and aft, note the nautical terms, illuminating the driveway and the lawn, and a single lamp left on inside, in the lounge. In the various rooms downstairs everything is mostly inert, except for the occasional scuttling insect, or is it a rodent, and the tiny expansions and contractions of the furniture. Pitter, patter, creak, crack.

But upstairs, in the bedrooms, there is a flickering going on. Pa's mattress is a raft, tossing on a current of uneasy dreams. He has taken a sedative prescribed by Dr Raaff, and it keeps his head just under the surface, looking at images refracted from above. His wife is in many of them, but altered somehow, a bit squiff. A trace in her of another person altogether, someone he doesn't know. How can this be? he cries to her, You're dead. That's an unforgivable thing to say, Manie, she tells him, I'm very hurt. His heart is wrung like an old rag. I'm sorry, I'm sorry.

Through the wall beside him, just an outstretched arm away, Astrid ripples in her sleep. She has recently lost her virginity, to a boy she met at the ice rink, and sex flows through her like a golden wind. She has forgotten the pain, though it's part of the shimmer around the faces of young men, with their bristly beards, and in this dream around the face of Dean de Wet in particular, whose mouth is a pink colour it doesn't have in waking life, thrilling her deep inside, down where everything meets.

In the guest bedroom, Tannie Marina dozes and starts, dozes and starts. She achieves only the beginning of a dream, in which she's on a picnic with P. W. Botha at an old fort somewhere, and he's feeding her strawberries with thick white fingers, before she gets woken by a kick. At home in Menlo Park she doesn't share a bed with Ockie, who lies twitching beside her like a hit-and-run victim, waiting for medical assistance. What a thought, Marina, sis on you, but you can't help what you think, it's only human, and far worse has gone through your mind, oh yes it has. Her husband's foot touches hers, she pulls her foot away. Terrible to flinch from what you once, briefly, loved, or thought you did, or wanted to think you did. But are shackled to, regardless, for life.

At the other end of the chain, Ockie jerks like a dancing bear. He doesn't dream, not exactly, unless the shallows he splashes through are a sort of dream, but nothing quite happens, there is just the question of colour changing all the time. A bubble rises from the seabed, becomes a breaking of wind against the flank of his wife, who stiffens and flares her nostrils in protest.

And in her bedroom at the end of the passage, Amor lies sleepless, hour after hour. Not unusual for her, believe me, every night before she drifts off her mind must move outward from where her body is based, on its back in bed, to reach out and touch certain objects in particular places, in a specific order. Only when she's done that can she relax enough to let go. But tonight it doesn't work, other images from the day are too powerful, they come jostling in, Miss Starkey's pressed-together lips, Lukas's stick hitting the ground, the sore place on her arm where her aunt pinched her, so much rage in her fingers, sending out its little pulse of pain into the universe, notice me, I am here, Amor Swart, 1986. May tomorrow never come.

Who is to say, perhaps all these dreams might merge together, making a single, larger dream, a dream by the whole family, but somebody is missing. At this very instant he's stepping out of a Buffel in a military camp south of Johannesburg, wearing army browns and carrying a rifle. He used the rifle yesterday morning to shoot and kill a woman in Katlehong, an act he never imagined committing in his life, and his mind has done little since except turn that moment over and over in wonderment and despair.

Swart.

Ja, Corporal?

The chaplain wants to see you.

The chaplain?

He's never spoken to the chaplain. It can only be, he thinks, that the man knows what he did and wants to talk to him about it. His sin has somehow transmitted itself, he has taken a life, he must pay. But I didn't mean to. But you did.

She was throwing a stone, she bent down to pick it up, a flash of rage passed through him, concomitant with hers. He didn't think, he hated her, he wiped her away. All in a few seconds, an instant, over and done. Never over, never done.

So that even after the man has told him, he still believes he's responsible. My mother is dead, I killed her. I shot and killed her yesterday morning.

We've been trying to get hold of you, the chaplain says. We sent a radio message. We thought you received it.

He is in the chaplain's office, sitting in front of his desk. There is a Christian poster stuck with Prestik to the wall, I am the Way and the Life, but aside from that the room is drab and ordinary, too ordinary to contain the feelings that have been let loose in him.

I was in Katlehong, he says. There was a situation.

Ja, ja, of course. The chaplain is small and fussy, with hair growing out of his ears. He has the rank of colonel, but is wearing only a tracksuit right now, his face blurry with sleep. Having done his painful duty, he's keen to get back to bed, it's 0300 hours on the clock.

Here's a seven-day pass, he tells the conscript. I'm sorry about your mother, but I'm sure she's at peace.

The young man doesn't seem to hear him. He is staring out the window, into the dark. We had to bring things under control, he says slowly.

Ja, of course, that's why you're here. That's what the army is for. The chaplain has never struggled in his soul with questions of this nature, the answers have always seemed obvious. He wonders vaguely if this boy is a subversive type. Would you like a longer pass? he says. Ten days?

Oh, the young man says. No, I don't think so.

All right then.

My mother turned Jewish, you see, or went back to it, rather, and they like to bury their dead quickly. Same day, if possible. But they'll wait for me to get home and do it tomorrow.

36

I see.

It's all been planned like that. She's been dying for months. Everybody just wants it over.

All right then, the chaplain repeats uncomfortably.

The young man gets to his feet at last. My parents should never have married, he says. They were not alike.

He wanders back to his tent through the dark roads of the camp. Under canvas, hundreds of others like him, stacked in rows. My mother is dead. The portals through which I entered the world. No way back, not that there ever was. I shot and killed her yesterday. But I didn't mean to. But you didn't do it, you did not kill your mother. Somebody else's mother you killed. And therefore mine must die.

He is very tired, no sleep for forty hours and no prospect of it now, not till he's home. Crackle and burn. The fuse is lit. There's a smell in his nostrils perpetually, of rubber on fire, rising from somewhere inside him. He comes to his tent, where his bed waits for him, but keeps on walking, liking the sound of his boots on the road. Slumber, little soldiers, while the minotaur stamps by. Slouching towards Bethlehem in the Free State.

At the furthest edge of the camp, a soldier is on guard. A troepie like him. What do you want? he says, sounding scared.

I want your gold and your women, Anton says. Speaking Afrikaans for some reason, though he can hear the other guy is English. My father's tongue, forever foreign to me. No, I've changed my mind, I come in peace. Take me to your leader.

You're not supposed to be here.

I know it. I've known it since the day I was born. He hooks his fingers through the mesh and lets his weight hang down. Yellow floodlights send strange shadows across the tar. On the other side of the fence is a lot filled with military vehicles, many of them Buffels like the one he was in when it happened. Yesterday, only yesterday. So much life still to get through.

I have lost my mother, he says.

Lost her?

I shot her with my rifle, to protect the country.

You shot your mother?

What's your name?

Payne.

Oh, wonderful. He switches to English. We've met before. Are you an allegory? Are you real? Do you have a first name?

My first name? What do you want to know that for?

He holds up his hands. I surrender, Private Payne.

Are you all right?

Do I look all right to you? No, I'm not all right. My mother is dead. Thank you for your company, Payne. I'll see you down the line.

He lurches away in the direction he came from, and the conversation disappears, as most do, into the air, or into the earth, it sinks or it rises and will never come back again. Four hours later, Rifleman Anton Swart, nineteen years old, stands at the side of the road near Alberton in a military pickup zone, hoping for a lift home. He is haggard, he is pale. A handsome young man, brown eyes and brown hair, something in his face that will never be at ease.

He calls the farm from a phone booth in Pretoria. Eight thirty in the morning. Pa answers, sounding dazed. He doesn't recognise Anton's voice. Who is this?

It's me, your son and heir. Can you send Lexington?

He loiters outside the State Theatre, near the bust of Strijdom, till the car arrives. You come in triumph, he says as he gets in, an old joke on his part, referring to the make of the car, the only one Lexington is allowed to drive, although the family sends him on numerous missions into town every week. Lexington, go to the shop. Go and pick up my curtains. Drop this off at Madam Marina. Lexington, fetch Anton in Pretoria.

I'm very sorry about Mrs Rachel.

Thank you, Lexington. He stares out of the window into the white throngs on the pavement. A city of moustaches and uniforms, Boer statues and big cement plazas. After a while, he asks, Is your mother alive?

Yes, yes, she is in Soweto.

And your father?

He's working on a mine in Cullinan.

Unknowable lives. Lexington himself is a hieroglyph, in his chauffeur's cap and jacket. He has to wear them, Pa says, so that the police can see he's not a skelm, he's my driver. And for the same reason Anton must ride in the back seat, so that the divisions are obvious.

Why are you driving this way, Lexington?

Because there is trouble by the township. Your father told me I must go by the long road.

I'm telling you not to.

Lexington hesitates between two authorities.

Look, he says, hefting it into view, I have my rifle. He lays it across his lap. His uniformed lap.

What he doesn't say is, My rifle has no bullets. Without bullets, my rifle is nothing, a shell. It is there only to send out the bullets, like the one I put into her without thinking yesterday, the instant at which she began to fall a fracture line through my life.

You want I must go back?

Yes, Lexington, please.

Nothing will happen. And he is so very tired, he cannot face the long way around. No more long roads for me. Even the direct road wearies him, the familiarity of it, yellow grass between brown rocks. How I hate it, this harsh, ugly country. I can't wait to leave.

By the time they get to the Atteridgeville turn-off, he has finally started to drift off, first taste of sleep in two days. The small crowd at the side of the road seems like an image from a dream. Are they waiting for a bus? No, they are running, they are shouting, something is happening somewhere, yet all of it is weightless.

What isn't weightless is the stone that suddenly comes at him, hurled from the hand of a man who leans out of the scene, bloodshot eyes fixed only on me. The world becomes real in an instant. The side window shatters, the impact cancels him out very briefly, then he wakes into the streaming ribbon of road, Lexington speeding away.

Shame, Master Anton, hayi.

(Never called me master before.) Just drive, Lexington, drive.

A wetness running into his eyes, which turns red when he touches it. Only now putting the pieces together, to make sense of what just happened. And only now feeling it, the raw bloom of pain from one corner of things.

Jesus H. Christ.

You want we must go to the doctor?

The doctor? He starts to laugh, the sound quickly becoming convulsive. Doesn't know what he's laughing at, there's nothing funny in any of it, maybe that's the joke. He often cries when he laughs, hilarity and weeping almost one thing. Dries his eyes and says, No, thank you, Lexington, please take me home.

His father is in some sort of conclave with his aunt and uncle in the lounge. They jump up when he comes in, because of the blood, which he's forgotten about, though it continues to run down his face and drip onto his uniform, as well as the rifle, the useless, empty rifle.

It's nothing, he says, a stone, I'm not badly hurt.

I'll call Dr Raaff, says Tannie Marina. You need stitches.

Please don't make a fuss.

Damn it, I told him to take the long road around, Pa says. Why didn't he listen?

I told him not to.

Why? Why must you always disobey my orders?

I thought it would be safe, Anton says, laughing again. But even here the restless natives are fighting their oppressors.

Man, please don't talk rubbish, Ockie says, which makes his nephew laugh harder.

No mention of what has brought him here, just confusion and commotion, out of which Dr Raaff does eventually appear, presumably by the long way around. Marina is right, Anton needs stitches, and these are administered in the kitchen, out of sight of the squeamish. And there are little splinters of glass from the broken window that have to be picked out with tweezers.

Dr Raaff wields his tweezers with more-than-usual dexterity, he and the instrument are suited. His movements are precise and angular, his clothes scrupulously

41

clean. His fastidiousness is pleasing to his patients, but if they only knew the daydreams of Dr Wally Raaff, few would submit to being examined by him.

He says, not without relish, Two inches down and that could have been your eye.

Anton says, We switched to the metric system in 1971.

Dr Raaff glares coldly at him, mouth thin and tight, like one of his sutures. He's had more than enough of the Swarts lately and wouldn't mind dissolving this particular young man in a bath of sulphuric acid. But in public one must observe the proprieties, unfortunately.

Only after the good doctor's car disappears down the drive does quietness fall. By now it's late morning and the spring day is unseasonably hot, a buzzing of insects envelops the house.

I baked some milk tart, Tannie Marina says to her nephew. Don't you want some? She pinches the skin at his waist and adds coquettishly, You're very thin.

Later.

We have to go to that Jewish funeral place now, to sort out some things. Do you want to come along?

I must sleep, Anton says. I have to sleep.

He has to sleep. Enclosed in a sort of white tunnel, voices reaching him only faintly from outside, he climbs the stairs to his room. Undresses slowly, throwing each item of clothing onto a chair, like a piece of himself. He showers, some of the last two days washing off, but can hardly stay upright. Climbs into bed still damp and is almost immediately asleep, switched off like a lamp.

Only now, too late, when everyone else is awake, does he contribute his dream to the mix. Out of time, lost, its tendrils rise from his head, sketching in smoke. He is lying in a bed not unlike his own, in a long room filled with many identical beds, and from a doorway on the far side his mother emerges. She advances towards him slowly, threading her way between the beds, and when she arrives she bends down to plant a cool kiss upon his forehead. Thus in dreams do the dead return to you.

The spirit of Rachel Swart, née Cohn, lingers around the house in a state of confusion. She becomes almost visible at certain moments, when the light or the mood is right, but only to those who are willing to see, and then only obliquely, at the edges of things. She peered at Amor out of the mirror not long ago, though what she was really gazing at was the scene of her final exit, a fact she finds hard to take in. It's not uncommon, the dead are frequently unable to accept their condition, they resemble the living in that respect, but they have forgotten what they're nostalgic for, much is lost in the crossing over, and when they see you they do not know you.

Tojo the Alsatian observes her coming and going without difficulty, because he hasn't learned that it isn't possible.

She lifts the kitchen curtain to sneak a glance at Salome, just for a second, a peripheral shimmer.

Astrid thinks she hears her calling from her room down the passage, needing help again, always at the worst possible moment, but of course it's just a loose window hinge in the wind.

She rattles the small change in her purse, the way she used to, but when Manie calls out from the bath she doesn't answer.

Presses her cold lips to Anton's forehead while he sleeps.

Eventually she tires of the house and becomes noticeable in the streets of Pretoria, in places she liked to visit. She paddles in the pond at Magnolia Dell, drinks tea at a cafe in Barclay Square. Looks through the fence of the Austin Roberts Bird Sanctuary at a sad blue crane, pecking something shiny on the ground.

You get the idea. She touches down where her spirit was once thick, but she's no longer solid, a watercolour woman. In the crowd she is just another face, not much evident. She crosses large distances as if going from room to room, looking for something she's lost. In these appearances she wears different items of clothing from her wardrobe, an evening gown, a flimsy summer dress, even a shawl she bought on appro once from Truworths and took back the next day. She looks real, which is to say, ordinary. How would you know she is a ghost? Many of the living are vague and adrift too, it's not a failing unique to the departed.

Eventually she fetches up somewhere she certainly hasn't been before, except there she already is, lying naked on a flanged metal table, the spitting image of herself, but grey and cold, like somebody dead.

She is somebody dead. She looks at herself on the table and begins to understand.

An elderly female volunteer has been working on her for a couple of hours already. There's a limit to what can be done, given the prohibition on chemicals, but cleaning the body is most important. Then the pouring of the water, to purify the flesh, and the drying that follows. It is required, both the ritual and the cleanliness. And there is great respect and tenderness in doing it, which brings peace to this older woman, whose name, according to

44

the tag she wears on her lapel, is Sara. One day soon, somebody will do this for me.

Plain and clean and simple, that's how she approaches the job. The human form, reduced to what it is. She has dressed the body in the tachrichim and wrapped the avnet around it, but the knot that she's tied is just slightly wrong. It's meant to be in the shape of Shin, denoting one of the names of God, but her fingers are especially arthritic today.

Let it go, or else sigh and redo it. Much of life consists of sighing and redoing, particularly with Sara. The material world resists. Patience is a form of meditation. She has been a volunteer with the Chevra Kadisha, preparing the dead for burial, since her own husband died twenty-two years ago. To serve is to worship. Also, it passes the time. Also, you meet new people.

She decides to let it go. So God's name is a little bit wrong, does it matter? Nobody will see, everything is hidden in the aron. And symbolic anyway. How terrible is it? She has more important worries, like working on the face. She doesn't like to use make-up on them, more deceitful in death than in life, but this one's condition is quite bad. She was sick for a long time, poor thing, sores on her arms, not much hair left, gums blackened, very gaunt. Seems disrespectful not to improve her, you can see in the instamatic print you asked for that she was beautiful once. All human life is like grass upon the earth.

In her other, public life, Sara is not above a little vanity, she wears the occasional piece of jewellery and likes to put some colour on her cheeks. Long ago, before she was old, she too exerted an attractive force. Men noticed me, yes, they did. Sometimes a nostalgic mood comes over her and she takes out her own make-up box, to repair a bit of damage. There, my lovely, yes. A bit of rouge, a dab of powder. Doesn't want to do much more, truth matters and in her case truth was suffering. Over at last. A blessing. Goodbye, my dear. Rest easy now.

Lastly she brushes the thin hair on the woman's scalp. Gently and rhythmically, a part of the ritual she usually enjoys, but today a few strands come loose. Soft, almost substanceless, like something not there. She collects them in her hand, to be put into the casket later. All of it matters, every drop, every filament.

In the end the severe expression is gentled, becoming kinder, more accepting. Even Rachel's ghost is drawn by her own resemblance, she stands next to the body on the table, gazing wonderingly at the face it wears, trying to place it. She takes care not to get in the way, though she's picked up as a weak place in Sara's vision, swimming with spots. Maybe the onset of a migraine. She is prone to these, when the flesh she kneads is especially unwilling. See what you've done, she tells the woman on the table, but silently, inside. You've put me off my work, looking for the truth. The truth, Rachel answers, just as silently, is that who she is? I thought I knew her from somewhere.

Yes, definitely a migraine, Sara retreats, pulling off her rubber gloves, fumbling for her suppositories. They sometimes help if you can catch it in time. No need to dwell on the image of the old woman with her knickers around her ankles and her finger up her fundament, at such moments she feels very far from God.

In the room next door, just two bricks away, the shomer waits on a hard chair, Book of Psalms in hand.

A tall, bony man of asexual appearance, he wears a yarmulke and prayer shawl over ill-fitting clothes of a conservative cut. His duties begin shortly, but for the moment he's in that pleasing period of preparation, trying to empty out his mind, which is busier than most.

And in the room on the far side of him, the dead woman's family is in consultation with Rabbi Katz, who'll be conducting the levayah ceremony tomorrow. He instructed Rachel spiritually on her return to her own people, so it's only fitting. But this is the first time he's actually meeting the goy husband and sister, although Rachel talked about them a lot, and he has to say, excuse the lack of tolerance, but nothing has prepared him for how obtuse they turn out to be.

Starts out well enough. Manie is warmly greeted by Rachel's older sister Ruth, who's flown up from Durban this morning.

Hello, Manie, she says. You remember Clint.

He does, unfortunately. Clint is a big, meaty fellow, who used to play rugby for Western Province and now owns a steakhouse in Umhlanga Rocks. Howzit, Mannie, he says, shaking hands with unnecessary force. You look all right.

Manie, his wife corrects him, with the weary tone of one who does a lot of correcting. It's good to see you.

Ja, you too.

And it's not untrue. Of all Rachel's family Ruth is the easiest to deal with, because she also married out of the faith and was exiled for a while. Though she seems to be back in the fold these days.

But Rachel's middle sister Marcia and her husband Ben are also there and things with them are much more strained. Antagonism on both sides, the sense of some old wound, the details forgotten but the injury not. Nor does it help that Ockie said Congratulations instead of Condolences when he bumped into them outside, and that since then Manie has kept blaming them for his wife returning to her religion.

Look, the rabbi has told them twice already just in the past half-hour, it's really not the Levis' fault. This is what she wanted. It's what Rachel requested.

What she was brainwashed into, you mean, Manie says.

Calm down, the shiksa sister tells him. Remember what Dr Raaff said.

I didn't brainwash anybody, Rabbi Katz says. She came to me, of her own free will.

Because of these people, Manie insists, pointing at Marcia and Ben, who shift uncomfortably on their chairs. First time they've all been in the same room in years. They're the ones who arranged this meeting, supposedly to defuse tensions before the interment tomorrow, but see how that's worked out.

No need for that kind of talk, buddy, says Ben, without looking at Manie.

Honestly, Marcia says, what are we doing here? I thought we were all making an effort, or am I wrong?

The Levis are part of our congregation, Rabbi Katz throws in. It's natural they'd approach me.

Hand on heart, Marcia says, I can tell you that all of it was Rachel. She came to me out of the blue. I hadn't spoken to her for ten years —

Because of you, buddy. So be nice.

Do you know, Marcia says, we've taken this week of mourning on ourselves. It's supposed to be in her own house, Rachel's house, that the mirrors are covered and the candles lit –

There is plenty of mourning in our house, Manie tells her. But we do it in our own style, not like heathens. Then he subsides, like a tent without a supporting pole. He knows that they're right, Rachel found her way to them, they didn't come looking for her. And Marina lectured him the whole drive here about how important it is not to get worked up when he sees the Levis, and he agreed with her. He still does. They're not to blame.

The shiny little rabbi isn't responsible either, but Manie would like to do something to him anyway. He's seething over the injustice of all of it, but this morning especially over the plain pine box these people are going to put his wife into, she who deserves so much more, after he's paid for years into a funeral policy she turns out not to need.

Please understand, Marina says to nobody in particular, in her most soothing voice. This is difficult for my brother.

Yes, I'm sure it is, Marcia says. It's been hard for us too, believe it or not. Do you think we like being here?

Marcia, her husband says warningly.

All I want, Manie whispers, is for her to lie next to me in the family cemetery. Is there any way we can arrange something? If I make a donation . . .

The rabbi sits up straight. I'm afraid not. If she wants a Jewish funeral, then it's not possible. You can't buy our traditions, Mr Swart.

She wasn't really Jewish, Manie says. Not in her heart.

Ah, you know that, do you?

Ja, I do know, actually. My wife found many ways to torture me, it was a talent of hers.

Maybe you should have treated her better and she wouldn't have turned against you, Marcia says, taking her purse out of her handbag for no particular reason and then putting it away again.

Marcia, Ben says.

No, really.

We are not getting anywhere, the rabbi says, feeling close to tears. His sense of fairness has not been taxed this far since he first engaged morally with the question of Israel.

Manie, let's go, his sister says. You are upsetting yourself for nothing.

Ja, come on, vamonos. By now it's clear to all of them that the meeting is a waste of time. Rachel will be buried with her own people and Manie one day with his. Better for the Swart side to go back to the farm and get ready for tomorrow.

And as they drive away, Rachel's body is already being lifted into its final container and the lid screwed down. For ever. The shomer is in attendance and when the other assistants have gone he continues to sit in his lonely chair against the wall, chanting the tehillim. For the dead must have company all the way to the end. The psalms stand in for the whole Jewish people, words are magical in that way, but he is the sole human representative and takes his job seriously, like any good ambassador.

Sometimes he can detect the presence of the departed, as a rustling and pressing against the edges of his senses. Then he tries to chant the words directly to them, from his heart to theirs. But today, although he strains his mind outwards, he can pick up no other signal. The room feels empty to him. He recites regardless, and who is to say where the words travel to?

See the words fly, through the door of the room, down the passage, out the window. Watch them rise over the city and wing their way in a little psalm-shaped flock to the farm, in search of the woman to whom they are chanted. They circle the koppie and dive down to the lawn, they enter the house through the back door and pass on stilted legs through the kitchen, like a change in the light.

Anton glances up from where he sits at the table. What was that? he says.

Hmmm? Salome is at her usual station, in front of the sink, and her reflection looks back at him in the window glass.

Nothing. I thought ... He's still stupid with sleep, and is drinking a mug of strong coffee and eating a slice of Tannie Marina's milk tart. Soon the sugar will kick in, fire him up. He touches at the stitches on his forehead, bothered by their foreignness, the pulse of pain they emit.

The silence between the two of them is comfortable, unfraught. She has seen him grow up, from a tottering infant to a golden boy to this, whatever he is now, tending to him every step of the way. When he was little he used to call her Mama and tried to suck on her nipple, a common South African confusion. No secrets between them.

A sudden spasm of anger comes over him, and he pushes the plate violently away, the remains of the sickly-sweet milk tart on it.

(Yesterday I killed a woman just like you.) When I'm done with the army I'm leaving this country.

Ja?

I'm going to wipe this place off the bottom of my feet and never come back.

Ja? The clink and clash of cutlery. Where will you go?

Oh, he says, less sure about this part of his plans. Everywhere.

Ja?

I'm going to study English literature. Not here, overseas somewhere. After that, my main ambition is to write a novel. I might go into law later, or maybe just make a lot of money, but first I want to travel the world. You don't want to see the world, Salome?

Me? How will I do that? She sighs and starts to dry dishes with a big cloth. Is it true, she asks, that I am getting my house?

Huh?

Lukas saw Amor on the koppie yesterday. And she told him your father will give me my house.

I don't know anything about that.

Okay, she says. Apparently unperturbed, though she has thought of nothing else since the words were spoken. To have her own house, to hold those papers in her hand!

Better ask my father, he says.

Okay.

He watches her inscrutable back, which bore his infant self innumerable times, as it moves to and fro along the kitchen counter, carrying the stacked plates to the cupboard.

Yes, he says, absently. Better ask him.

The question about the house has travelled from his mother to his sister to Lukas to Salome and has now been planted in him, a tiny dark seed just starting to sprout. It comes back to him a couple of hours later, in another room on the far side of the city, at an almost arbitrary moment, doing up his shirt.

You know what my little sister said to Salome?

Who's Salome?

The woman who ... Our maid.

This conversation happens in a bedroom on the upper floor of a large house in a leafy suburb. He's speaking to a bosomy blonde girl, still in her last year of high school, with whom he's just animalistically and explosively rutted. Witness the tangled bedclothes, the state of half-undress, the pleasing afterglow in the groin.

What did your sister say to her?

That my father promised to give her a house.

Did he?

What?

Promise.

I don't know, Anton says, standing in front of the dressing-table mirror and straightening any giveaways, loose zips and untucked shirts, all clues in the suspicious eyes of Desirée's mother, due back from the hairdresser any minute. He leans in to examine his stitches, impressed by the wound all over again. Now I look like a soldier.

Don't let him give a house to the maid, Desirée says, indignant. She'll only break it.

I think it's broken already. But that's not the point.

From outside, the unmistakable sound of the old lady's Jaguar purring into the drive and pulling up below in a little spray of gravel. They're on the second floor,

53

fortunately, because the curtains are open and she might otherwise be able to look in on her daughter writhing back into her blouse while her boyfriend does up his flies. Not much to mistake in that tableau.

Hurry, she's here.

You go and talk to her! Say I'm in the bathroom.

Okay. He jerks the bedcover straight, casting a backward look at her, but she's just a blonde blur, closing the bathroom door. No match for the image he's carried around to lonely places these past months. Desirée's brother Leon is a friend of Anton's from high school and she remained in the background for quite a few years as a mere and irritating younger sister before certain glandular changes caused an alteration in perception. The need to fuck like bonobos is uppermost these days and he certainly came here today for no noble reason. Only one thing on my mind since hearing about Ma, funny that, just how it works, Eros fighting Thanatos, except you don't think about sex, you suffer it. A scratchy, hungry thing going on in the basement. Torment of the damned, the fire that never goes out. But still, despite bodily appetites, he feels that he's chasing some emotion he can't quite name. Might even be love, though that would surprise him. She's given him comfort today, for sure. Yes, to lie a long time among her plump undulations, that would be peaceful.

Instead he pads, alarmed and half tumescent, through the well-upholstered passages of the upper floor, glimpsing other bedrooms and bathrooms on either side. Then a study, edge of a desk showing, a Persian rug, a standing lamp. Why does furniture always look innocent, no matter what happens on it?

54

He's not supposed to be up here, too personal in every way. He lost his virginity to Desirée, she will always hold a special charge for him, but she's not the only thing that excites him on his visits. Desirée's father is an important cabinet minister, a physically as well as morally repugnant person with the blood of innocents on his hands, and Anton would like to hate him unequivocally but finds himself secretly stirred by the outward trappings of power. The mean-looking guards in a booth at the entrance, the busts and oil paintings of colonial criminals from a highly selective history, the casual mention of well-known, fear-inducing names, all of it is terrible but thrilling, and his most memorable thunderclap of an orgasm took place in a chair where the buttocks of the Minister of Justice had only recently rested.

The wife of this urbane and awful man, Desirée's mother, roils him in a completely different way. Like an older, Aryan doll, pretty but hard, all her surfaces washed and powdered and lacquered and fixed, so that you can't help longing to pierce the brittle veneer. He shoots down the stairs and into the kitchen just ahead of her, and is leaning against the counter when she comes in through the back door, high heels striking sparks on the tiles.

What a surprise! I thought it was your cute little car outside. She lets him kiss her coolly on one cheek. But what happened to your head?

The wounds of war. Just a stone, not serious.

So you're on sick leave?

No. My mother died yesterday.

Oh, Anton! It finally happened ... I'm so sorry. She allows the enamel to crack a little, enough to simulate a genuine emotion, hairdo vibrating with the strain. At least her suffering is over.

Yes, at least there's that.

She puts a hand up to his cheek and he almost, actually, weeps. Where does it come from, this little chink of weakness? Luckily, his lapse is covered by the return of Desirée, freshly sheathed, sprayed with perfume, lipstick reapplied.

Maman! / Mein Schatz! Kiss-kiss! Since a recent European trip the two of them affect foreign modes of address. They are the same kind of creature, and Anton recalls a night out in Johannesburg last year, the two of them feeding spoons of ice cream to each other, fluttering and cooing like pigeons on a ledge.

For her part, Maman quite likes Anton this evening, or feels sorry for him, at least. She wouldn't mind massaging his shoulders, but settles instead for chivvying him along. Would you like a Valium, for your nerves? I have some in my cupboard. And I was just going to open a bottle of wine. I know it's a sad day for you, so I'm sure you'd rather not ...

Actually, he says, I'd love a glass.

He should be at the farm. He didn't tell anyone where he was going and he took the Triumph without permission and he knows his father will be very angry and these are all good reasons not to hurry home just yet, but to stay and pop a Valium and have a glass, or maybe two.

And at the farm, at this moment, a braai is just beginning. On the way back from the meeting with those people this morning, Pa felt the need to slaughter some living thing. Now a table has been set up at the bottom of the lawn, while the sun sinks bloodily over the veld, not unlike the chunks of meat marinating in bowls. At the fire itself, Ockie tends to his coals. This is his contribution! Chops on a grid, beer in hand, then a man can be at peace. Salads are a woman's job and if you listen you'll hear Marina's voice giving orders in the kitchen, Wash this, Slice that. Who put her in charge of the world?

Here, too, somebody has opened a bottle of red and almost all the adults are partaking. A curious scene, this low-key festivity just a day after Ma has died, but on the other hand people have to eat, life goes on. They'll be drinking and making bawdy jokes soon after you go too.

It's not only family in attendance. There are a couple of hangers-on, among them the Reverend Simmers and his helper. The dominee is in a relaxed and chatty mood, beaming vaguely and throwing out little bon mots in all directions. Everyone likes the personal touch. Trouble is, almost nobody likes Alwyn Simmers, aside from Pa and Tannie Marina. He sits flanked by the two of them as the braai gets going, eyes masked behind those bulletproof glasses, under the kapok tree in the dusk, the sizzle and smell of meat on the air.

On the other side of the table, Amor watches and listens, but says little herself. She still has a bad head, two days down the line, as if she's wearing a dark hat of some kind, too tight for her skull. Next to her, Astrid is pushing back her cuticles and jiggling one sandalled foot.

From a little way off, Pa muses on them, his two daughters. But where is the other child? The first one, the boy, can actually not remember his name for a second. They should all be here, his offspring, lined up in a row, birds on a wire. All their names starting with A, what were he and Rachel thinking? We just liked the sound of it, his wife always told people, though the sound of it is what most embarrasses him now. If the first one's name had been different ...

Where is Anton? he demands, suddenly irked.

Astrid sees a chance to make trouble. He sneaked out in the Triumph. I saw him.

Going where?

She shrugs suggestively, but speak of the devil, here are the wan headlamps now, coming over the ridge. Though it must be later in the evening, because everybody has food on their plates, clearly visible as the lights float slowly down towards the front of the house and fix the gathering for a moment in their beam. They go out, the engine cuts, car door opens and closes, and Anton walks in a studied, loose-jointed way over the lawn towards them. His knees don't quite straighten, he wears a bleary grin.

The same condition afflicts some of the gathering. Get yourself some meat, Ockie calls to him, too loudly. Come and join the other sinners! And Tannie Marina pats the chair next to her. Here! She can see that her crazy nephew, the mistake, has been making some mistakes of his own lately and might be in need of a guiding hand tonight.

Manie's stare hasn't wavered since Anton came into view. He nods grimly, recognising his earlier, fallen self. Nice. Ja. Very nice.

What now? He drops the car keys on the table.

Your mother died yesterday, but you have time for wine and loose women. Nice.

Loose women? Ockie says hopefully, casting around, amazed. Dominee Simmers mutters something prayerful and Anton slides into a seat, quaking silently with laughter.

Ja, mock. Sneer at me. Every sin is written in the ledger and on the last day –

Your sins too, dear Father. The women and the wine.

Those days are past. And I have emptied my heart, I have asked for forgiveness, and I have moved on. But look at you!

On the other side of the table, Dominee Simmers gives an imperceptible sigh. He'd been conversing with Manie just before the damned son came back, and the talk was going well. In just a little moment he was going to nudge the topic around to the important question, he could feel that the mood was right, but now an off note has entered in. Something about that boy, can never remember his name, Andre, Albert, something about him is otherwise.

Your father is upset today, he offers helpfully. Because of the Jewish funeral.

You should have seen the coffin, really cheap-looking, Tannie Marina says. And with wooden handles!

After he's been paying for a policy, Ockie says excitedly. For twenty years already!

What I want, Manie moans, the only thing I want, is to lie next to my wife for eternity. Is that so much to ask?

Instead she'll lie in the Jewish cemetery, Marina says.

It is very unfair, the dominee observes.

Why is it unfair?

What your father is saying, he would like your beloved mother to be buried here on the farm. With the rest of the family, next to him. Where she belongs.

Where her home is, Pa adds.

By a real minister.

Meaning you, Anton says.

A silence opens, pierced by the hishing sound of fat dropping into the fire.

That is what your father would like …

But it's not what she wanted.

The dead don't want anything! Pa says, or rather cries, for he loses his decorum briefly. A silence falls as the talking stops, making the sound of chewing uncomfortably loud. There's a feeling of mild shame upon the gathering, with no obvious focus, and it takes a while for conversation to resume.

Manie offers no further contribution to the discussion. He sits slumped, apparently without conviction, though it should be remembered that he went down to the barn this afternoon and slaughtered the lamb that they are eating now. Yes, he cut its throat, a small flowering of violence in the midst of his helplessness, oh it felt good. So people will pity themselves, soaked in sadness over what they've lost, with no awareness of other losses close to hand that they have brought about. The grief of mother sheep, what is that? Yet it marks the air like human grief, it can't be washed away.

Amor puts down her fork.

Are you not going to eat that meat? Astrid wants to know.

She shakes her head, feeling she might kotch. For the past two days she's been feeling scratchy and nauseous, on the edge of some undefined rebellion. She keeps remembering something she saw at her father's reptile park recently. Feeding time at the crocodile enclosure, and she's tried to erase the image, but can't, of a kindly old uncle in a safari suit, throwing handfuls of white mice to the primitive drifting shapes in the water. Snippety snap. Tails hanging out of a grinning mouth like strands of dental floss. What are we, that we have to eat other bodies to keep going? With disgust, she watches Astrid reach over to her plate, stuffing bits of flesh and fat into her working, glistening mouth.

That's Ma's bracelet, she says.

No, it isn't. It's mine.

Ma wore it all the time.

Are you calling me a liar?

Anton puts his plate down and wipes his fingers carefully on a paper napkin. By the way, he says, I hear you're giving Salome the Lombard place.

What? Pa says, though it rings the faintest bell.

Hah! Tannie Marina snorts. That'll be the day.

Anton turns to look at Amor, who shifts on her chair. Pa said . . .

I said what?

You said you would give her the house. You promised.

Her father is stunned at this news. When did I say that?

That girl isn't getting a house, Tannie Marina says. No, no, no. I'm sorry. You can forget that story right now. She busies herself with tidying away, although not everyone has finished eating yet, the sound of clashing cutlery like the gnashing of teeth.

Pa tries to explain. I'm already paying for her son's education . . . Must I do everything for her?

Amor falters in confusion, while her brother smiles and smiles. He leans abruptly towards Alwyn Simmers. Could we talk honestly for a moment?

The minister opens his palms. Of course, Alan, he says. Please go ahead.

My mother was terrified of dying and couldn't accept it was happening. But even so, she was very clear about what she wanted. It wasn't much. Just a few things. One of them was to go back to her religion and be buried with her own family. She specifically said that.

Honesty is very important, the minister says, his voice hoarse.

Pa becomes suddenly very hot. What is wrong with you?

I ask myself that all the time.

Don't you ever worry that you might burn in hell one day?

This is the worst possibility he can come up with, but Anton reacts, as he often does, with merriment. I'm already there, he says, wiping away tears of hilarity. Can't you smell the braai?

I'm her husband! I know better than you. I know what my wife believed.

Really? I hardly know what I believe myself most of the time. All I'm saying, not looking for a fight, just trying to keep it simple. You should do what she wanted. All of it. Which includes giving Salome the house, if that's what you promised.

I never did, Pa says. I never promised anything!

Amor blinks at him, genuinely startled. But you did, she tells him. I heard you.

What is wrong with all of you? Pa shouts, then gets up, for some reason with difficulty, and walks off on stiff legs into the garden, bellowing incoherently.

Tannie Marina twists her necklace till her voice sounds strangled. He's crying, she says. Are you happy now?

Happy? Anton says, considering the word. No, I wouldn't say that. But we all might be closer to it if I say goodnight.

When he goes, he leaves behind him an abruptly disordered company, people turned at angles to each other amid small sputterings of argument. Often what remains in his wake of late. Ascends to his room, a space cluttered with books and papers, walls festooned with quotes and notes to self. From there, via the window, onto a ledge and thence by means of a tricky manoeuvre onto the roof. The spot where he likes to sit is on the very top, a warmish wind moving over him, looking out on the dark land, pricked here and there by lights.

Under a loose tile he's stowed a plastic bag, from which he now retrieves a roach and a lighter. Fires it up and puffs on it, savouring even before he stubs it out the sensation of his mind relaxing, expanding. Ah, yes. Thank God. I am almost somebody else.

Anton the firstborn, the only son. He is anointed, to what he doesn't know, but the future is his. What is it you want? To travel, to learn, to write poems and lead nations, he wants to grab hold of everything, all of it is possible, he wants to eat the world. But a tiny sourness at the back of his throat seems always to have been there, though his life is pure and mild as milk. Wherefrom this curdling? There is a lie at the heart of everything and I have just discovered it in myself. Spit it out. What is wrong with you, man? Nothing is wrong with me. Everything is wrong with me.

Down there around the fire, he can still see figures gesticulating and talking. The last ripples of the commotion he set off, not yet subsided. How you flounder, how you flail, when you try to keep your footing.

In the aftermath of the family fallout, Alwyn Simmers lost his glasses as he struggled to his feet, upheaval all around him, and in his panic now he hears them snap under his shoe, like a breaking bone. He's blind as an earthworm without those lenses, the fabric of things a misty blur.

Siebritz, he cries. Siebritz!

He is calling for his assistant, whom he otherwise detests, but Siebritz will not reply. Upset by the scene that played out at the braai, which reminds him of his life, for in crisis as in harmony everything is connected, at this moment he is halfway back to town in his car. He is done with that family, he is done with the Church and, most especially, he is done with the dominee. No more!

Siebritz! Siebritz!

Thou art forsaken in the hour of thy need, Alwyn, where is thy succour now? It is only the just man who is tested, remember! Help will come if you wait.

If he could only make her out, there is one figure sitting very still close by. Amor. She hasn't moved from her place at the table, though everybody else has left. Hasn't twitched a limb or a brow, in fact, for the past couple of minutes, so sunken is she in thought, or something else.

She is contemplating her brother, Anton, who is regarding her from the rooftop in return. But her reflections are internal. Amazement, in a way. That he could speak like that. Could say what he did. It must be wonderful to be a man! She has a peculiar longing to take him by the hand. Not to lead him anywhere, just to hold on. Or maybe to be led.

She's used to being treated as a blur, a smudge at the edge of everybody's vision. Too young, too silly, to be taken seriously. And strange too, a strange child. Unusual and maybe tragic, easy to overlook. But tonight her brother, from his high place, seemed to notice me.

Nearby, Alwyn Simmers has at last been rescued by Tannie Marina, offering her fleshy forearm and another plate of home-made potato salad. No, thank you, where is my driver? He seems to have disappeared. The dominee just wants to go home now, flatulent and disappointed, to the little house he shares with his sister. He wants it so ardently that he even stamps one foot on the grass.

It's soon established that Siebritz has departed. Lexington can take you, Marina says, clapping her hands, so that her bracelets clash noisily. Lexington! Lexington!

Lexington comes hurrying from the back of the house, putting on his cap. Ja, Mrs Marina? Take the minister back to his house. The dominee leaves in triumph and soon they are bowling down the highway towards the glimmering yellow lights of Pretoria, which only the driver can see.

Tell me, the minister asks him, how long have you been working for those people?

Twelve years, sir.

What do you think about them, that family?

Lexington hesitates, smiling broadly out of nervousness, to no effect. They are good to me, sir.

They are good to you, yes, yes. But what do you think about them?

No, I am not thinking about them, sir. I am only doing, not thinking.

The statement is untrue, but Lexington cannot answer truthfully. He senses that the minister wants something, but to give him what he wants might endanger his position. It is not always possible to please two white people simultaneously.

Well, I think things about them, the dominee answers. I won't say what, but I think things. About that son especially, whatever his name is. Adam.

Yes, sir, Lexington says, keen to be agreeable.

Something is wrong with him. You mark my words. He's a wild donkey of a man. His hand is against everyone and everyone's hand against him!

Dominee Simmers is vexed this evening, he has a crimp in his soul, which always brings out the biblical in him. The Lord's creation is amplified when you use heightened language to describe it.

This country! he exclaims. He's not sure why the country is to blame, but he repeats it anyway. This country!

Yes, sir, Lexington answers, and for a moment the two of them are in genuine accord, South Africa troubles them both, though for different reasons. Alwyn Simmers feels emotionally joined to his black compatriot, it seems to him that they are equals in God's eyes, although they should always sit on separate seats in the car. God decreed it so, just as He decreed that Rachel should die at the hour she died and that her house should be filled with those who mourn her, it is His wish too that in other rooms the sons and daughters of Ham should be toiling on behalf of their masters and mistresses, hewing wood,

66

drawing water, and generally making life liveable for those who bear the heavy yoke of leadership. A burden that some might prefer to decline, Let this cup pass from me, but if the cup is yours, you must drink from it, no arguing with God, no matter how bitter the dregs.

Laetitia keeps a spare set of spectacles at home for her brother, in case of emergencies like these, and by the next morning, his remaining sight restored to him, stirring his first cup of coffee, Alwyn Simmers feels altogether in a better humour. The more he muses on the events of the previous night, the sunnier his prospects seem. The disarray has worked to his advantage, perhaps the Lord wanted it this way, because Manie is now further estranged from his ungrateful children and might be more inclined to show his generosity elsewhere. But it's important to make a move soon, before the situation changes. Today, if possible! Except Manie's wife is to be buried today. Come to think of it, what is the time, it could even be happening right now, as we speak.

Yes, no denying it's happening. The little room is as bare and simple as her coffin and filled with people. Rachel was a sociable person, she had a lot of friends, but the benches are mostly packed with the Jewish side of the family. Like Afrikaners in that way, blood is the thickest glue of all. For years she didn't see or speak to most of them, so they were invisible. But here they are today, throngs of faces you haven't seen in years, a few still with names attached, aunts and uncles and cousins, with their offspring and familiars. Rachel's mother, your arch-enemy, turns sharply away when she sees you, no quarter given, even now.

Manie hunches his shoulders against them all. Too much has happened to pretend it doesn't matter. He prayed long and hard last night and he believes the Lord wants him to be here, to show grace and set a Christian example. Faith means you have to wrestle with yourself, can't just hate them and be done. But it's hard for him, much harder than he imagined, to be sitting among these people, who have taken her away from me, with their strange customs. Why must they tear their clothes and make me wear a black ribbon over my heart and a skullcap on my head? Why do they keep wishing me a long life? He doesn't want life to be long, not today, he wants it shorter, he's had enough of it. In particular, he would happily give up the next few hours from his allotted time, take them, keep them, I don't want them.

His own tribe is a much smaller group. There's his partner from work, Bruce Geldenhuys, and a couple of other friends from church. Plus the family, obviously, though Manie has deliberately put Marina between him and his own children, to keep his son at a distance. He can't even look at Anton. What happened last night at the braai is still warm with Manie, still troubling him inside, like a fizzing in his bowels.

There's been some praying in Hebrew and now Rabbi Katz is giving the eulogy. He's decided on an expansive theme for his hesped, in an attempt to heal the divisions in this family. Rachel came to me, he tells them, six months ago, when she knew she was dying. She had been away from her own people, her own faith, for a long time. Years. And she didn't expect to return. But life works in peculiar ways. And sometimes it's only when you know life is ending that you can finally give it a meaning. So it was with Rachel. I believe it would have made her very pleased to see all of you here today, both sides of her family, Jewish and non-Jewish, English-speaking and Afrikaans. It would have felt right to her that everybody should come together for her sake. The world is imperfect, yes, but at moments like these it can be whole ... etc., etc. You see his point, how Rachel made short-sighted choices, which left her dissatisfied, but at the last she journeyed back to where she began, and thus closed the circle. The rabbi is fascinated by mathematics, geometric forms in particular, and for him the circle is so obviously perfect that all divisions should fade away before it.

While he speaks, he waves his stubby hands around in a repetitive way, but his voice is reassuring, with a calm, even tone, like that used by dentists and air hostesses, and it's conducive to reverie. Many of those assembled in front of him have drifted sideways in their minds, far from what he's saying. To counter the paganism around her, Tannie Marina is reciting the Lord's Prayer quietly, under her breath. She feels her faith swelling in her almost physically, like a tumour. Ag, sis. It's a tumour that killed Rachel, Ockie has often thought about it, what would it actually look like, if you lift it up, into the light? A clot of rubber and blood, like something that blocks the sink, or is it more subtle? A foreign object penetrating your body, the memory of it so recent that it stirs your very cells, and Astrid shifts on the hard pew, feeling moist and restless. She had sex yesterday with Dean de Wet in one of the stalls down at the stables, and it was beautiful, despite the smell of fresh dung. The horse stamped and huffed in a neighbouring stall, rustling the straw with his hooves. Shit, that's what it is, thinks Anton, all of it is horseshit, everything you're saying, not one word of it is true. I killed her. I shot and killed her in Katlehong, it wasn't God who took her, before her time. But you think there's an order, you think your actions matter, that they'll be weighed and judged in some final reckoning. But there is no reckoning. For each of us, death is the last day.

And so, for Rachel, the rabbi concludes, knowing that she was going to die was the beginning of a new life.

At the end of the row, pressed between her brother and sister, Amor is alone. That's how it feels to her. Never been more solitary than in this forest of people. Nothing around her, nothing and nobody except that wooden box, and inside it, but don't think about that, don't think about what's inside. The box is empty and it has four sides, no, six, no, more, but what does it matter when it's going into the ground?

The truth is that my mother is dead and she lies inside that box. As she thinks it, the solid world comes undone, starts to liquefy. She feels it slide. Clenches herself, presses her thighs together. Make it stop.

Now everybody is on their feet to sing. But Amor sinks back to the bench, feeling suddenly faint. Leans first towards Anton, then sharply the other way, to her sister. Tugs on Astrid's arm, to pull her down.

What is it?

The first time she tries to say it, she sounds like a puncture.

What? Astrid hisses back, screwing up her face.

I think I might be ...

What?

You know. Bleeding. Down there.

Astrid blinks slowly. Oh, you can't be serious. Don't you have something with you? She glares at her little sister, then leans the other way to pull their aunt down into the picture too. Whispers to her.

What? Tannie Marina says. Shhh.

Astrid hesitates, then tries again. This time she hisses a little too loudly, so that a woman behind them, an acquaintance of Rachel's from schooldays, has her nostalgic reverie disturbed.

Marina's mind takes a few moments to fix on what is being said to her. The last menstruation in her case is far in the past, soon after her last child was born, and these days it's unpleasant to imagine such a thing is even possible. But apparently it is, it's happening right now, at the worst conceivable moment.

I must say, she whispers furiously, this is very selfish of her. Doesn't she have a . . . ?

Astrid shrugs. She is not her sister's keeper!

Now everybody is starting to shuffle around and cough, and the pall-bearers are going to the front to pick up the coffin. Seems the service is over and there's a procession outside to do the burial part. Marina knows she ought to help her niece, but leaving now would be terrible, it would be like when Ockie erased the who-shot-JR episode of Dallas from the VHS player by mistake before she'd seen it. She takes hold of Astrid by one elbow and whispers to her instead. Take her outside and look after her. We'll deal with it after this.

Me? Why must I do it?

Because she's your sister.

Astrid is amazed. She has never thought of Amor as a possible adult, somebody with breasts and blood and opinions, much less with the power to expel her from their mother's funeral and to shame her in the process. Yet here they are, while everybody is chugging along in one direction, the two of them heading in the other. Outside, she turns on her sister. How could you do this? she says.

I can't help it, Amor says, and at this moment feels a cramp go through her, a hot wringing close to the core. It's like when she stepped on a nail that time, running in the grass. How she'd wailed. Ma, Ma, please help me!

With a pinched face, Astrid casts around. Nothing to be done, she decides. Sit over there till it's over.

She means a bench by the front entrance, but Amor finds a cloakroom nearby and goes inside, into a greeny sharp-smelling space, and finds a cubicle, and withdraws. The drip and mutter of water everywhere, a broken pipe maybe. Another cramp rising from the depths. The scene flickers around her, like a black-and-white film. She can't believe this is happening, that she's cooling her forehead on a wall tile in a public toilet instead of accompanying Ma's coffin on its last few steps, through the thickets of gravestones. A fine spring day, light sifting down through the bud-heavy trees. The levayah proceeds slowly, pausing for the recitation of Psalm 91, then lingering a little before shuffling on again. There's a snory sound of bees, jacaranda blossoms pop absurdly underfoot. Till just a short way further the same pause is repeated, the same singing of the psalm, and it seems this is how it will go on, in stages towards the grave, but Amor isn't here for any of it. She's doubled over, thinking,

I need a painkiller, I must have a painkiller. But what will kill the pain of not being there while the casket is let down into the grave? Or not being one of those who step forward now to take hold of the spade and throw a shovel-load of earth onto the box?

Whack! The thud of soil on wood is very final, like a big door slamming closed.

But where is Amor? Where is Astrid?

Anton turns in bewilderment, unsure whom to hand the spade on to.

They had to go somewhere, Tannie Marina hisses. Give that thing to your uncle.

Where did they have to go? The question keeps bothering him, while the line of people goes slowly past, each tossing their quota down into the hole. Bit by bit, the coffin disappears, as if the ground is taking bites out of it. Not so different from our style. Whack, goodbye, good riddance.

Astrid watches from a distance and when the Kaddish is finally done and the small crowd starts to disperse, she bangs on the toilet door and yells at her sister to come out. Amor staggers forth, clenching her thighs together, grateful to be wearing black. As the family draws closer, the questions that will be asked draw closer too, Where did you go, What happened to you, and there seem to be no answers to hand.

But Tannie Marina, at last, has seen and understood, and makes sure she's there before any of the men arrive. Don't worry, I'll take care of it. She has a long-practised mode of imparting confidences and instructions, mouth close to the submissive ear, in this case those of her husband/son/brother, and then Ockie and Wessel go off

73

with Manie and she's steering her nieces towards her own car while she squeezes her hands into those little white golfing gloves. Well, I don't mind telling you, I'm very glad that's over.

Though in fact it isn't over, because everybody is expected at the Levis' house for the after-party or whatever these people call it. Marcia caught Manie at a wobbly moment just after the interment, her face whetted and purposeful, but he still can't believe he said yes. Nor could she, it was obvious. Thought she could count on his antipathy. Well, we're still in the same place. I'm sure you remember how to find us. He does, of course, wishes he could forget. But we're not going for long, he tells Ockie as they get into the car. Just showing ourselves for a while, then our duty is done.

But where are Astrid and Amor? Anton is still bewildered, not least at being pressed up against his unpleasant cousin Wessel, who always smells unwashed. Manie's buggered if he'll answer any question from his son again, so it's left to Oom Ockie to explain. They're driving with Tannie Marina, he says, but offers nothing else. A mystery! Why have people changed cars? What could make two girls walk out of their mother's funeral, just at the important moment?

They're driving with Tannie Marina to the same destination, but they have to make a little detour on the way. They find a shopping mall a few blocks away, rows of cars twinkling merrily in the sun. Just going to double-park, we won't be long. She counts out money from her purse into Astrid's hand. I'll wait here. You can bring me the change. There's a queue at the entrance to the mall, everybody's bags being sent through a metal detector in case of bombs, then a long walk to the pharmacy at the other end. Amor has to stop twice along the way for the cramps to pass, leaning on the wall. Then she's with her sister in a queue at the pharmacy, among shelves groaning under the bounty of products to help people with their bodily functions, staunching this, alleviating that, sanitising something else, while she turns the soft packet fearfully in her hand. Astrid slips her the money, Here, you pay, it's for you, isn't it? The wait isn't long, a minute or two, but the cramps are coming regularly now, in waves. And all this time I thought I was sick about Ma. She looks down at her feet, allowing them to become the whole world, till she's at the counter and the woman in the white coat is looking sympathetically at her.

And they should really sort it out at the mall, but she can't face another public toilet today, so just keep going, keep going. Do it when we get there. Marcia and Ben live in Waterkloof, in a sprawling double-storey amid two acres of foliage. They're used to entertaining, though that's not quite the word today, and have employed their regular caterers. Marriage, funeral, whatever, people have to eat. Two long tables have been set up on the back patio and tea and coffee and some light snacks provided. All very restrained and tasteful. Marcia is something of a society hostess and knows how things should be done.

And here again, as soon as they're through the front door, Tannie Marina does her conspiratorial head-bend and speaks into Marcia's ear, and Astrid and Amor are quickly directed down a side passage. There are candles burning all over the house and even in the guest bathroom the mirrors are covered, which has the creepy effect of making you feel observed. As if Amor needs to be more self-conscious!

Okay, I'll wait outside, Astrid says. Been years since they've seen each other naked and even the thought of it is horrible.

Help me, Amor whispers.

No, no. Her little sister will never be beautiful, no, not like me, and Astrid doesn't want to watch her doing what she has to do. No way, she says. Don't be a baby, just stick it in your panty, it's a sanitary pad, even you can work it out, just look at the instructions! I'll wait for you outside.

She goes out, closing the door behind her, leaving Amor alone in the bathroom. Alone in the world. Where is Ma? She's supposed to be here, right now, at this very moment, to help. But she went away, while I was gone.

Every surface in this house is made of some expensive material, steel or marble or glass, and if a bit of wood shows here and there it's been sanded and varnished into smooth submission, and Astrid wants it, she wants the whole world to be made of fine, sculpted surfaces like these. Makes you realise how rough everything is at home, how full of sharp edges and angles. Authentic, Pa would call it, but who needs reality? This is much better. Astrid trails her fingertips over the wallpaper, feeling the raised ridges of its patterns.

A man comes down the passage and stops uncertainly nearby. Is it occupied?

Yes, my sister's inside.

He loiters, his eyes going over the shape of Astrid's body, especially her breasts and legs. He's an old guy, forty at least, and not attractive, bald with bad skin, but she can't help responding to his stare. Shifts from one hip to another, tucking a strand of hair behind her ear. Funny how you can always sense male attention, especially when it's concealed, and she thinks that this old man wants to say something to her, he has a dirty word he wants to speak aloud, and part of her wants to hear it too.

After a little while she knocks on the door. Hurry up!

He keeps on staring, not saying his word, but Amor emerges just then. She's done what she had to and can feel the alteration, like a faint pressure at the centre of her body. A strangeness within, around which the rest of her has been composed.

Are you finished? Astrid says, speaking too loudly. Is that it now? I hope there's nothing else important I have to miss because of you. She goes ahead of Amor, swinging her hips.

The lounge is jammed with people, humming like a hive of bees. Astrid plunges right in, while her younger sister stops. Better to hang back in the doorway. The threshold seems like the place to be, not here or there, not one thing or another.

Anton sees her from across the room. He's been standing there for a while, observing the gesticulant scene unfolding, like events in an aquarium. There are my relatives, near and far, come to pay respects to my mother. There is my father, who turns his head away when he sees me, and there is my little sister in the doorway, but something about her is different. He can pick it up right away.

Did you change your hair?

No.

Did you change your top?

No.

Anton looks her over again, intrigued. He knows he's right and he can see she knows he knows. She twists and turns in her discomfort, but outwardly shows calm. She has learned to do that, to keep hidden what counts.

You changed something, he says.

This is later, outside the house, while Pa has gone off to find Lexington, who's parked around the block. Astrid is also there, but she's speaking to Tannie Marina, leaving Amor and Anton alone. All the goodbyes said, the rites conducted, our mother underground.

Where did you go?

When?

At the funeral. You and Astrid. Where did you go off to?

Again the twisting and turning. Something happened. He doesn't understand, or only half, or only half wants to. Better not to know! Or to know by other means.

In any case, here comes the car at last, Lexington at the wheel, Pa glowering beside him. He leans over to press impatiently on the hooter and they fit themselves into the back seat, the two older children on either side, Amor in the middle, huddled forward over the bed of hot coals she holds inside her body, and then they are driving away in silence, the remaining Swart family, each of them tired and grieving and complicated in their own particular way, back towards the farm and the house they call home.

The house is empty at this moment. It's been deserted for a couple of hours, apparently inert but making tiny movements, sunlight stalking through those rooms, wind rattling the doors, expanding here, contracting there, giving off little pops and creaks and burps, like any old body. It seems alive, an illusion common to many buildings, or perhaps to how people see them, filled with mood and expression, windows like eyes. But nobody is here to witness it, nothing stirs, except for the dog in the driveway, leisurely licking his testicles.

Not even Salome is around, as she normally would be. You might have expected to see her at the funeral, but Tannie Marina told her in no uncertain terms that she would not be allowed to attend. Why not? Ag, don't be stupid. So Salome has gone back to her own house instead, beg your pardon, to the Lombard place, and changed into her church clothes, which she would have worn to the service, a dark dress, patched and darned, and a black shawl and her only good pair of shoes, and a handbag and hat, and like that she sits out in front of her house, sorry, the Lombard place, on a second-hand armchair from which the stuffing is bursting out, and says a prayer for Rachel.

Oh God. I hope You can hear me. It is me, Salome. Please welcome the madam where You are and look after her carefully, because I wish to see her again one day in Heaven. I have known her a long time, from before she was a madam even, from when she and I both were young women, and in these past days we were sometimes one person. I am sure You understand because it was You who gave this great suffering to her, so that I could look after her. For that she promised this house to me and for that I thank You. Amen.

Perhaps she doesn't pray in these words, or in any words at all, many prayers are uttered without language and they rise like all the rest. Or perhaps she prays for

79

other things, because prayers are secret in the end, and not all to the same god. But in any case, after some time has passed, which is certainly true, see how the shadow of the anthill has moved, for the sun is no longer at its highest point, she gets up slow and stiff from the chair and goes back inside. When she emerges again, after another unmeasured interval, she is wearing her usual clothes, her ragged dress and slipslops, a cloth tied over her hair, and she sets off along the footpath around the koppie.

It might be any day. She walks this path every morning and back again at night, and often a couple of times in between. All lights and all weathers. Hard to tell one journey from another. When she gets to the back door she leaves her slipslops outside and proceeds barefoot. Her uniform hangs in the pantry, blue dress with white doek and white apron, and she's allowed to use the bathroom for two minutes to change. Then hangs her own clothes out of sight, round the corner in the pantry.

Only now can she go further, into the deeper reaches of the house. The family has returned, or maybe they never left, they give off an air of rootedness, of being dug in.

Let's say they are sitting around the dining-room table. Or standing at different angles in the lounge. Or out on the front stoep, one party down in the driveway and the other in the more commanding position above. It doesn't matter. The following exchange takes place between Manie and his eldest child, somewhere.

I have thought about your words the other night, Pa says, and I am very angry.

At moments like these he likes to model his tone on the Old Testament god, and expects therefore to be obeyed.

Yes?

Not for my sake, but for the sake of others. That you were rude to me is nothing new. I expect it. But the way you spoke to the dominee! A holy man, a preacher.

Anton sniffs and smiles. A fool and a charlatan.

That's enough! The disrespect stops today. Listen now and hear me well. If you don't apologise to him, you are out of this family. I will never speak to you again.

For Manie has brooded upon the events of the previous evening, like a hen upon a huge black egg. You have offended my marriage and my religion, and you shall pay.

You must know, Pa, that I can never do it.

Can't help you. Between you and your conscience.

I won't say sorry to that man. For what? I only spoke the truth.

The truth? Manie is outraged afresh, even the bristles on his chin standing out like little spikes. About my wife? About promises I didn't make? Choose your side, it's up to you. But if you do not humble yourself, you are out in the wilderness.

Only when their father has gone, making a loud and righteous exit, does his younger daughter show herself, emerging from behind a pot plant like a character in a farce. Anton, Anton. I heard what he said.

What is it, Amor?

He speaks irritably, for she is spoiling what might otherwise be a high, clear moment for him. To be cast out from the family, to be free of all this!

I heard what Pa said to you, and it isn't right.

What isn't right?

He did promise. I heard him. He promised Ma he would give Salome her house.

Her little face is lit from within by its sureness.

Amor, he says gently.

What?

Salome can't own the house. Even if Pa wanted to, he can't give it to her.

Why not? she says, puzzled.

Because, he says. It's against the law.

The law? Why?

You are not serious. But then he looks at her and sees how serious she is. Oh, dear me, he says. Do you have no idea what country you're living in?

No, she doesn't. Amor is thirteen years old, history has not yet trod on her. She has no idea what country she's living in. She has seen black people running away from the police because they're not carrying their pass-books and heard adults talking in urgent, low voices about riots in the townships and only last week at school they had to learn a drill about hiding under tables in case of attack, and still she doesn't know what country she's living in. There's a State of Emergency and people are being arrested and detained without trial and there are rumours flying around but no solid facts because there is a blackout on news and only happy, unreal stories are being reported, but she mostly believes these stories. She saw her brother's head bleeding yesterday from a rock, but still, even now, she doesn't yet know who threw the rock or why. Blame it on the lightning. She's always been a slow child.

One thing, though, perturbs her.

But why? she says. Why did you tell Pa to give Salome her house if you knew he couldn't?

He shrugs. Because, he says. I felt like it.

And it's exactly then, in the tiniest way, without even knowing it herself, that she begins to understand what country she's living in.

The next day she's dispatched, with her suitcase, back to the hostel. Just for a few months more, Pa tells her when she tries to protest. Till things settle down. She knows better than to argue, she can hear from his voice that it's useless. Even though he promised, and a Christian never goes back on his word, her needs are minor, she doesn't matter. So Lexington drives her to the school and drops her by the fishpond, and she must slowly ascend the narrow stairs to the dormitory, with its cold linoleum floors, the beds in their regulated rows, identical, and hers in the corner, unchanged.

Her brother leaves the next morning, or is it the morning after that, the early hours are all alike in the springtime. He carries his military bag and his rifle and he wears his uniform, ironed for him by Salome, though he's polished the boots himself. Nobody there to see him off. Astrid is asleep and Pa has already gone to the reptile park to work. Lexington brings the Triumph to the front steps and Anton loads his bag into the boot. Keeps his rifle with him, for the look of it, just in case.

Goodbye, house. Goodbye, Pa, though you will not answer. Dawn is welling up like a wound as they jounce down the track. Anton gets out to open and close the gate and then they head off, away from the city, on lonely roads.

There's a spot, a military pickup point near Johannesburg, from where he can make his way. Two other troepies there already, waiting for a ride. He unloads his bag from the boot and leans in at the passenger window. Cheers, Lex, go in triumph. Goodbye, Anton. See you next time.

Close to noon, he approaches the military camp where he's stationed. His last lift has set him down half a kilometre away and he has to walk a long suburban street towards the front gates. Through a tall fence topped with barbed wire he can see the shapes of tents and prefabricated bungalows, rows and rows of them, other young men like himself moving between them, washing clothes, smoking cigarettes, talking.

One of these figures detaches himself, comes over to the fence. Hey, he calls. You!

Takes Anton a second to remember. Late at night, shadows on the tar. Payne! I told you we'd meet again.

Where've you been?

Home, for my mother's funeral.

Still joking about that?

For Payne has thought about that bizarre encounter a few nights ago, when he was on guard duty, and decided that his visitor wasn't serious. Seen by the light of day, with a fence between them, he's a very ordinary young man, possibly insignificant. Certainly no one to fear.

Anton holds on to the fence with one hand, squinting down its length towards the front gate and the two sentries he can make out there. It has become plain to him in this very moment that he cannot go back in through that gate again, cannot rejoin the scene inside. Cannot do it. And cannot say why. Something has happened, that's all he could tell you, if he were asked. Something has happened to me.

You are witness to a significant moment, he tells Payne.

Huh?

You are watching my life jump from one track to another. You are seeing a huge change happen.

What's that?

The Big No. It's taken a long time to get here, but I've had enough. I'm refusing at last.

Refusing what?

All of it. I'm saying, this far, no further. No, no, no! He thinks about it and adds, You could come with me, of course.

Come with you where? I don't even know you.

That would soon change.

You're crazy, Payne says, laughing. What a joker this guy is. First he kills his mother, then he's going AWOL at the moment he comes back to camp! Ho ho ho! He knows for sure Swart will keep walking towards the gate like everyone else and they'll bump into each other later, probably in the mess.

But that isn't what he does.

Hey! Where are you going?

Back in the direction he came from, apparently. Payne has to jog along the fence to keep up.

You're a joker, he says. They'll catch you. They'll put you in detention barracks! Hey! What's going on? This isn't funny. Are you all right? Wait. Don't do this. Don't you know there's a war on? Don't you care about your country?

Anton doesn't answer because he doesn't hear. He is pushed from behind, as if with a giant hand, by one simple, blind desire, to get away.

In this endeavour, the uniform is both a danger and a great help. Picking up a ride is easy if you're in the army, but you're also a target for the military police, who'll want to check your papers. Best to make a change soon, and a few hours later, at an all-night shop next to a highway heading south, he buys a cap to cover his head. Sunny South Africa, it says on the front. Looks stupid on him, but it definitely covers the hair and some of the stitches on his forehead. In the bathroom of a Wimpy next door, he changes into civilian clothes, jeans and a T-shirt and jersey and casual shoes. Looking at himself in the mirror, he thinks he's passable, a young man on his way somewhere.

Sunny South Africa. He has some such idea in his mind. Throbbing in his thoughts from the moment he walked away from the camp this morning is an image of a pristine white beach, cows standing around on the sand, chewing and lowing. In the background, misty cliffs rise out of a thick green carpet of trees. Not a part of the world he's ever been to, but he heard some older boys at school talking about the Transkei once, about living rough in the jungle and catching fish and surfing and smoking ganja, and he has the notion that he might do that for a while. He has almost no money and no plan and he doesn't know a soul, but all of that is part of what pulls him and he believes it's the sort of place you could disappear in if you were so minded.

First, Anton, you have to get there! By now it's late, close to midnight, not so many cars on the road. Away from the street lights the darkness bulges in, crammed with emptiness and threat. Behind the garage next door is a muddy field, a ditch full of weeds running along the edge. He throws his rifle into the ditch, followed by the bag with his military clothes inside it. He's kept only a few of his own shirts and pants, what he had with him, stowed in a plastic bag. What I've just done is a crime, he thinks, and yet it felt so weightless.

He chokes down a momentary dread, feeling how very big the world is, and trudges to a likely spot near the off-ramp to the highway. Showing himself in the fluorescent glare, one hopeful thumb outstretched. Got to have some faith! It might take a while but sooner or later, if you just keep trying, someone will stop for you.

PA

HE'S JUST COME OUT OF the shower when the phone rings. It's not his apartment and the call is probably not for him and there are a few people he's actively trying to avoid, but he goes ahead and answers anyway. A feeling he has inside, like an outline of something.

Astrid on the line. He can hear it's her, though only bits of words are coming through. Probably on that new mobile phone of hers, so proud of it, useless heavy brick with buttons. Not an invention that's going to last. I can't make out what you're saying, he tells her. Drying himself in the lounge as he speaks. Can't you call on the landline?

Hisses and squeaks. He puts the receiver down in irritation. She's one of only two or three people who have his number, but she makes excessive use of it. Astrid has taken upon herself the silences of the family, she has made herself the messenger and bringer of news between them. It's a role she needs and resents, and for which she's needed and resented in return.

Anton dresses quickly while he waits. It's the middle of the day and the Johannesburg sky is flawless, though the air has a midwinter bite. He's pulling a jersey over his head when the phone rings again. Still no complete words coming through, but this time it occurs to him that she isn't actually speaking. He can hear her making a strange sound. Like a whimpering, almost.

91

Hello? he says. What's wrong?, just as a cloud covers the sun, and in the shadow that follows he has an intuition, like a funnel down which he can see a bright, tiny picture of the future. One of those moments, hard to explain, when time seems to move in the wrong direction.

When she does talk at last he listens intently as she tells him what he already knows, not only the facts of it, their father/this morning/poisoned/in that glass cage, but her fear too, he hears as clearly as if she's describing it Astrid's unhinged terror that what happened to him will happen to her too. As if fate is infectious.

You don't think of it enough, he says, when she finally goes silent.

What?

That's why you're so scared. To come to terms with something you're afraid of, you have to imagine it enough.

What am I afraid of?

Death.

But he isn't dead, she says, starting to make that whimpering sound again.

Not yet. This too is part of the picture he saw, a tiny window on the future. But for now all they know for sure is what she's told him, that Pa is unconscious in the ICU at the H. F. Verwoerd Hospital in Pretoria.

I'm going over there right now with Dean, Astrid says.

Right.

And then a silence falls, with a question underneath it.

I don't know, Anton says at last. Speaking perhaps to himself, though she hears it differently.

It's time, she tells him.

I don't know. I have to think.

92

Anton. It's time.

I'll decide that, he says, angry but almost unable to get the words out. His voice is pale, a ghost voice. I don't know if I can.

Just come and see him. He's unconscious, so you don't even have to speak.

It's been nearly ten years, Astrid.

Exactly! It's enough. Oh, whatever, do what you like, you always do in any case.

Ten years, almost, of estrangement, in which he's been through some terrible things, far away on the outer margins. And is this how it concludes, by rushing through to the bedside of his snake-bitten father, to ponder where it all went wrong? And what's the point? To demonstrate blood loyalty? I do not love him. He does not love me.

He's upset Astrid, he can hear, but she'll be all over him otherwise, like a crowd of hands. Neediness and anxiety don't know any boundaries, and Anton likes his boundaries. Have you spoken to Amor? he says, to change the subject.

I left a message for her. If she's still at that number. I haven't heard from her in ages.

Did you also tell her it's time? Did you order her to come home?

I never ordered you, Astrid says. And it's different with you and Pa, obviously. You know it is.

When the call ends, he goes on standing there for a long moment, staring at a crack in the windowsill from which a line of ants relentlessly emerges. How many of them? More than you can count. Any meaning only in the multiplicity of dots. Why is that comforting?

Astrid is right, it's time. He's always known the moment would come, one way or another, but pictured it happening differently. Didn't think salvation would be so ambiguous and so unsure. Maybe it can't be otherwise. Every day since he left home has been imprinted on him as a visceral, primal endeavour and he doesn't dwell on any of it, nothing to be savoured there. Survival isn't instructive, just demeaning. The things he does recall with any clarity he tries not to, pushing them under the surface. Part of what you do to keep going.

You keep going because if you do there will eventually be an end. South Africa has changed, conscription stopped two years ago. Jesus, what he did by deserting the army, he's a hero, not a criminal, amazing how fast that changed. Except that nobody much cares, one way or the other. It's history already. You're just one more ragged figure who went on the run for a few years, hiding out in the wilds of Transkei and then in Johannesburg, hard to know which jungle was worse. But when it comes to survival you do what you gotta do. Even at the expense of, you know, your dignity. Ha, please, Anton, dignity was the first to go, you dropped it like a dirty rag at the side of the road, and that was only the first station of debasement, much worse followed on. Images of dirty acts in filthy rooms, pains to hurt the soul as well as the body, performed without hesitation, all just to keep on breathing another day while doing nothing, absolutely nothing, with the finest years of your youthful life ... So what, who gives a shit? Others have suffered way, way more than you have, though that's somehow true of every experience. In the end, all you can say is that you got through this far, far enough for things to change and become easier, no need to hide any more. Holding on, holding out, an old South African solution.

He paces the apartment restlessly for hours, looking out through bare branches at the Yeoville streets down below, opening cupboards and closing them again. He appears to be searching for something, but isn't, really. He's already made up his mind and now he's just going through a kind of inventory, a summing up. None of this belongs to him, bar a few items of clothing and some books. All the rest is the property of a woman, quite a bit older than him, with/off whom he's lived in these few rooms for many days. Too many days, as both of them have known for a while.

He writes a note to her and leaves it on the kitchen table. Dearest / In an effort to challenge the Holy Ghost to a bout of Russian roulette, as well as an ill-fated ambition to break a Guinness world record for living among poisonous serpents, my fool of a father has landed himself in a coma. I rather fear the worst. As you know, he and I haven't spoken since my mother's funeral, but I've decided it's time to go, well, home. I may be a while. / I'm sorry about this and a lot of other things besides. Including another request, the very last, I hope, for money. I know I said, but you'll appreciate the circumstances, etc. Though I truly am desperate and this turn of events means that I may very soon be able to pay back everything I owe you. My acc details as always. / In the face of most of the evidence, I do still love you, A.

He has to call around and ask a few people before he finds somebody who'll drive him through. Leaned too hard on almost everyone he knows, they're all wary and weary of him, he can hear it in their voices. Even the guy who does agree to run him has a reason to do it, which he brings up almost as soon as they're on the highway out of Joburg. Don't like to mention it at a time like this, but I'm under serious pressure right now. So whenever you can, I'd very much appreciate . . .

I understand, Anton tells him. I'm going to repay everybody I owe, but I swear that you're the very first in line.

He's made the same promise to a couple of other people in recent months and always meant it fervently, but he especially means it today because this really is a turning point and he can feel it. He made a terrible mistake when he exiled himself. Return is the only solution. Not if, but when. And already, as he draws closer to the source, he can sense his future swelling with promise, like a melon ripening under his hand.

The world glows as a result. It's the first time he's driving this road to Pretoria since his mother's death. Nine years ago! And see how much has changed, how the brown veld is bursting forth with bounty, new developments all along the edge of the highway, offices and factories and town houses, economy in full flow, the blood of the land pumping again. A new, democratic government in the Union Buildings! He can see those venerable sandstone facades against the ridge as they come into town, lit in the distance by mild wintry sun. Wonder if Mandela is in there right now, at his desk. From a cell to a throne, never thought I'd see in my lifetime. Weird how quickly it's come to seem ordinary. When before, Jesus Christ.

He's dropped outside the main entrance to the hospital and has to find his way like a little germ through miles of intestinal passages. What an image, but in its way appropriate, given the setting. Always such sad, wrecked people sitting around in hospitals, and those are just the visitors. The patients are much further gone, obviously. The only reason to come in here is because you or somebody close to you is sick or hurt. No cheer in these confines.

The ICU is the worst of all, in a zone of greeny undersea gloom, no windows anywhere in sight. The same mournful army of worriers outside, though here, of course, there's more to worry about. He spots Astrid at the same time she sees him, her wide face widening further with surprise.

I'm so glad you came, she whispers into his ear as she hugs him, squeezing too tight and leaving behind a sickly phantom of perfume. He's seen Astrid a few times over the years, she's helped him with money and been his one link with the family, but he's amazed all over again at how she's transformed into a thickened version of her adolescent self, never got her body back after the pregnancy and now she's a globular echo of her husband, round little Dean, who bobs closer, one short-fingered hand extended. Howzit, Anton, good to see you.

Look at this, Oom Ockie exclaims. Jirre hey. My goodness.

His tone is jocular and astonished, at how much his nephew has changed. But he himself has become an emphysemic husk of what he used to be. And all of them are different, of course they are, time has played its tune on all our faces.

97

Of everybody Tannie Marina is the least transformed, a little weaker, perhaps, and somewhat less certain in her convictions. Where he's concerned, Anton knows she's taken his father's side in the rift, no surprise in that, but you can tell right away that she's got no stomach for a fight today. Her little baby brother, felled in his prime, the trailing vulnerable afterthought in the family, who should outlast them all! She's been weeping and her warpaint has run. He pecks her on the cheek and gets a whiff of cold cream and salt.

Then they're standing there with not much to add, and the big scene is over. His arrival merely a minor sensation in the end, the prodigal returning, a drama everybody has seen before. Boredom sets in quickly. You come back after long vanishment and the surface closes as if you were never gone. Family quicksand.

Anton hasn't quite focused yet on the figure of his father, so close to hand. How is he doing, actually?

Not so well, Dean murmurs. He stopped breathing for a while last night.

But he's stable now!

It got him in an artery, Dean says. Unfortunately. That's what Dr Raaff told us. And he's had some kind of allergic reaction ...

I don't blame the snake, Marina says firmly. It's the dominee that killed my brother.

But he isn't dead, Astrid cries, shivering. Why does everyone keep saying he is?

Can I see him?

Visitors are only allowed in four at a time for ten minutes, once in the morning and once at night. But there is a nurse in charge of the ward, a shaven-headed no-nonsense type, who takes a sort of formal pity on him.

You're the son? she says, sounding angry. You can slip in for a minute.

He takes this as a bad sign, time might be short, but follows her as instructed, wearing a surgical mask and gloves, into the sepulchral, humming grotto of the inner chamber. A sense of quiet industry, centred on the afflicted bodies lying in their beds. Pa is in the far corner, all sorts of tubes running into him, though they give the impression of running the other way, out, sucking the vitality from inside him to power some different system. He looks like something crumpled, shucked-off, under the green sheets. Not just skin, but close to it. More battered than I remember.

Hello, Pa. It's me. It's Anton.

Does he say it aloud? He's knocked, anyway, by an unexpected backwash of emotion. Something in me cares, he's astonished to discover. Yes, something in me really gives a fuck.

I'll just leave you for a minute, the hard-looking nurse says.

She twitches the curtains around him, but not enough to block out the whole ward. Anton can see a black man in the next bed, bandaged up like a mummy. Verwoerd must be spinning in his grave, can't believe they haven't changed the name of the hospital yet. The man groans aloud from inside his wrappings, not quite a word, unless it's in a foreign language, the language of pain. Apartheid has fallen, see, we die right next to each other now, in intimate proximity. It's just the living part we still have to work out.

Hello, Pa, he says again.

Then sits there, waiting. For what? No answer will ever come. It's me who has to do something. But the thing he has to do, the thing I came here for, I don't know what that thing is.

Listen, he says to his father. They've left us alone together because I'm supposed to say something to you. I'm supposed to say I'm sorry. But you will never get those words from me. Do you hear?

(I do not hear.)

I was crazy when Ma died. For a while I actually believed I killed her. Things were not good with my mind. But I meant everything I said. You were an alcoholic shit to my mother before you found religion and after that you were a sober kind of shit. You owed her, but even after she died you thought it was the other way around. You got it wrong with her, and you got it wrong with me, and I will never say sorry to you. Do you hear me?

No, he doesn't hear. Nothing will reach Manie again. Although he lies at the middle of the scene, none of it exists for him, not the hospital, the bed, the curtain, his son, and certainly not the words that are being spoken to him, they are not where he is. Though where he is is harder to describe.

Picture a tunnel underground where no light has ever shone. Something like that, a crack in the bedrock of himself, is where Pa has retreated. The passion, no, the poison in his blood has driven him down there. And will drive him further still. Riding the fumes of evil, toxic dreams. Accompanied by the last flicker, the last ember, of a voice. Saying what? Saying nothing. I am, I was, nonsense like that. Occasionally a crude form surges past, half recognised, gone. My life. That time. Shadows of shadows. Down to the grainy truth of things. And in.

Herman Albertus Swart dies at 3.22 in the morning on 16 June 1995 and the waiting room is empty. His family have all gone home to their various beds, where they snore and fart and mumble and toss their way towards dawn. The only person present when he goes is a Muslim nurse named Waheeda who secretly recites a verse from the Koran over him, Inna lillahi wa inna ilayhi raji'un, but whether this intervention has any effect on his soul is impossible to say.

The news is passed on to Astrid an hour later. She wakes out of deep slumber to her Nokia ringing, a sound she's not used to yet, only had the damn thing a couple of weeks, doesn't know how all the buttons work, and it takes a long blundery minute to put the light on and find her way to answering. By then she knows what's coming, why else would they be calling at this hour, and all she can do is protest, as if that will change the outcome. No, it isn't true! But it is true, it always will be now.

Her husband gives her a hug, he's pretty sure that's the required gesture at this point. Astrid looks pale and weak, so he decides that a cup of tea with sugar might be the correct next step, and shuffles off to the kitchen in his long johns to make it, failing to see that his wife finds herself in the middle of a storm.

Yes, at this moment, Astrid is being carried by a high, horrible wind, all force with no form, which has plucked her loose from solid objects. How she clutches and cries out as she flies! Till she finds herself blown against a door, at the end of a passage, and knocks on it as hard as she can, though she has no power.

Hello?

Her brother's voice, quiet and calm. As if he's been waiting for her to come.

She can almost not get the knob to turn, so small is her strength. Anton is sitting up in bed, the lamp on, a notebook in his lap. He watches her try to speak and fail.

It's happened, he says.

She nods wildly, then throws herself across the bed, convulsively gathering handfuls of the coverlet. Finally manages to talk, though the wrong words come out. We are all orphans now!

He regards her equably, his mind elsewhere. When?

When? I don't know. The hospital just called. We should have been with him! Why did they send us home?

What difference would it make?

What difference? How can you ask that?

Not the first time her brother has amazed her. It's like looking at him through the wrong end of a telescope. Though from his point of view, she is suddenly in very clear focus. I was with him only yesterday, Astrid is thinking, he was alive and breathing, how is it possible that he's neither of those things now? But Anton can see once more inside his sister, cold and clear as the clapper of a bell, that it's her own death she's feeling. If it can happen to our father, it can happen to me. This nothing, this state of Not. She mourns herself in terror.

Her husband discovers them like this when he wanders down the passage with a tray of tea, his distraught wife stretched out over her brother's feet in the spare bedroom. While Anton, who is in Dean's opinion a deeply odd person, has chosen this moment to jot something in a notebook.

(...)

He requested to come and sleep over last night with Astrid and Dean in their shabby little house in Arcadia, rather than go back home. Didn't feel ready for the return, but it also seemed preferable to being at the farm with Tannie Marina and Oom Ockie, who are staying there in Pa's absence. But he's experiencing now, at this very moment, a pull towards some undefined centre, while everyone is dazed.

It's all right, he murmurs soothingly to Astrid, stroking her hair with a distracted hand. If he could have chosen an exit, it would be this.

What, bitten by a cobra? And what for? He didn't even get close to breaking the record. He was only on day six!

His sister, it's obvious, is inconsolable, or determined not to be consoled. Which reminds him, there is still another sister to be informed.

Did you ever get hold of Amor?

She never called back. And I didn't try again, there was no more news to give! Someone will have to tell her now.

I'll do it, he says. Give me her number. A way of extricating himself from this weepy scene, though he detects in himself a genuine, therefore interesting, need to pass these tidings to his youngest sister. Make a note of it in the journal, to be pondered later. Meanwhile, get out of here. By now the whole household is awake. The twins, Neil and Jessica, seven years old, have picked up their mother's distress and are both wailing disconsolately, while Dean hovers helplessly, urging everyone to calm themselves. Anton withdraws to the phone in the study, where it's quieter. Freezing in here, the middle of winter and the coldest hour too, just before dawn. Very early as well. Even earlier in London, a whole two hours. But it's in the nature of news, especially bad news, that it wants to be passed on, it desires transmission, like a virus.

Three rings, before a sleepy male voice answers, very English, clean and clipped. He tells it who he's looking for.

I'm afraid Amor doesn't live here any more. She moved out a month ago.

Do you know where I can find her? It's urgent.

Who's speaking, please? the voice says, turning chilly and sharp as the speaker wakes up. Do you have any idea what the time is?

This is her brother, Anton. I'm sorry to disturb you, but it's important.

She never mentioned she has a brother.

That's interesting. But it doesn't change the fact I am her brother.

Well, Anton, if she gets in touch I'll let her know you rang. If you're really her brother, I'm sure she'll call you.

He takes a breath. Please pass on that our father has been killed by a snake. A long silence follows, static on the line. Hello? Are you still there?

Is this a joke?

In the sense you mean it, I'm afraid not.

Well, I'm sorry, the voice says, softening its tone.

Why? You've never met my father. Please just tell Amor she needs to call home.

She calls the farm a few hours later, but there is nobody around to pick up. The phone rings and continues to ring. A lonely sound, made more lonely by the way it repeats identically, over and over, with no solution in sight. At one end the ringing, at the other end Amor. She has caused it to happen, from far away.

After a minute she gives up. Sits there for a little while, then tries again. She knows by now there will be no response, but she's after something else. She hears the tinny beep against her ear and it almost physically conjures for her the empty rooms and passages down which it carries. That corner. That ornament. That sill. She closes her eyes, listening. A commotion of longing and revulsion inside. How did it become so complicated? Home used to mean only one Thing, not a blizzard of things at war.

It's the first time that Amor has thought about the farm in a while. She has learned, or perhaps has always known, that if you want to move forward it's best not to look back. All she's done since leaving South Africa is keep moving forward, or at least keep moving, not always sure of the direction, changing rooms and cities and countries and people, all of it smearing past like a landscape at speed, something in me unable to stop.

Though she has, apparently, stopped. There she is, quite stationary, if you discount the sobbing, in an armchair. Near a window looking out on a foreign street, in the wrong hemisphere. All of it feels suddenly very still and fixed to her, and somehow upside down. What am I doing here? she thinks, though perhaps not in words. Not a girl any more, a woman, the shape of her body transformed. Only a few features still recognisably the same, including the burn marks on her feet, faded but still visible, and which for some reason are hurting now, an old signal from the past.

105

That same night, she's on a plane back to South Africa. Return feels like a condition more than an act, one for which she's in no way prepared. The suddenness of it, every last little piece of it, is like a great white concussion, a sort of impact. Inevitable, but also unbearable. She can't sleep on the flight and finds herself pacing in a galley area at 3 a.m., ten kilometres in the air above Chad. How ordinary and how strange human life is. And how delicately poised. Your own end might lie just in front of you, under your feet. This plane breaking up into a million flaming pieces, one moment from now.

Doesn't happen. A few hours later she is in the back of a taxi, being driven to the farm. She has negotiated a special fare with the driver, Alphonse, a middle-aged man who has recently come here from the Congo in search of a better life. He shouldn't have taken this route, he doesn't know the city well and gets tangled in the streets in the centre of town, for which he keeps apologising in French, but she doesn't mind, the delay is a relief, she likes the feeling of being between two places, recently departed and not yet arrived.

The view from the taxi window is a bit amazing. She doesn't consciously know it but there is a somewhat festive air outside, because yesterday was a public holiday, Youth Day, nineteen years since the Soweto uprising, and today it's the Rugby World Cup semifinals, South Africa is playing France later, and the pavements throb and throng with bodies. Never did the middle of town look like this, so many black people drifting casually about, as if they belong here. It's almost like an African city!

But then you come to the road leading out to the farm and when the buildings fall away the old earth shows itself beneath its petticoats, bleached and bare. The day itself has a bony sheen to it, light pouring down from a hard, bright sky. All this you know of old, but when you're past the township and at the spot where the farm begins, your eye goes straight to the tip of the spire on the big, ugly church building. Still seems like a shock and an intrusion, even though it was already built before she left. The First Assembly of the Revelation on the Highveld, though what exactly was revealed to Alwyn Simmers has never been made apparent to anybody else. Nevertheless, there's a sizeable crowd outside the church and the sound of hymns is painted on the air.

She's alert now to the possibility of change, but nothing else seems different. Not the gate, the gravel road or the top of the koppie, marked by its black, contorted tree, which instantly pulls your eyes. Now that's a spot you have returned to, in thought and dream, while you were gone.

Something familiar, too, in the knot of cars around the house, an unsettling throwback to a moment she can't place at first. Then she can. Ma, dead, that day nine years ago. How much has changed since. My body, my country, my mind. I ran from all of you as hard and as far as I could, but the past has its little claws, it has dragged me back.

Stop here, she says. At the bottom of the drive. She pays Alphonse and uses the trees as cover to slip round the side of the house and in through the back door, to avoid having to talk to anyone. But in the kitchen she meets her brother. Both of them stop dead still.

Why, I do declare, he says at last in a bad Southern accent. It's Missy Amor.

Anton.

A lot happens in the silence that follows.

Honestly, I almost didn't recognise you.

Well, you look the same.

Not quite true. He's always been lean, but he seems to have been whittled down further, towards some essential core. And his hairline has receded a little, making the old scar on his forehead more noticeable. But in other ways the outside form is what it was, though the content might have changed.

This is the moment when they're supposed to embrace, but neither acts and the moment passes.

Welcome home, he says. Of course the circumstances could be better.

Yes, she says. I suppose they could.

It's a fact of life, in Anton's opinion, that the circumstances could always be better, but he's full of unnatural fury right now. He's only recently arrived, an hour ago, and hasn't yet got over the corner of the farm given to Alwyn Simmers' spiritual/capitalist project, something Astrid mentioned but he failed to take seriously. The sight of that horrible church, squatting there like a, like a, well, comparisons can't convey it, but he's been greatly troubled. And then he's got to the house to discover that his father has been using his room for storage, every available surface piled with junk. At this moment he's holding in his hands a cardboard box filled with paraphernalia from the reptile park, books and pictures and flyers and an old stuffed lizard with glass eyes. He gestures to it with his chin.

Trying to clear out my bedroom, he says.

Hard not to assume it's deliberate, there's lots of other space, after all, but Pa wanted to bury me. Piece by piece, Anton has been uncovering himself, carrying each box/object down to the garage and dumping it there. The familiar furniture emerging gradually, bed and desk and chair, the topography of childhood. Long way to go still.

What about my room? Amor asks. Is that also full?

Yours? No, no. As you left it.

He knows because, naturally, he's been to check.

Okay, she says. I'll go and settle myself.

But doesn't, not quite. Both of them hovering.

Are you here to stay?

I don't know, she says. I've only just arrived.

Well, you left behind a broken heart in London. Wouldn't believe you have a brother.

Oh, she says, feeling her cheeks heat up. Sorry about that. Who is he?

Nobody. (James.) Just a person I know.

Ah, first love. Always so touching. Stay silent then, international woman of mystery. Need help taking your rucksack upstairs?

I've carried it around the world. I think I can manage.

He watches her climb up to the second floor, a twitchy smile twisting his lips. Well, well. Turn your back for a few years and the sphinx becomes a minx. Astonishing transformation. My little misfit of a sister was always somebody else, apparently.

For her part, and though she keeps her face empty, Amor feels all churned up inside, in a few stray seconds. Big brother always had the knack. She proceeds down the passage, past door after door, to her room. Where everything has stayed the same, as far as she can tell, though a thin pelt of dust has settled on every surface. Nobody has cleaned in here for a while. She lowers her rucksack to the floor and stands, looking around. In no hurry to unpack, not yet. No need to rush the moment of touchdown. Let the illusion linger that you're still in motion, still without a home.

Though soon, of course, you have to go downstairs. A moment she dreads, but a shower and fresh clothes will help. When she catches sight of herself in the bathroom mirror it's with a sense of wonderment that those features could ever belong to her. She's been told a few times recently that she's beautiful, but doesn't believe it. She remembers too well a podgy girl with greasy skin, who answered to her name. But that girl has yielded up another somebody, who doesn't feel like me, but is. At least, I live in her.

She's always misjudging her looks and choosing the wrong clothes or haircut or necklace or perfume. Her solution is to keep things simple. What comes most naturally is to go without make-up or jewellery or the expected female flourishes, presenting herself just as she is. There are times when nakedness feels like the most truthful solution, though you can't go forth in that state, unfortunately. Some covering is always necessary. When she's showered and dried off, she puts on a blue cotton dress. She would like to wear sandals, but doesn't want to display her damaged feet, the missing toe especially, so chooses a pair of closed shoes from her cupboard instead. Her hair is long and she prefers to tie it back, out of the way. The overall effect, to her eyes, is one of plainness and bareness, not displeasing.

Nevertheless, she can sense her appearance registering almost physically among the small crowd in the lounge as she walks in, like a ripple in a pond. Ooh, my word. How she's changed! Can you believe it? There is a contraction, an indrawing, in her vicinity, in which no one is more excited, or more alarmed, than the women related to her.

My golly, but look at how much weight you've lost! Tannie Marina breaks momentarily from her despondency to give her a squeeze, sneakily testing how much flesh she's lost. We'll have to fatten you up! Have a chicken pie.

I don't eat meat, Amor reminds her.

Still not? Oh, I thought you'd grown out of that …

Marina resents afresh that her niece, for no good reason, turned vegetarian all those years ago, to the consternation of the adults. Ever since that terrible braai! It seems to her in some vague way like a communist sentiment, part of the general unease in the family around the time that Rachel died, which now appears to have infected the whole country.

Animals don't feel pain, she explains. Not like we do.

She could go on, but at this moment her other niece, who has been circling like a satellite, suddenly falls to earth.

Amor, Astrid says, almost inaudibly. My God!

It's hardest of all for Astrid, and her face, even under its make-up, shows signs of internal struggle. How did it turn out like this? She can't be my sister, this is an impostor, except.

I can't believe, she says. And just look. Your hair. Your skin.

111

They embrace, holding each other with their fingertips, pointing with their mouths rather than kissing outright. But still, Astrid can't keep herself from touching, and might actually wail, if the twins didn't rescue her by starting to fight and howl in her stead, allowing her to seize them each by an arm and drag them bodily into a less populated part of the house, where she does break down weeping after all. Dean has followed her and she thrusts the two children into his arms, like a double accusation. Here, she cries, you must be good for something, and rushes off to lock herself in the bathroom.

Astrid on her knees over the toilet. She hardly needs her finger to make it happen today. Horrible, unnatural, never get used to it no matter how many times, and it's not even working any more, putting on weight all the time, can't stop it, and her teeth are a mess because of all the gastric juices, have to stop doing this, have to, have to, but at this second it's a fitting punishment for eating all that milk tart, why didn't you stop yourself, and for looking so bad next to Amor, my God how does she turn out that way, used to be porky, never what you'd call sexy, but something happened while she was gone.

Amor slips out of the lounge, away from the crowd. She has greeted everyone, but the required small talk is beyond her. Not her strength. Better to retreat to the kitchen, in search of somebody you truly missed.

Salome. / Amor.

They hug easily, without effort. Warm hands, strong hold. Soft rocking. Release.

How are you?

I don't know. The first honest reply to this question today.

Ag, shame, Salome says.

She is noticeably older, the lines in her skin more deeply scored, especially around her mouth and eyes. An expression of disappointment has started to harden on Salome's face, like the calluses that thicken the soles of her feet. She still wears no shoes. In this house, she never will wear shoes.

I'm sorry, she says, and it doesn't have to be explained what she means. Though she isn't mourning Manie exactly. He didn't always treat her with respect and not once in the time since Mrs Rachel died has he brought up the matter of her house, though maybe that will be different now.

(Will you help me?)

It isn't spoken aloud, but Amor hears it as if it is. The question of the Lombard place and her mother's last wish and her father's promise, really several questions although they feel like only one, has followed her around the world, bothering her at particular moments like a stranger importuning her in the street, plucking at her sleeve, crying out, Attend to me! And she knows she must, one day she will have to answer, but why should one day be today?

We'll speak more, she says to Salome.

She's somewhat distracted, there's a commotion in the lounge, some raised voices, she hurries through. Despite the sombreness of the occasion, the TV has been switched on in the corner, the volume turned low, and there's a noticeable edging in that direction. It's all very tense because for a while it looked like they'd actually have to cancel the match, the rain is that bad in Durban, and if we don't play today we're out of the World Cup. Still

113

storming away, the lightning sizzling over Kings Park Stadium, but the game is happening at last, two teams bashing and grinding gladiatorially at each other in the glutinous, apocalyptic mud.

The mood is feverish and patriotic, the whole country is behind the Springboks, even though most of the players are white. There's a huge crowd watching, despite the pouring rain, a lot of black faces among them. It's hard not to feel caught up in a big, roary oneness, all of us united, a year into democracy! Even Ockie has a warm glow, only partly due to Klipdrift, and God knows he took the new South Africa hard. But he has to admit, it's nice to be able to play international sport again. Gives us the chance to donner people from faraway lands and, man, we really fucked up those Samoan floppies a couple of weeks ago.

But Tannie Marina doesn't approve. Who switched that on? Is that now really necessary?

Ockie sighs. The universe is somehow always set at an angle to his wants, but this is not the moment for resistance. He turns off the television.

It's true that Manie has died at a very inconvenient time. If we get through this knockout round we'll be in the final, one week from today. It suddenly occurs to Astrid, who seems by default to have taken over the planning of the funeral, that the date really matters. It can't clash with the match! There'll be a serious drop in attendance.

There's a thought, Anton says. We could save on catering costs.

Her spasm of grief dispensed with, Astrid has returned to full strength and composure, but she doesn't have the strength right now to be shocked by her brother. Give him a taboo and he feels the need to break it. Always been like that, as long as there's an audience. So irritated by him today. He's been playing to a small gallery in the corner of the lounge for the past quarter-hour, on a theme he returns to now, namely the culpability of Alwyn Simmers in the death of his father. So culpable you could almost call it murder.

Ooh now, Dean says uneasily. Murder is a big word. Dean is an accountant and he does the books for the reptile park and the precise facts do matter, in his opinion. Manie was bitten by a snake. It was an accident.

More than one snake in this story, Tannie Marina murmurs.

He agreed to it. He signed the contract, and all possible precautions were taken …

I can confirm that, says Bruce Geldenhuys, Manie's business partner. He's an older man with a handlebar moustache and a sorrowful expression, very earnest and softly spoken. He has come out to the farm today specially to have this conversation, to make sure they're all thinking the same way. Last thing Scaly City needs, a lawsuit by the family. We had the right anti-venoms, everything was done by the book. He had a bad reaction, it couldn't be helped.

A bad reaction to a cobra bite, Anton says. Not so unpredictable, is it? What was my father doing in that glass cage anyway? Testing his faith in public, and failing, obviously, but what for? To raise funds for the church! Trying to break the world record for dwelling among serpents! Sponsor our true believer while he wrestles with Satan in a nest of vipers! Just like Daniel in the

115

lions' den! A cracked, crazy notion, all of it, a greedy, stupid stunt in support of a sham ministry. My father would never have thought of it himself.

Not wrong there, Bruce says, catching the general drift of things. No problem blaming the dominee, if that's what they want to do. Come to think of it, they actually have a point, poor old Manie was manipulated ...

Well, Dean says uneasily, it was still his choice, wasn't it?

You'd better get over it, Astrid says. She's talking to Anton, because she can see there's something he doesn't know. It's legally arranged that Alwyn Simmers does the funeral.

What do you mean?

He's burying Pa.

Takes a lot to startle Anton, but this sudden blankness is like shock. Oh, no.

Well, he is.

No, he isn't. Over my dead body, pardon the phrase, is that Voortrekker shaman burying my father.

But now everyone is looking at him and not saying something they're thinking.

What? he says. What?

Erm, Dean says unhappily. There's more. You need to talk to the lawyer lady.

What lawyer lady?

The family lawyer has recently retired and his daughter has taken over the firm. Cherise Coutts is in her late thirties, with something of a ruined bullfroggish beauty to her, hard to overlook. She's here partly to pay her respects, her father and Manie were in cahoots for a long time, but also because Marina Laubscher requested her presence today, to pass on an important message.

116

What message is that?

Well, she says. I'm sure you're the last person who needs an explanation about the long-standing family dispute ...

Not a dispute. A disagreement, you could say. Around the time of my mother's funeral.

Dispute, disagreement, she says. Call it what you like.

She and the difficult eldest child have withdrawn to Manie's study, off the lounge. The room is small and a lot of space is taken up by a wooden desk, so they're somewhat cramped into a corner. Every movement that she makes is underscored by a soft clinking and clashing of bangles and pearls and to this sibilant soundtrack she extracts some papers from an efficient-looking black briefcase and squares them up on her lap, using the tips of her manicured green nails. One page in particular, which bears Pa's loopy signature on the bottom, seems to be the document that counts right now.

Anton's knee drifts against hers and he jerks his leg away. Excuse me. He's aware of a stale, reflexive desire uncoiling inside him. Something intriguing about her indolent haughtiness and the pebble-cold eyes behind her diamanté reading glasses. Also, she appears to be somewhat relishing the news she's about to break, a tiny crack of cruelty in her professional armour, and he's perversely stirred by it. Hurt me, baby, I can take it.

She reads the document aloud in a monotone, then takes off her glasses and puts the page down. Looks at him expectantly.

No. Fucking. Way.

That's your choice, obviously, she says. As long as you understand, if you refuse, you will not inherit anything from your father. The instructions are very clear about it.

That is so low. Is it even legal?

I drew up the document myself. I can assure you it's perfectly legal. It's your father's bequest, he can set any terms he likes.

He jumps up to his feet, as if about to exit, but instead paces the confined free space left, a short track round the desk to the door, up and down, fired by nameless anxieties that course in him, searching for outlet.

She watches him, intrigued by his anguish. I don't understand, she says at last. Say you're sorry and it's over. It's just words. Why does it matter so much?

You're a lawyer. You should know that words are everything.

In a courtroom, maybe, but that doesn't apply here. Nobody else will even hear you.

He stops his pacing and stares at her. His voice when it emerges has a faint, strangled quality, coming through layers of resistance. Do you have any idea ... But he can't finish, the sentence narrows away. How to express the gnawing, relentless hunger for ... for what? You don't even know what you want, Anton.

Instead he counts the charges on his fingers. First, the land for his church. Next, he's to bury my father. Then you tell me he's a beneficiary of the estate. And now I have to humble myself before him. Is there nowhere that man doesn't have his greedy, grasping hands?

All of it is what your father wanted.

What he was manipulated into wanting! I'll bet you even my punishment was devised by that thief. He sits again abruptly in his chair, which exhales a blurt of dust from its seams. Just can't do it. Sorry.

Whatever the trouble between you, she says, your father never gave up on you. Can I smoke in here? She goes to the window and inserts a menthol into a long porcelain holder and lights it, stands puffing and watching him sidelong. He could have cut you off completely, but he wanted you to have a chance.

To humiliate myself.

If you see it that way.

How I see it, how it is. My father got his ideas about sin and punishment from the Bible, believe me, I was there when it happened. He knew what he was doing. I have to abase myself before I'm forgiven. Making me go down on my knees in front of that crook! No, no, that's a line I can't cross.

The crook he refers to is Alwyn Simmers, who cuts a venerable figure these days, ever since he struck out on his own. The Lord has been good to him in recent times, and he has a fat flock who regularly pay their tithes. His plumpness sits comfortably on him now, filling out his new charcoal-coloured suit, overflowing his cuffs and collar. His hair has also silvered nicely, or so he's told by Laetitia, who brushes it tenderly every morning. Of course, he can't see it for himself. His eyes have completely gone now, or so far gone that he's close to blindness, only a shadow or two moving in the murk. He has invested in a new pair of spectacles with near-black lenses, their big square frames a pleasing shape to his fingertips. Not to mention his most prized new acquisition, a talking wristwatch.

Beep beep, the watch says. The time is eleven thirty.

Sorry about that, he says to his visitor. I should have switched it off.

Anton is fascinated and appalled, everything about this man is grotesque in his eyes, and nothing more so than that big, ugly, vocal watch. He wills it to speak again, but he'll have to wait fifteen minutes.

They're sitting in the lounge of the minister's new home, a sunny north-facing room in Muckleneuk that looks out on a rockery. Alwyn and his spouse, sorry, his sister, no disrespect intended, have long since left behind the damp little quarters at the rear of the Dutch Reformed Church, now that God has willed prosperity on him. Much has changed. He no longer calls himself dominee, he's a pastoor these days, peddling a softer line in salvation to his customers, ahem, that is to say, his flock, so that everyone benefits. The minister has never cared overly for worldly goods and chattels, whatever those are, but my, they do make life comfortable.

He's very comfortable, too, with the scene that's unfolding. He knows why Anton is here, he's been advised ahead of time, and there is a sweet taste to this revenge that he's determined to savour.

Just three spoons of sugar today, he tells Laetitia, who is pouring the tea.

When she's finished stirring, she withdraws to let them speak. But only as far as a chair near the door, in case she's needed. Presses her hard knees together, sipping fast and furtively, like a bird pecking.

I'm here to say sorry, Anton tells him.

For what, my boy?

(You know very well what for.) For the way I spoke to you nine years ago. I was not in a good state. I didn't mean what I said.

Anton has had to rehearse, even going so far as to practise a neutral expression in the mirror, though that seems superfluous, considering. His teeth, bared in a light smile, are biting back how he really feels.

Ag, no, the dominee/pastoor decides at last, that was a long time ago.

Nevertheless.

God forgives everything, he declares, momentarily confusing himself with his creator. Don't think about it another second.

All right. Anton is only too happy to comply, though he suspects he'll be thinking about this for quite some time to come. Keeping his back to the sister, he pulls a twisted face, half fearing that the dark glasses are a decoy, but the pastoor doesn't skip a beat.

The father loves the prodigal, he says, more than the dutiful son.

Always seemed unfair to me. But it's the way of the world.

The Lord is never unfair! Come now, Andrew, pray with me.

Andrew/Anton/aka the prodigal can't quite bring himself to kneel as the minister does, but goes so far as hunching over in his chair, trying to look supplicant. He keeps his eyes open throughout, staring at the orange carpet, while thanks are given to the Almighty above for returning the lost lamb to the flock, for softening hard hearts and changing anger into humility, etc., etc., and inside himself Anton suffers, he suffers. Fire and ice at the same time. You speak with forked tongue and so do I. I am not lost or soft or humble. My heart is still hard towards both of you, not-fathers one and two. Harder than ever. I am the wolf, not the lamb. Remember.

Beep beep. The time is eleven forty-five.

Ag, sorry, man, the minister says, mid-prayer. I should have switched it off.

And shortly afterwards Anton is in his father's Mercedes, driving away at speed from his little act of surrender. There, 'tis done, and the lawyer lady was right, capitulation is easy. My mouth tastes of gall. No, in truth it tastes of nothing, because weakness has no flavour.

Money is what it's all about. An abstraction that shapes your fate. Notes with numbers on them, each a cryptic IOU, not the real thing itself, but the numbers denote your power and there can never be enough. Power might have saved you, Anton, got you out of the country and put your aspirations in reach. Not too late to redeem yourself, though it may take a while for the numbers to climb again. Meanwhile, you have to dig in, suss out, keep on.

He stops at an ATM, not with much hope, but against all expectations she has put some money into his account. Two thousand rand. Not so much, not so little either. Why is she always so kind? Hot tears spring into his eyes, till it occurs to him that this time she might be paying him to stay away. Mentally genuflects towards her regardless as he slides the grubby notes into his wallet. You have my gratitude, if not my body. Must phone you later when I'm brave. But actually, it's Desirée he's been thinking about.

One more stop to make, or not. He does get as far as a parking space directly outside the Winkler Bros Burial Services, where at this very moment Pa is being prepared for burial. He's been told that today would be a good day on which to view his father, if he'd like to. He doesn't know the answer to that question. Do I want to commune with my dead father one last time? What will either of us get from such communion? Even now, sitting outside the low brick building, which looks more like a municipal office than a funeral parlour, he doesn't know.

Then he does know, and starts the engine. The sound, even as it diminishes, carries into the nearby room where Fred Winkler, eldest of the three brothers, has been working on Manie for a couple of hours already. All the basics done, the orifices cleaned out and corked up, to stop the leakage. There's a lot of letting go at the big moment, same way you came into the world you make your exit again, incontinent and howling, but don't tell anybody. Part of the evidence that has to be washed away, to conceal the crime. What crime is that? The crime of death. Nonsense, Fred, there is no crime, you are providing a service, that's all. His late father, also Fred Winkler, who taught him and his brothers this business, being a mortician is a family sort of thing, who would do it otherwise, his father said to him long ago, You have to make them look peaceful. That's what the family wants to see, that their loved one is at peace. Bullshit. What they really want to see is that their loved one is alive. They want to believe that Manie is only sleeping. It's the family that wants to be at peace.

You do your best. A lot of tricks you can use, plumping up collapsed cheeks with cotton wool, sticking down loose ends with glue. All sleight of hand. He's the sensitive one, could have been a painter, or perhaps a homosexual, but instead he wields his make-up brushes

123

on cadavers, remarkable what you can hide under powder and colour. Not to mention his perfumes, generic bottles of scent he keeps in a little mirrored cabinet on the wall. People stink even when they're alive, but afterwards it's much worse, and in Manie's case there's something especially off with the leg. The leg is where the snake got him and it's really bad. Lucky it wasn't the face. Not much you can do with it, except cut the pants short that side and hide it away. As long as he fits into the coffin.

Manie's final receptacle has not yet been chosen, though this delicate process is currently under way in the front office, two bricks away, where the dead man's two daughters are in consultation with the youngest brother. Perspiring and pudgy, with thinning blond hair, too tightly squeezed into his trousers, Vernon Winkler is showing them the range in the catalogue, actually a ring-bound folder of plastic sleeves holding dot-matrix printouts and cheap instant photographs.

I don't like those fittings, Astrid says. What do you think, Amor?

She sighs. Does it really matter?

The fittings? says Vernon. You mean the flowers? You're not getting those ones. You have to choose your corsage from a different catalogue.

Not the flowers. The handles. I don't like those cheap plastic handles.

Astrid is furious, but too sad to show it. Even though Pa had a funeral policy, she's outraged at the prices charged by these solemn-looking criminals for what is, when you get down to it, just a wooden box. She doesn't want to be here, in this featureless office with grey carpeting underfoot, also a kind of box, with a desk and telephone in the corner. The telephone rings frequently, there are always fresh dead in need of burial, never any end to sorrow, and indeed, in two of the other straight-backed chairs that stand in random clumps against the bare walls, a young couple sits holding hands, sobbing inconsolably.

We can change the handles, Vernon Winkler says. He's bored with this hissy older sister, but quite perked up by the pretty younger one, he likes them quiet, he can almost imagine, except no, he mustn't, not here, and not in these pants. Embarrassed himself like that in a public situation once.

In the end, after all the fuss, Astrid opts for the top-of-the-range Ubuntu casket, very popular right now, a brand that goes well with the times. It's described in the catalogue as having the warm glow of highly polished meranti wood and generous dimensions befitting the giving and open nature of Africa. It features a traditional Zulu bead design in the middle of the lid upholstery, while the interior is snugly quilted, and coloured with the subtle palette of the savannah. The silver full-swing bar grip handles, locally made, are also very pleasing.

Less pleasing is the attitude of her younger sister, who's barely said a word on the entire outing. Really, Astrid only brought her along for some input. What's the point?

I'm sorry, Amor says. I don't have a strong opinion about things like handles.

She doesn't mean this sarcastically, she is in fact ignorant about the smaller workings of the world, but Astrid says, Well, it's too bad if you think my universe is petty, but somebody always has to decide about handles.

125

Amor ponders this statement. I don't think your universe is petty, she says at last.

This is in the car, Astrid's little Honda, on the way back to the farm. On the edge of town, in slow traffic. The mood between them has softened, Radio 702 playing some strummy, plucky thing in the background. The day has been too much for Astrid, the kids causing havoc from the crack of dawn, Dean working on her G-string too and now this saga with the coffin. But it's not just today, or even the past few days, the truth is she hasn't felt all right for quite a while. Not for years.

Actually, she says in a different voice, I do think my universe is petty.

Amor listens.

I don't know how I ended up here, Astrid says.

Why is she confessing this to her younger sister, whom she doesn't like? There's something about Amor that makes you feel you can. What used to seem blank and stupid in her, almost like brain damage, now seems like the opposite, silence and attentiveness, a kind of intelligence. She's somebody you can tell things to.

We didn't use protection and I got pregnant and instead of doing the sensible thing I ran off with Dean to the magistrates' court and bang, there goes the rest of my life. Same as Ma! I didn't think about what I was doing, I just did it. My body did it, you could say. My mind was somewhere else. Now I've got two children and I'm exhausted and I don't feel young and beautiful any more.

She frowns. What's the hold-up in front? She toots the horn. I love Dean, she says. I mean, I'm fond of him. It's not that I'm not. But we're very different.

Amor nods thoughtfully. (You want to leave him.

Oh, no, no! I could never.) Astrid contemplates her future through the windscreen, while a light changes. But I did have an affair, she says, almost in a whisper.

Amor nods again. Who with?

The man who came to put in our security.

Impossible not to giggle when you picture it. Really?

Yes, really. Astrid giggles too, lightened by the unexpected release of talking about her sin. She does, actually, think of it that way, as a sin, and would like to be absolved. The security man she had the affair with, Jake Moody, is a Catholic, and she was fascinated by his description of how confession cleansed him of his transgressions and failures. Even this one? she'd wanted to know. Yes, he'd told her, even this one, but not yet.

The thing is, she finds herself saying, the thing is, he's just so different from Dean. In every way! Even his name ... it's a manly name, you know what I mean? And so apt. He really is moody, he was madly jealous about me, I miss his jealousy ...

The thing is, she tells Amor, I'm not over it. I've been thinking of calling him.

But now she's said too much and Astrid feels suddenly queasy and claps a hand to her mouth. How did that happen? Her sister isn't a priest!

You're not to repeat any of it, she hisses through her fingers. Any of what I told you, not to anyone!

Of course not, Amor says. Why would I?

You can see she means it and Astrid is briefly calmed, but soon after they've arrived at the house she feels the need to withdraw to the bathroom to purge her inner turmoil. She really wants to turn herself inside out today. Poor, mistaken Astrid! You can't puke up the thought which pains you most, namely that you and your sister have somehow changed places, and Amor is on a trajectory that by rights should be yours.

Not true. Not how Amor sees it, in any case. For she too has her little pains, and they wear her out, though she does not speak of them, or is not asked, and when they show themselves it tends to be when she's alone. On top of the koppie soon afterwards, for example, sitting on a rock. Her favourite spot, the scene of her enfeeblement. Why does she keep coming back?

Look through her eyes. The whole picture seems much smaller to her than the way she remembers, the koppie itself much lower, the burnt tree just a spray of dead branches. The roof of the Lombard place is a geometric shape down there, barely noticeable.

Yet the colours pierce her, as if they're sharp, and the sky is huge and unmistakable. Below her, the farm itself spreads infinitely away into hills and folds and fields, merging with a brown distance beyond, and she does feel the world as big, very big. She has seen some of it herself. The countryside looks the same but the laws piled on top of it, the invisible, powerful laws that people make and then lay down at angles across the earth, pressing down heavily, all those laws are changing now. She can feel, almost as if it's part of the picture in front of her, that she has come back to the same place, but it isn't the same place any more.

The family has done nothing, of course, about Pa's promise to their mother. Nobody has mentioned it since Ma died, except Amor herself, and that not for a long time. She is thinking about this problem right now, and she very much wants to mention it. She believes, or perhaps only hopes, that a provision has been made in Pa's will to set the matter right. But it would be best if they could all agree on what to do before the will is read.

In the dining room that evening, everyone around the table eating, is an obvious moment, and she's about to ask the question, the words are actually in her mouth, their individual syllables completely innocent (Can Salome have her house now?) ... and look, the scene from outside is so convivial, the room filled with friendly light, a fire burning in the grate and the family gathered at their repast ... What harm can such a question do? Send it out into the warm room, perhaps the answer will surprise you.

Whaddah! The impact is like a soft punch, releasing a collective cry of fear and relief, everybody turning at the same time. Amor's question drops to the floor, unasked. But no, that's not what made the sound. Something else, something quite material, has flown into the glass door very hard from outside.

What is it? cries Dean, terrified. A bat? No, a bird, those pigeons are very stupid, observes Ockie. That was my mother's spirit, Astrid thinks, irrationally. Why was it flying around at night? Marina wants to know. Must've been attracted by the stoep light.

A dove, not a pigeon, lies dying on its back on the slate, amid a tiny blizzard of feathers. A thin thread of blood leaks from one nostril. Small creature, small death. One claw stiffens and convulses. The little body cools.

Shame, go and bury the poor thing, Astrid urges her husband. She wants it removed from her sight. Dean goes out dutifully and lifts the bird up gingerly by one wingtip. He casts about for a suitable burial site and finds a spot in a disused flower bed under a thorn tree. Digs a hole with his hands and tips the creature in. Covers it up again. Stands there for a minute, dwelling on the death of his father, way back when he was still a young boy. The bird took him there. One thing conjures up another. All events joined somehow, at least in memory.

The bird lies in its little grave, just under the surface of the earth, for only a few hours before it's dug up by a jackal, one of a pair that has taken up residence near the koppie. They have become much braver since Tojo died and when the house goes quiet they come prowling and scavenging around. The dove is a gift, the reek of its blood coming up through the soil, only the end of one wing stained with human scent. The two jackals tear it apart with high, gibbering cries, till Astrid can't bear it any longer and throws open a window and screams at them to stop.

They pass on through the dark landscape, stitching from shadow to shadow, following a path they themselves have worn down around the base of the koppie. The landscape is luminous to them and the air swarming with messages. Tracks and traces and happenings far off. Near the electric pylons they pause, alerted by the humming of current in the power lines overhead, and throw back their heads to send out wobbling howls in reply.

Salome hears them in her house, beg your pardon, the Lombard place, and quickly closes the door. She is receptive to signs and portents, and the howling of jackals is like an evil omen to her. Some kind of troubled spirit abroad. And with their elusive liquid movement, pouring from one spot to another, they do seem insubstantial and their weird chittering calls other-worldly.

They trot across the floor of the valley in the direction of the highway, north. But stop far short of it, at the outer limit of their territory. It is necessary to renew their markings, using bodily juices, to lay down the border. Beyond here is us. Written in piss and shit, inscribed from the core.

Now they move east, heading for another outpost where their signature has faded. But are brought up short after only a little way by a disturbance that has occurred since they were last in this spot, almost exactly twenty-four hours ago.

The ground has been opened up, in the place that stinks of bone. The earth exhales odours when it's torn, undetectable to the human nose but to Canis mesomelas, oh, it speaks in tongues. The wound is big and raw, and the smells of the diggers are in there too, the metal edges of their claws, as well as their sweat and saliva and blood, though they themselves have gone. Perhaps this is their attempt at a burrow. Perhaps they will come back to finish it.

They come back the next morning. Two young men wearing overalls, carrying spades. Their breath a visible vapour on the cold air. It is still early, just after sunrise, and the shadows of the gravestones stretch out pale across the ground. The jackals have long since departed and other creatures have taken their place.

A caterpillar ripples its way along a leaf.

A meerkat sneaks through the grass, like a wisp of smoke.

A beetle spindles by, stops still for an instant, resumes.

Lukas and Andile dig and dig. A person is not a bird and can't just be thrown into a shallow grave, where a jackal might be able to reach them. But a hole six foot deep and the size of a grown man is hard labour to excavate, much more so when there's frost on the ground. Although the chill is like metal in their bones, they are both gasping and perspiring, and happy to take a break when Alwyn Simmers arrives.

He has come to get a feeling, quite literally so, for where he's to conduct the funeral. It's all right in a church, everything flat and tame, no chance of tripping. But out here in the rough, that's another story. And Manie has requested a Dutch Reformed service, which throws the pastoor a little, because he's already forgotten the Calvinist ways.

Lukas and Andile lean on their spades in the half-dug grave, watching with unconcealed curiosity as the Toyota Corolla lumbers up the dirt road and parks next to the wrought-iron gate of the family cemetery. It's driven by a womanish-looking man who, when he clambers out, reveals himself to be a mannish-looking woman instead. She's wearing a white blouse and a long brown skirt above meaningful calves and flat shoes, on which she hurries around to help the poor, blind, bad-tempered minister into the world.

Other arm, Laetitia! He's breathing heavily. How many times must I tell you?

Sorry, Alwyn, sorry . . .

It's a constant refrain between them, admonishment and apology, and each seems to relish the part they play, while hating it too. In this case, brother and sister are merely names that sit on top of a much deeper entanglement. Thus they hobble, entangled, over the uneven ground, through the rusted metal gates and between the gravestones, canted and crumbling, the gravestones, that is, not the twosome, though in their way they are canted and crumbling too. Where are we? cries Alwyn Simmers. Almost there, Laetitia Simmers replies.

From inside the rectangular hole in the ground, Lukas and Andile watch them approach.

Are we there yet?

Yes, Alwyn, now we are there.

This is where I'll stand?

Yes, that is where you'll stand.

He sniffs the air, turning his head from side to side, like a monarch surveying his domain. Who's there? he calls suddenly, sensing a presence close to his knees.

It is us, Baas.

Who is it?

Andile and Lukas, Baas.

Andile is the one speaking, Lukas would never use the word baas, at least not any more. He has an air of proud reserve, or perhaps it's disdain, seeming somehow to be looking down on the white pair, even though he's half submerged in the ground. While Andile bobs his head and grins obsequiously, if it were possible he would bury himself completely.

Let us go home, Laetitia. I have seen enough.

Yes, Alwyn, she replies meekly, though across her mind there flashes the nasty desire to say other words to him, What do you mean, Alwyn, you can't see a thing. She frequently has cruel impulses but squashes them down, except those pertaining to herself. For under her long skirts and sleeves, Laetitia carries some self-inflicted wounds.

The two whites get into their car and drive away, the two blacks go on digging. Really, this interlude has served no purpose, we could have done without it, yet it's repeated in reverse just four days later, when the Corolla returns with the brother and sister inside it. But this time they have a hearse travelling behind them, a black Volvo, somewhat modified from its original design. It has followed them all the way from town and now comes rocking and lurching its way up the dirt track, the corpse of Manie Swart in his Ubuntu coffin in the back.

The name of the funeral home, Winkler Bros Burial Services, is stencilled in unimaginative white lettering on the rear doors of the vehicle, and Fred himself is at the wheel, a man who looks much older than he is, completely bald at thirty-seven, the lines of his face drooping in tandem with his big moustache. His vest and his under-pants are too tight, which shows as a tiny, vexed frown between his eyes. Over them he's wearing his standard black suit, not a dab of creativity in the man, though it's been a while since it was dry-cleaned and the fumes of his own sweat, from other, hotter days, come winding up to Fred's nostrils as he drives, making them dilate.

There is also, or so he imagines, a faint tincture of decay on the air, leaking from the coffin at the back. It can't be, the lid is down tight, but he keeps picking up a smell. Maybe some residue on his hands? He wants this farm funeral to go well, he knows it matters to Alwyn Simmers, whose church he belongs to. Actually, he does quite a lot of work for the pastoor, you could almost say they have an understanding, to their mutual advantage. Deo volente, of course, but you can count on the Lord to understand, He's not averse to a bit of profit in His name, as long as your innermost soul is pure.

Fred Winkler feels his soul dangling deep inside himself sometimes, like a stalactite. No, more loose and trembly, like a bat in a cave. Will I ever, in some grainy twilight, break free and fly? Somehow he thinks not.

He parks next to the cemetery. A little early, but a few mourners are already around. Alwyn Simmers and his peculiar sister have pulled up nearby.

Beautiful day, the minister observes, lifting his face to the sky. He can feel the sunlight and the receding frost, but in truth he isn't thinking about the weather. He is anxious about what lies ahead, because it could be tricky. This family. The Lord sent them to try me. That trouble with the son all those years ago, what is his name again, and now they want to blame me for their father's death too. Not my fault if his faith was insufficient. Just need to get through the next couple of hours without a scene. He's hit the right note in his eulogy, he thinks, to keep them at bay. Got to beat them into line. Money brings out the ugliest aspects of human nature, he's seen it over and over, to his great sorrow. So tragic and so unnecessary. Truly, men have made an altar unto Mammon.

His melancholia has almost reached a pleasurable pitch when Marina Laubscher descends, fake pearls vibrating. So great is her agitation that he can't make out what she wants. Or he can, but doesn't believe he heard correctly.

Say that again?

I want them to open the coffin.

But why?

I want to be sure it's my brother inside.

Of course it's your brother inside, he cries, his own hysteria suddenly matching hers. Whose brother would it be?

135

But she will not be deterred, not today. Since Manie's death something inside her feels unhinged, and has found its focus in a Huisgenoot article she read last week while she was on the toilet, about a dodgy funeral home on the edge of Johannesburg where they'd discovered decomposing bodies piled up in a shed. She didn't completely understand, something about using and reusing the same coffins, and in many cases, the article said, the wrong person had been dispatched at the funeral and in a few instances two bodies had been squeezed into one coffin. The story had disturbed her at the time, enough to render her constipated, but since Manie died it's all she can think about. What if it's not her brother in the box? What if he's in there with someone else?

He's by himself, Fred Winkler protests, his moustache bristling. I closed it personally this morning. (Watched Jabulani do it, actually.)

Well, open it again.

I don't know if I brought the right screwdriver. I thought this was a closed-casket service.

It is, but I must see for myself. Open it immediately!

Do what she says, her husband urges in the background, sounding like a hostage. He just wants this scene over.

Do you have the screwdriver? Alwyn Simmers asks the air.

Fred scrabbles in the back of the hearse, in the compartment where he keeps the tools. He's frantic to the point of gasping, sure already he'll be found guilty, guilty, guilty, but praise be, the right implement is to hand.

Do it quickly, Pastoor Simmers tells him. Don't let anybody else see, for Christ's sake.

The blasphemy slips out, like a gobbet of snot, too late to stop it. Everybody pretends they haven't heard, especially the minister himself. Fred Winkler keeps his head down, looking very intently at the screws as he unwinds their thread, anticlockwise, turning back time. Jesus raised Lazarus from the dead. Did he stink? I wonder. And there is, there definitely is, a sweetish reek coming out of the coffin. Very noticeable in the cramped, upholstered space at the back of the car. Much worse still as the lid comes off. Don't think about food, especially not food going bad, starting to liquefy and rot. Please don't vomit, not here. No room for tricks. Hold your breath and concentrate, as if down a tunnel, on what's revealed. The face, nothing more, and keep it that way, eyes closed, mouth ajar, seen in profile. The shape is right, but there's something about the colouring. And the size ...

He looked bad, Fred says quickly. Much worse than this. I did a lot of work on him. But he was swollen up and the veins went a bit funny. (You should see his leg.)

This is the moment when Astrid's twins wander past the open back of the hearse and see the body of their grandfather/someone not their grandfather lying there. The full knowledge of death comes to Neil and Jessica de Wet, shocking them rigid, before Astrid seizes them both and drags them off, and the incident sinks away almost immediately in the general disorder. Close it up, Marina orders the man from the funeral home, with his ridiculous moustache, and he's only too happy to comply.

Marina is definitely unhappy with the way her brother looks, if it really is Manie she saw. It seemed like him, more or less, but also not. As she broods, it becomes

137

increasingly possible that she just looked upon a swollen stranger in that box.

Open it again!

She's come clattering back, not five minutes after she left. Fred Winkler has just started putting in the last screw, and the halitosis of the grave has finally dispersed.

Ag, no, Marina, jissus, man, absolutely not!

Ockie's had enough. He's completely, totally, hundred per cent had it up to here with Swart family kak! Wanting to open the coffin again! Since his brother-in-law died in this incredibly stupid way, he doesn't recognise his wife.

In this moment, she doesn't know him either. It's been years since he shouted, least of all at her, and she suddenly sees him anew. My husband! Married more than half my life!

I'm sorry, Ockie, I'm not myself today.

That's all right, my little penguin, he says, immediately tender. Have you taken your drops?

Fred Winkler turns the last screw. A measure of sanity returning. He's perspiring even in the winter cold, like somebody sick, which perhaps he is.

He's not yet a free man. Only when the coffin is finally lowered into the earth will he be able to leave. He has to stand through the interminable service, with his bladder full and pressing out against his too-tight underpants, while the pastoor, who's technically gone back to being a dominee today, delivers one of his more orotund addresses, gilded with praise for the character and faith of Manie Swart.

In the awkward corner space of the graveyard, everybody standing, the assembly has formed of its own accord

138

into three rings around the minister. The inner circle is the family and the second is made of loose friends and associates, almost all of them, come to think of it, people Manie knew from church. That includes a hefty older lady called Lorraine, much in favour of perms and cardigans, who's been his discreet companion the past five or six years. And she is weeping today, because she misses Manie, of course, but also because he always promised he would make an honest woman of her yet he never did take that step, and what now? Allow her this little moment, because soon she will be leaving this place and the other lives clustered upon it, with not very much to show for her sojourn aside from a modest bequest, to be mentioned again at the appropriate time.

Behind them, a step back, is a handful of workers from the farm, who, in keeping with the new expansive spirit abroad in the country, have been allowed into the enclosure of the family cemetery itself. Not buried here, though, no, of course not! This place is for blood kin only. There's no official burial site for farm labourers, who are not attached to the land, not really, they are transient, even the ones who've lived here many years. In the end, they all blow away.

Some deaths are natural, Alwyn Simmers tells them. But when somebody dies by accident, it can feel like an injustice has occurred. That something must be set right. He glares sightlessly at his audience. It can be hard to accept that even an accident is part of our Heavenly Father's design.

No accident here. None. Just as the downfall of Adam and Eve was no accident either. Let's not forget that Satan took the form of a serpent, back in the Garden of Eden.

He brought about the downfall of the first people on earth and sent us, their descendants, into exile. Yet even this is a part of the Lord's design, brothers and sisters. For insofar as Satan will finally lose this great game, he too is only playing his role. In the end, the very end, all accidents will be meaningful!

The blind minister has found his rhetorical flow, his beautiful voice curling away between termite hills and tussocks of grass. Always had the gift of the gab, a way of singing when he speaks. There are moments of true inspiration when he's taken over by something beyond him, another driver behind the wheel. Please let it be the Lord Jesus, but sometimes he worries it isn't. In a brief lapse of probity forty years ago, Alwyn Simmers and his sister committed the sin of fornication, unfortunately with each other, and although neither of them has ever mentioned it again, he does occasionally feel the urge to confess it aloud from the pulpit. On days like these he fears he actually might. But no, keep telling the other story, the one we all agreed on, you know which one I mean, about salvation and humour and renewal and forgiveness, if we are truly Christians we won't ever fuck our sisters, the thought won't occur to us.

Beep beep. The time is ten thirty.

Ag, sorry, man, the minister says, I always forget to turn it off.

Everybody laughs and shuffles, their attention dissipating. The dominee has lost his place too. He'd intended to conclude by telling them about Manie's enormous generosity, even in death, but his thread eludes him. Time to wrap it up instead. He jumps to a little joke he had planned for the end, but gets the punchline wrong, so that a damp, baffled silence ensues. Claps his hands and reminds everyone they can still contribute to the fund Manie set up when he was alive, even though the sponsorship part doesn't apply any more. All manies, ag, monies go to charities doing good works in dark parts of the world.

Now the service is over, the necessary gestures made, and the gathering can unravel itself again, all the more uncertainly for being out here in the veld. You can really feel your smallness under the big, bright winter sky, no buffer between you and the universe, as you scurry out the gate. And Fred Winkler can pee at last. He trots a little way and turns his back on the graveyard and the people straggling from it, forgets they're there. Such release! Nothing joins a man to the earth more completely than an umbilical arc of hot yellow urine. For a short while there is only that single sensation of letting go, until it's time to shake off the drops.

When he goes back to the hearse, the last of the mourners is disappearing down the track and two black men are already filling in the grave. He nods to them as he trots by and one of them answers. Morning, Baas. What a strange job I have, reflects Fred, as he climbs back into his vehicle, not without self-pity. I make people ready to disappear. And all my work disappears with them.

After the long dark car has gone, Andile and Lukas resume their labour. Much easier to fill a hole than to dig it, but still it's toil, man is doomed to live by the sweat of his brow, or at least some men are. Some women too. Just the way it is, apparently, or so everyone in these parts seems to believe. What do you expect, a revolution? When they're done, they beat the earth flat with their spades and then sit under a thorn tree to share a cigarette.

Lukas says goodbye to Andile and takes the footpath to the Lombard house. Where I live. A crooked little building, something out of true at its centre. Three rooms, concrete floor, broken windows. Two steps up to the front door. Cross the threshold. Hello? Your own voice coming back at you. His mother is not at home. She seldom is. Tending the children of another woman, the white woman, over the hill. Leaving him alone in the three joined rooms, full of time and silence, dust motes spinning in the sun.

He takes a bucket, goes to get some water at the pump. Washes with a lappie outside the back door, stripped down to a pair of ragged red underpants. Afterwards he crouches down, drying in the sun. His long dark body is ridged with muscle, a pink scar zigzags across his back. Some private history there, don't know him well enough to ask.

He dresses in smart street clothes, ready for town. Spends a lot of time studying his own expression in a broken shard of mirror. He doesn't see the anger and pride, or the lonely sense of injury. Instead he admires his lip, which is becoming sensual and pendulous, and the long curving lashes on his eyes.

He's going to Atteridgeville, the township nearby, to visit a girl he knows. As he starts down the track, jaunty and perfumed, his route skirts the edge of the lawn behind the farmhouse, where the whites have congregated. Some kind of send-off for the man who died. Lukas knows his name, of course, but it seems separate from the person it designates, who in turn seems not like a human so much as a force.

The son of the force comes out of the house as he goes past. Hey, Lukas. Hello, Anton. Unsureness in how to address each other, now that adulthood has come.

What're you up to these days?

I'm working here on the farm.

I thought you had plans to study? University?

No, I couldn't do it. I got into trouble at school, I was expelled, I didn't finish. He shrugs and smirks.

So you're back here, working? Hang on ... Where are you going now?

To town.

How're you getting there?

I will walk to the main road. Then I will hitch a ride.

Anton is holding a glass of what might be whisky and is leaning forward as if to hear better. The warm glow has made him benign and optimistic, keen to solve the problems of others. Let me give you a lift, he says. I want to talk to you.

No, it's oraait.

I'm giving you a lift, friend. Wait for me one minute.

He goes off inside and searches around upstairs for the keys, which takes longer than it should. By the time he locates them and comes back outside, his glass is nearly empty and Lukas has departed. See him way off down the road, a tiny figure in the distance. Right, fokoff then. Anton raises a toast to him, drains the glass and hurls it forcefully into the veld. A silvery tinkle out there, briefly satisfying.

He doesn't want to rejoin the gathering on the lawn. Been thinking about Desirée and wishing he'd had the guts to ask her to the funeral. Though it's an odd idea, not a social highlight, after all, but an invitation hard to

143

refuse, which is really the point. In any case, too late for that now and just as well, you're not in great shape, are you, Anton, drunk and slanted inwardly, not a brilliant idea to talk to anybody, least of all the ex-girlfriend you deserted without a word and whose heart you reportedly smashed to pieces. Also, uh, not a good plan to mingle with the stoic prayer-sodden lot round the back.

Tea and sandwiches have been laid out on the patio by Laetitia Simmers and other church volunteers, while the guests mill around on the grass. Seen from upstairs, it's all hats and hairdos and bald spots, in aimless circulation. Laetitia herself is in attendance, bustling in crimplene behind the long trestle tables, pouring from a pot. Tea is her talent, and she smiles joylessly through the steam at her brother, remonstrating with himself near the clivias. Beep beep, just at the high point of his speech!

By now Anton is in Manie's bedroom, looking around. Ere yet the salt of most unrighteous tears, here I am, sniffing through his stuff. Some money under his socks. I'll have that, thanks. Quite like the look of that electric razor too. But dear Jesus, what is that inexplicable object?

He takes the cryptic thing from next to his father's bed. Turns it over, sniffs at it, pulling in a faint, old smell of fire. A piece of shell, some reptile, probably a tortoise. Pa was always obsessed with the cold-blooded sort, not so good with the mammals, humans least of all. He puts the piece of shell down again and just then sees the shotgun. Mossberg pump action, inherited from Oupa, nobody else allowed to touch it, though who'd want to, blunt, ugly, charmless thing. Family heirloom, supposedly.

Picks it up, holds it, feels the weight and substance. Real. Oh, yes. When you've claimed a man's gun, you claim the man too. Law of the frontier. Oh, balls, Anton, who scripts these thoughts for you? But he's excited by the weapon, something in him electrified and afraid. Thunder-stick make magic, make heapum big noise, make small man very dead.

Aims out of the window with it, at the distant figure of Dominee Simmers in the garden. Blam! See him jerk backwards into the flower bed, kicking. No, let him live. Gun isn't loaded anyway, but he remembers where he saw a box of shells just yesterday. In his own room, among the crap.

Goes there now and loads it, the way he saw Pa do it. Kachunk. And just then hears from outside a loud screaming and hullaballoo from the patio. He runs to the window, and can almost not believe what he sees, a troop of baboons arriving at the very moment he's taken the weapon in his hands, so unlikely as to be a dream, but be reminded that all coincidence is unlikely, Anton, that is the very nature of coincidence. Anyway, there they indisputably are, the shaggy minatory thugs, helping themselves to the sandwiches. At my father's funeral!

We rise out of nature into culture, but you have to fight to keep your lofty perch, otherwise nature pulls you back down. First time he's held a weapon since the army. First time he's fired one since then too. Since that day which by agreement with himself he does not contemplate, and will not now. Even though the jolt of power, the kick and clap of it, is instantly familiar and thrilling. Enough to repeat, and repeat, as he runs. Blam!

And Blam again! The noise rolls out in concentric rings, like the giant extent of my reach.

The baboons have long gone. Scattered wildly at the first shot, even though he missed/aimed high. Shrieking and commotion, then silence. Anton is far from the house now, out in the veld. Such a deep satisfaction in that quiet, walking crunchily upon your land. His rage like a hot gale blowing through him. Make no mistake, I am home.

The little gathering on the back lawn has been shaken. Can't blame them, first the baboons, then the shotgun blasts. An edge of chaos to things around here. Soon a few guests make their excuses and then the trickle turns into a flow. Not long after Anton pulled the trigger, all the visitors have gone.

Now the empty patio seems somehow larger than before, and the refuse scattered around takes on a significant air. The only figures left are those of Laetitia and another elderly white lady, cleaning up. Oh, and don't overlook Salome, washing plates and cups in the kitchen sink. She's in her Sunday clothes, what she wore to the funeral, for she was there too, why was it not mentioned before, yes, she was present, almost but not quite in the front, standing behind the family.

And the family is still here too, of course, nobody keen to go back to their own homes just yet. The farmhouse is big, there is room for everyone, and it's the first time in years that all three children have been together. Thus people wax sentimental even in grief. See how death has united us! Though it's also true that the lawyer is coming out here at lunchtime tomorrow to go through Manie's will with them, which might be another reason to hang around.

Cherise Coutts is wearing a faux-fur coat and hat this afternoon, which she must need, because even on this glinty winter's day she drives an open-top sports car, part of a recent divorce settlement that's left her lonely but well fed. She takes what is obviously her natural position, at the head of the table in the dining room, and after she's shed her outer layer, hands out her business card in a general sort of way to those deserving, between nails that are today painted gold. Cherise A. Coutts (BA LLB), Univ of Pretoria.

She's here to explain the contents of Manie Swart's will to them, which are fairly straightforward. Only two beneficiaries are unable to be present today, both send their apologies. One is Dominee, I beg your pardon, Pastoor Simmers, whose church commitments keep him away, and the other is Miss Lorraine Louw, who feels it is not her place to be here. Murmurs of insincere protest, She was Pa's girlfriend, Of course we know that, We're all civilised people, but when they hear she's getting a lump sum, not so small, everyone quietens down.

Manie, it turns out, has business interests and pieces of property all over the show, it's not just Scaly City that's kept him going, though the park continues to bring in surprising amounts of money each month. But pay attention, here's the part that matters. One. The proceeds of these various concerns are controlled by a trust, the sole trustee of which is the person addressing you now. Two. The income from the reptile park, as well as from Manie's various other interests, a full list appended hereto, shall be paid out equally to all the beneficiaries of the trust on a monthly basis. Three. The beneficiaries of the trust are the First Assembly of the Revelation on the Highveld, hereafter referred to as Manie's church, as well as his sister Marina Laubscher and his three children, all present here, and happily Anton is among them, having removed the small, uh, obstacle that might have disqualified him.

Four. The farm itself, which includes not only the house they are all sitting in at this moment, as well as the property on which it is built, but also the various other plots/properties immediately contiguous which have been bought up over the past thirty years, is not part of the trust. Manie intended it to remain intact, as a home/refuge/base to the aforementioned three children, as long as any one of them wants to live there. No part of it may be sold off except in the case of financial emergency and then only with the unanimous agreement in writing of the three children.

Ms Coutts, whose professional demeanour is very close to boredom, squares the pages neatly with those amazing golden nails. Everyone has noticed them by now. This woman has powers! She looks at them all with disdain, as if peering down from a ledge. Any questions?

Amor, appearing half asleep, winds her way slowly upright to a single question. Um, what about Salome?

Excuse me?

Salome, who works at the farm.

Until this moment, everyone in the room has worn an almost stupid air. But now a tremor runs through the group, as if a tuning fork has been struck on the edge of the scene.

That old story, Astrid says. You're still on that?

It was sorted out a long time ago, Tannie Marina says. We're not going backwards now.

Amor shakes her head. It was never sorted out. When my mother died, it wasn't possible for Salome to own the land. But the laws have changed and now she can.

She can, Astrid says. But she's not going to. Don't be stupid.

Is there any mention of her in my father's will?

Why would there be? Tannie Marina snaps. She has an urge to pinch her niece, but she's too grown up for that, unfortunately.

Any mention of who? the lawyer says. I'm afraid I'm lost.

My mother wanted Salome to have the house where she lives and the plot of land it's on. My father promised he would do it, but it's never been given to her.

Cherise Coutts makes a show of paging through the documents in front of her, though she must have drawn up their contents herself. Meanwhile Tannie Marina reaches into her cleavage to pull out a tissue, unfolds it like origami, cries viciously into it. I don't care what you say, she tells them, while she dries her eyes. Whatever your principles may be, you're supposed to stand with your own people! What she means by this isn't altogether clear, at least not to anybody present, though she has an air of bitter satisfaction, as if she's had the last word. She puts away the tissue where she found it, and all apparent emotion along with it, deep between her breasts. Wanting to give land to the maid! Have you ever!

Anyway, Cherise A. Coutts (BA LLB) says. It's not mentioned here. I don't know anything about it.

There you are, Tannie Marina says, as if that settles the matter.

It's time, Ockie says, and in a second everybody gets to their feet and starts heading to the door. For a few minutes already there's been an itching and straining in that direction. The meeting started late and went on longer than it was supposed to, which means we might miss the kick-off at Ellis Park if we don't hurry.

South Africa! The name used to be a cause for embarrassment, but now it means something else. Truly, we are a nation that defies gravity. We're playing in the final of the World Cup today in Johannesburg and all over the country there's a giddy mood in the air. Boks versus the All Blacks, the eyes of other nations gazing hotly at us. From one in the afternoon there's been almost nobody in the streets, supplies of beer have been stockpiled and faces everywhere are bathed in a fluorescent glow. In lounges and kitchens and backyards, in restaurants and bars and public squares, people look at nothing but the game. Even those who don't like rugby, due to whatever deficiency in their characters, are watching today.

It's no different on the farm. At the labourers' cottages, a black-and-white set has been propped up on a crate and the image flickers fitfully before an assembled audience. And over in the Lombard place, Salome stares at the unfolding contest with a frown. She doesn't know the rules, all of it is noise and spectacle to her, yet somehow it compels. From the doorway behind her, half in the next room, even Lukas pays grudging attention, hands stuck in his pockets.

At the main house, the mood is a queasy blend of depression and excitement, inducing nausea. Nor does the alcohol help. And the match is so tense and thrilling, it's enough to make you claw the furniture. Our boys

150

keeping it tight, not letting that meat mountain Jonah Lomu through, but we're not scoring any tries either, it's just drop kicks the whole way, points pushing against points, little grains of victory and defeat. Behind the striving are willpower and flesh in perfect union, straining and grunting and heaving but also great longing, for all its manpower rugby is still a spiritual pageant in the end, and when we're in extra time, and every centimetre and every second matter, oh man, there are no words. And then Joel Stransky! And it's us! And nothing will ever, ever be better than this moment, with everybody jumping up and hugging each other, strangers celebrating in the streets, cars hooting and flashing their lights.

But then it does get even better. When Mandela appears in the green Springbok rugby jersey to give the cup to Francois Pienaar, well, that's something. That's religious. The beefy Boer and the old terrorist shaking hands. Who could ever. My goodness. More than one person thinks back to that moment when Mandela came out of jail, fist in the air, just a few years ago, and nobody knew what he would look like. Now his face is every-where, avuncular, friendly, stern but forgiving, or beaming down on all of us like Father Christmas, just as he's doing right now. Hard not to shed a tear for our beautiful country. We are all as amazing as this moment.

But where is Amor?

I don't know, she was around a while ago . . .

Who asks the question, who answers it, all that is lost, if the question is asked at all. But it's certainly true that Amor isn't nearby at the big moment, she has slipped out and gone somewhere. Come to think of it, was she ever here?

Well, leave her then. If she doesn't want to be part of it.

It is definitely Astrid who says this, or perhaps Tannie Marina, they are almost the same person these days, but in any case they're not alone in this sentiment. Leave her, if she doesn't want to be part of it. It's clear to everyone, not just the aunties among them, that however much she's changed in other ways, Amor still holds herself aloof and apart. Always been an unusual girl, excuse me, woman.

She is sitting upstairs in her room at this moment, thinking about the meeting that's recently happened and what was said and what was not said, and her place in all of it. There seems to be no centre to the situation and it's hard to separate one thing from another, so that she feels tangled in little questions, each in need of an answer. She can hear her name being called amid the yelling and whistling going on downstairs, and there's a similar uproar from the labourers' cottages a short distance away, but all the cacophony of celebration is far from her, like a speech in a strange language.

Parties break out everywhere tonight, and the sound of revelry drifts over from the township, but here on the farm it feels wrong to celebrate too much. Not so soon after. One thing to drink, but let's keep the music down, out of respect. Though the mood stays happy, no doubt about it, at least for a few hours. And in the morning, of course, when the whole country wakes up with a hangover, like a compound fracture in the brain, it's no different with the Swarts, who are filled with greed and grief, as well as alcohol. A poisoned, unwell atmosphere overshadows the house, somewhere between melancholia and boredom, though the day has a glassy clearness and a crisp breeze is blowing.

Who belongs here now? The answer is no longer clear. Among the various people who've stayed over, there's now a general sense of restiveness, an itchy need to move on. A spirit of agitation flickers in the corners of the house. All the rituals are completed, why are we still here?

The goodbyes are said downstairs and then the family is at last moving in different directions. They were pulled together by a powerful vacuum, which has now turned inside out and expelled them again, Astrid and Dean with the twins back to their house in Arcadia, Tannie Marina and Oom Ockie to theirs in Menlo Park, and only Amor and Anton remaining on the farm. The zero point of death has begun to shrink behind them, nobody can live with intense emotions for very long, it's too exhausting, and everything that can be described can also be made harmless. A time will come when Manie's tragic exit is turned into an amusing family anecdote, Can you believe it, our happy-clappy daddy thought God would protect him if he lived in a glass cage full of poisonous snakes, but ho ho, he was wrong.

The snake that bit Manie is a young female of the species and at this moment she is lying on display in her tank at the reptile park. Look at the fat scaly awfulness of her, bulging with poison, a hard sheath full of grumous matter, and if she were lolling outside on some country pathway she would be beaten to death just for being what she is.

Why is it still alive? Astrid wants to know.

It was Astrid's idea to come. The three siblings on a visit to Manie's work. Some kind of bonding exercise, as well as a homage to Pa. This is two weeks after the funeral and Astrid's guilt is rising. She never did enough for her father, she never truly appreciated him! She wants to make up for it, in case of future punishment, but doesn't quite know how.

Bruce Geldenhuys, who owned Scaly City with Manie, is showing them around. He puffs ruefully and draws his eyebrows together and says, Well, it's a snake.

A snake that killed somebody, Astrid says. Don't dogs get put down if they do that?

Ja, but, I mean. Bruce is a stolid sort, not much hampered by frills and imagination. It isn't a dog, it's a snake. Everybody expects snakes to bite. And everybody knows they're poisonous. How can it help being a cobra?

Or a rat, or a cockroach, or a germ. You are what you are, even if ratness is your fate. Nothing to be done. If it's your lot to be hated through glass, then hated you will be, and in the eyes peering at her now, belonging to Anton and his two sisters, there's as much awe as revulsion. Whatever is hated is also feared, some consolation in that. No wonder she twitches under their gaze, then slides oozily away behind a rock to sleep.

The outing has turned curiously flat. The three Swart children wandering through the reptile park, looking at hard-shelled, cold-blooded creatures in tanks. Really, this enterprise keeps us alive? But yes, it does, the place has always been a smash hit, from the first day. At this very moment two more buses are pulling up outside, disgorging multiracial groups of children on a school excursion. How very heart-warming and depressing it all is.

You want a coffee? Bruce says as they pass the canteen. He's ill at ease with Manie's offspring and doesn't bother to hide it, so when they decline, his relief is obvious too. He says goodbye at the entrance. Nice to see you, stop by any time. Always here. No rest for the wicked.

Then they're on their way back to the farm, Anton at the wheel of the Mercedes. Been driving it every day since he got home and by now it sort of belongs to him by unspoken agreement. Thinking of letting Lexington go, no need for that expense any more. Also thinking, though it's a nasty idea, of kicking the workers off the farm. Let them live in the township, come in each day. With new laws in favour of tenants and squatters, you can't be too sure, can't let them build up any claim on the land. There's a lot to sort out on the farm, Pa was losing his grip, and if it's just him and Amor living there, no prizes for guessing who'll be doing all the work.

Count the telephone poles and on the third it will be safe to speak. One, two, three.

I've decided to leave, Amor says.

Back to London? Astrid says brightly.

No, I'm going to Durban tomorrow.

Tomorrow? Durban? What do you mean, on holiday?

No, to live.

To live? Her sister and brother stare in astonishment. Has she ever been there? Does she even know anybody in Durban?

My friend Susan stays there. She works as a nurse. After a moment, she adds, I think I might try it.

What? Nursing? Astrid yelps in disbelief. But you can't look after other people!

Why not?

155

Astrid flails, till a memory from way back provides an answer. You can hardly look after yourself!

I've been looking after myself for years.

It takes a second for Anton to locate the correct question. Why, he says, are you doing it at all? You could stay here on the farm, get a monthly income from Pa's trust fund ...

Yes, I could, Amor says. I thought about it. But I need to go.

Very simple, very plain. She has an intention and she's made it known. She'll be leaving tomorrow to go to Durban, of all places, to be a nurse.

We'll see about that. I mean, Anton says, you can always come back.

Yes. She nods in agreement, but she's looking out of the window.

Astrid says nothing, though mean little subtitles flicker within. No surprise, thinks she's too good for us. Well, leave her then, if she doesn't want to be part of it.

Anton takes her to the station the next day, from where the long-distance buses depart. She loads her rucksack into the boot and climbs in next to her brother and they move off together, more or less in tandem, across the landscape. Not much talk between them. Amor gets out to open and close the gate and they resume the drive, heading to town, somewhere in the long pale middle of the winter afternoon.

It's a worthless bit of property, he says suddenly.

She knows immediately what he's talking about, as if they're picking up an old conversation. If it's so worthless, why not give it to her?

Because Pa didn't want to?

But Ma did. And he promised he would do it.

So you say. Nobody else heard that promise.

But I did, Anton.

The road reels hissing under the tyres, pulling scenery past them.

You think Salome has such a bad deal? he says at last.

Not such a good one.

She has a house. She can live in it till she dies. We could make that official. Write it up as a legal document, saying she has the right to stay there for the rest of her life. Will that be enough?

No. She shakes her head. Fascinated by how obdurate he is, while he sees the same thing in her.

We can do it with her job too. A guarantee of employment till she's old, with a pension in retirement, as well as a roof over her head. Huh? A lot of people can't say that much.

I know.

And even if we do all that, no guarantee it'll make any difference. I saw that son of hers, Lukas, the other day. You know Pa paid for his schooling, because he's supposedly so bright, but it turns out he still didn't finish matric. Got into trouble somehow and dropped out. He's working as a labourer on the farm.

She nods. Yes, I heard that.

You understand, he says, people don't always take what you give them. Not every chance is an opportunity. Sometimes a chance is just a waste of time.

Yes, she says. But a promise is a promise.

The bus is already waiting outside the station, its engine running. A few other passengers are lined up outside, all of them, in Anton's eyes, marked with a common quality, of grime and desperation and too little money. Only those who're struggling and down on their luck travel in this way and he feels unexpectedly sorry for his little sister as he gets out to say goodbye.

Here, he says. Take this. Holding out a couple of notes.

No thanks. It's okay. But she does, all of a sudden, hug him hard, and he finds himself returning the pressure. Their first contact in years.

Anton's in an expansive mood, he had a glass of wine before leaving home and did finally find the courage to call Desirée. Found the right words too, falling off the tip of his silver tongue, how he's been thinking about her ever since he got home, and through all the lost years as well. Never spoke to her once in the long stretch of time he was AWOL, so he fully expected vitriol and vituperation, deserves it too, but instead she was pleased, more than pleased, to hear his voice. Couldn't he come over? He could, he can, he is, just as soon as he waves Amor off, and the musky dew of reunion dampens his body already.

Feeling dizzy and generous as they finally let go, he tells his sister, You know, we can work something out with Salome's house.

Really?

Sure, he says, smiling. This is South Africa, land of miracles. We can make a plan.

The last passengers are climbing onto the bus, the driver is getting ready to depart. She hesitates, but he waves her on. Remember, you can always come back, whenever you want to!

She looks at him through the tinted windows of the bus as it slowly pulls away. Singular figure, leaning on the air, one hand upraised. When he turns to go he does it quickly, and the city closes over him like a dirty brown river.

She settles back in her seat, feeling happy for the first time since she touched down. Salome will get her house. A boulder has rolled away from the mouth of a cave. Thin sunlight warms her through the glass, the dry blond hills of the city move past in slow cascade. Goodbye, railway station, goodbye, Voortrekker monument! The wheels thrum underneath her, like a giant heart beating in the middle of it all. Salome will get her house. Amor closes her eyes.

ASTRID

She gets back from the hospital to an impatient message from Astrid on the answering machine. Really, really wish you'd get a cell phone, like a normal person. Call me, I want to tell you something.

Amor can hear in her sister's voice that the something isn't urgent. It's a vain or self-important something, and though it matters to Astrid, Amor doesn't have the strength for it now. Later. She'll have that conversation later.

There's a certain time of day she tries to keep for herself and that's the hour or two after her shift ends. Morning or evening, the ritual is the same. She fills the bath and lights a candle on the edge of it. Then she takes off her uniform, item by item, always careful to do it in the right order, because if she gets the sequence wrong she has to dress again and start from the beginning. Lying in the warm water, while the light in the room changes, she can often forget herself for a while. Or become herself so completely that everything else ceases, including the hard, long day behind her. But she's unsettled this evening, something jangled at the heart of it all.

Susan comes in later. A heavyset woman with short black hair, maybe. By then Amor is out of the bath and making supper in her dressing gown. They kiss, without much heat.

While they're eating at the kitchen table, Astrid rings again. Querulous tones in the next room. Where are you, damn it? Been trying all day. Call me back, I have something to tell you.

Aren't you going to pick up? Susan says.

Amor shakes her head. A heaviness even in the small gesture. I'll ring her later.

What's wrong?

I don't know.

Did you lose another patient?

Yes. But that's not unusual, is it? Not if you work in the HIV ward.

No, Susan says. Then it wouldn't be so unusual.

She holds Amor's hand while they eat. They don't talk more but it's as if a conversation is taking place, one they've had many times before. Susan used to work with Amor in the same ward but gave it up a couple of years ago, because it depressed her. These days she's a health consultant to a big company. She doesn't think Amor's job is good for her, doesn't understand why she keeps on doing it, even when the cost seems obvious.

Most of their conversations are in the past by now. They've reached that stage in proceedings and both of them know it and don't speak of that either. But there is still great softness in two hands linked together on a tabletop.

The table stands in a modest, two-bedroomed house in the Berea area of Durban. Susan's place. There's a root-edness, a permanence, to the look of the house, the look of the life in it. In the lounge, where Amor sits down soon afterwards to call her sister back, the couch is an old one, well used, and the cushions on it are worn. Likewise the carpet and the pages of the books on the shelves. But nothing in this room belongs to Amor, the look of permanence has been borrowed too. She didn't used to think about it but these days she does, more and more.

Astrid answers immediately, twitchily. Where were you? I tried and tried . . .

I was at work, Amor says.

Astrid huffs audibly. Since she married a rich man, she finds the notion of work distasteful, especially when it's a job. Running a house and raising a family is bad enough, but that's why you have servants, to help you. It seems to Astrid that her little sister has chosen the life of a servant instead, and what for? To punish herself?

Anyway, she says, I wanted to tell you about the inauguration.

The what?

President Mbeki's inauguration. I mentioned weeks ago, don't you remember, that we got an invite? You forget everything.

Oh yes, I remember, Amor says, though she has wiped it away till this moment.

Astrid's husband Jake is in partnership with a well-known politician, let's not mention names, no need for indiscretion, but he's a popular, powerful guy, and black, obviously, which is what counts these days. Just luck that it happened, they're neighbours in the same gated community, and both of them saw a chance to make money, which they do. Lots and lots of it, big bucks in security these days, with crime rates through the roof. And if it's that business association which got Astrid and Jake their invitation, so what, the way of the world, not only here, everything depends on who you know.

Most thrilling day of Astrid's life! She wants to tell Amor, like she's been telling everyone, about the crowd at the Union Buildings, with their outfits and their hats! Famous people, man. That actor, can't think of his name but you'd know him if you saw him, and Fidel Castro and Gaddafi! Most of them were only a blob in the distance, but they had these giant TV screens and on there they were blown up big.

The inauguration was scheduled to coincide, down to the day, with ten years of democracy in South Africa, and you could see it in the crowd, such a happy, easy mix of races, everybody so ... I don't know, so lubricated, somehow, so slick. Because, I mean, let's face it, these are people who like their lives for a reason. All of them are rich, but what does it matter, as long as they're on the right side? The whole extravaganza was so inspiring, so uplifting, with the live music and the bright African colours and the fly-past overhead, and of course the party deserves it, just won such a huge majority of the vote, they can afford to be pleased with themselves.

Personally, Astrid says, I don't know about Mbeki. He seems to have only two facial expressions, have you noticed? One where he just looks wooden, and the other where he lifts up his eyebrows and looks surprised.

Through the window of the lounge, Amor can see the tiny strip of back garden, mysterious in its dark rust-lings, and beyond it the lights of the city and the harbour. The night is still and cold and clear, no humidity in the air. Perfect autumn weather. Nicest time of year in this part of the world.

He gave a great speech, Astrid says. I must admit, my mind wandered after a bit, but he does do the hopeful message very well.

166

And the choirs and the bands and the parties all over the show ... Such a festive atmosphere, the loosest Pretoria has ever been, you wouldn't have recognised it ...

But now here's the thing. Astrid's voice drops and points, exactly as if she's next to you, leaning her head in to whisper. At one of the gatherings, a dinner party at the State Theatre, she'd seen Mbeki from up close. And she has to admit, despite that thing with the eyebrows, he's a good-looking man. And she thinks, she's almost sure, Astrid tells her sister, that he noticed her.

What?

Mbeki. He looked at me from, oh, six feet away. And there was just a, I don't know, a kind of electric jolt that passed between us.

Oh, Amor says.

I think he wanted to ask for my telephone number, Astrid says. Couldn't do it, with all those people. Maybe even his wife in the crowd. But I think he wanted to.

Well, Amor says. You are living the life. She doesn't know what else to add, because she's supposed to envy Astrid and she doesn't.

But Astrid has already sensed that her little anecdote has failed to impress and is making conversation-ending sounds. Don't know why I bothered, my sister has no clue about things like social status. No clue about much, actually. Always been like that, though I used to think it was an act.

Susan is already asleep when Amor goes through to the bedroom, or she'd tell her about the talk with Astrid. Or maybe not. She doesn't tell Susan everything these days, it doesn't always help. But it's still a comfort, a deep, quiet comfort, to lie behind your companion in the warm dark, one arm around her and a human heart beating in your hand. Doesn't matter too much any longer that it's Susan in particular you're holding. Just a body and a presence. Not alone.

Because in the morning you must get up and dress in your uniform, item by item, in the correct order, and go back to the hospital. To the ward in the hospital where you work. Where every day, literally every day, there are more and more sick and dying people, whose needs you must attend to, whose needs you cannot attend to, because the man with two facial expressions, who might or might not have wanted your sister's number, doesn't really believe that they're sick.

Susan is right, it isn't good for her. And she's right, Amor is driven to do it, something compulsive in how she seeks out suffering and tries to ease it. Because you can't, not in this particular battle, you can't win. So why impale yourself, over and over, on a spike that will always be there, no matter what? Do you want to hurt yourself?

Maybe that's why. Maybe it's a way of punishing myself.

But even as she says it, Astrid knows it's not true. On her knees in the confessional for the first time in half a year, and she's lost the talent for telling the truth.

For the past year, approximately, she has been having an affair with Jake's partner, the politician who now more than ever shall remain nameless, no need for indiscretion, and incidentally she suspects that it's this liaison, rather than the business ties, which landed them the invitation to the Union Buildings. But so what again, if you think

168

about it, that's how the system works, favours for favours, and life is going very well for Jake and Astrid Moody these days. Really, her husband ought to be grateful she's having the affair, if he ever finds out about it.

That's not why she's doing it, though, of course not! Truth is, Astrid finds him, i.e. the politician, almost unbearably sexy, her nostrils quiver when he comes near, her body wants to cleave for him. And it was never like this with a black man before! Not for her, anyway. The opposite, actually, Astrid always used to find blacks un-attractive, but she's noticed lately that they've started to carry themselves more confidently, they dress and cut their hair in their own style, and she has to admit, it has an effect. Plus they're not prejudiced against heftier women no longer in their first bloom of youth and are open to flirting with her.

Even so, the idea of kissing one was just too much, you couldn't do it, not till this guy came along. He's something else, he makes you see the world differently, the feel of his muscles sliding under smooth dark skin, the stare of his heavy-lidded eyes. The way he says your name a little wrong, with the stress on the second syllable. His cock, so solid-looking, not pink and breakable like white men's penises. His gold Rolex on the nightstand beside the bed. The fine, soft grain of his tongue.

This has to stop. You gave me your word!

I know it does, she says. Then quickly adds, But why?

Why? You ask me that. Don't you see how far you've fallen?

Fallen from what, Father? She isn't arguing, she likes the inflated tone he takes, his language as ornate as the fittings in his church.

From the righteous path, the priest says, and sighs. Astrid. Astrid. I thought you'd put this behind you half a year ago, after we spoke.

Yes, Father.

You can't see him behind the screen, except as a shifting presence, so his voice is everything, but she knows him well enough to pick up the drop in tone that happens now. The intimate note. It was Father Batty who presided over her conversion and her subsequent marriage to Jake, and their closeness hasn't faded from that time. Plus she was here six months ago to confess all of it to him, the affair and its sordid repercussions, and he'd made her promise she would end it. She'd meant to, her promise was sincere, but she didn't do it, not even close. Wasn't ready for that step, as it turned out. So she's stayed away from church since then, to avoid exactly the scene that is playing out now, with its tortuous tassels of guilt. A mistake to come!

She's only here because she told Amor about going to the inauguration and she could hear that her sister didn't approve. Approval matters greatly to Astrid, and it's been troubling her that God might not approve of her lately either.

Both you and Jake have shared your struggles with me, Father Batty says. You opened your heart to me and told me what had gone wrong. Earlier, when you were with, with …

Dean, she says, a fresh pang of guilt passing through her. Who lives now in Ballito with his new wife Charmaine. Poor little man, what I did to him. Those were my lost years, Father.

Yet here you are, repeating them.

But it isn't the same! She thinks about what's different, which leads to another concern. Do you think it's more of a sin, Father, to commit adultery with a black?

Father Batty has complicated and contradictory feelings about this particular parishioner. He has spent many hours in her company, more than the usual convert requires, but then she is more needy than most. Indeed, it has occurred to Timothy Batty before now that Astrid's needs may be like a furnace that consumes whatever you throw into it and then requires more. He decides that a severe approach is required, to put out the fire.

Adultery with anybody is a mortal sin! We discussed this in your catechism classes, why should I have to remind you? You promised me that behaviour was behind you. It was a sign of weakness in your marriage, you said. I worry that it's a sign of weakness in you instead.

Finally, Astrid begins to weep. Always a purging moment. Temperamentally speaking, Astrid took to Catholicism easily, or the other way around, her conversion felt natural. Her new faith, which she experiences as a kind of waterproof garment she's buttoned down over herself, doesn't stop her acting on her fears and desires, but it provides a way of washing them off afterwards. She will receive her penance and the karmic clock will be set again to zero and she will swear to the priest that she will follow his instructions, that this is the last, last time she will ever stray, and she will deeply mean it.

But Father Batty isn't having it this morning. It's no good, this endless repent and repeat. You must quit it, this very day!

I understand, Father.

Do you? I told you last time you must put an end to this before you can receive communion.

I haven't taken communion since.

And you're proud of that, are you? Timothy Batty is in his sixties and has been in this game, beg your pardon, this calling since he was a young man. By now his moral discoveries have long since hardened into rigid, habitual forms. He doesn't especially care about the weaknesses in Astrid's character, but he does care that she's strayed beyond his reach. Her last confession was six months ago and she hasn't been returning his telephone calls and now is the moment to be strong. No penance for you today.

But I've confessed!

This is not a true confession, because you're still in a state of sin. You are not repentant.

I am, Father, but I'm also weak. The little booth is suddenly very close, Astrid can't breathe, she wants to escape. I will end it, Father, she says, hoping to hurry things up so she can get away.

We'll see. Father Batty is pallid and lightly freckled, but his imagination has its vivid patches. It has conjured Astrid at times, always a more pleasing experience than the real thing, though the priest likes plumpness in a woman, a sign of rude good health. He would never touch her, not actually, not with his hand. But a man may dream. God looks into your heart, he tells her sorrowfully. Never doubt it. You may deceive yourself, but you will never deceive Him.

I don't want to deceive Him!

Good. That is very good. Now go and ponder what you've done and set things right in your marriage.

Remove this stain on your life, and when you are ready, come back and you'll receive absolution.

She emerges from the confessional in a state of unease, far worse than when she went in. No penance to ease the burden! She knows she must end the affair but doesn't think she can, a common human dilemma, not only related to romance. Shouldn't have gone to the priest, not before she was ready. Who knows what she wanted when she went in there, but certainly not this outcome. Now she's having a crisis.

There are still a couple of hours before she has to pick the kids up from school, and to comfort herself meanwhile Astrid decides to go to Menlyn. She's always at her least unhappy in a shopping mall. The density of the shopfronts pressed together and the masses of bodies in slow turbulence, like a roiling lava lamp, serve to hold and contain her. Nothing terrible could ever happen to you there. Though she did see a man having a fit once, maybe even a heart attack, in the pet food aisle in the supermarket. Imagine, your last sight in this world, a bag of dog food! But still, it's where she feels safest.

Astrid's fears haven't eased with time. If anything, they've got worse. When the blacks took over the country she thought she'd have a cadenza, people were stockpiling food and buying guns, it was like the end had come. And then nothing happened and everyone just went on like before, except it was nicer because there was forgiveness and no more boycotts. It's not wonderful worrying about your safety all the time, of course, but the upside is that Jake's business is booming. Never been better. And at home, it goes without saying, they've got the most upmarket protection.

She pushes her laden trolley out to the car park and piles the packages into the boot. Bounty and abundance! Sometimes she invents reasons to go shopping, the sensation is so pleasurable, but there's always a feeling of disappointment when it's over and you have to reverse out of your parking place and get in line at the exit boom. A peppermint clinking enjoyably against her teeth, she drives out of the mall and into the next line of cars, waiting at the traffic lights.

It's unusual for Astrid to be less than vigilant, but she's still vexed inside by what happened in the confessional and has failed to pay proper attention. This is the only explanation for how a man, a stranger, could suddenly be sliding into the seat next to her. She looks at him in astonishment. Despite his pocked and dented face, he is well dressed, he is calm. He's even smiling, as if he's been waiting for her to pick him up. Howzit, he says to her by way of greeting, showing a gun.

Who are you? she asks. What do you want?

The questions are not unreasonable, though in a certain sense Astrid has been waiting her whole life for this man.

My name is Lindile, he says. I want you to drive.

His name is Lindile, but that's only one of his names, he's also known as Hotstix and Killer, he's that sort of person. At present he lives not far from here, but he's lived in lots of places, he doesn't stay anywhere for long, he touches down for a moment then floats on, he rolls and drifts through identities and cities, or they move through him, like a current of air. Nothing permanent about him, nothing that lasts.

The fear has at last reached Astrid, the certainty that what cannot possibly happen is actually happening. To her.

Drive, says Lindile, and she drives.

He doesn't care about this hysterical white woman, she is only the means to an end, namely the BMW she's steering. An order has come through for just such a vehicle, down to the exact colour, steel grey, and she happens to be at the wheel. Nothing personal. Though if she continues to wail and gibber like this, in a way not unfamiliar to him, she may become a liability and then he won't be so polite. He pushes the weapon into her side, tells her that no harm will come to her if she does what he says. He knows it's what she wants to hear and almost immediately she calms down a little.

He makes her drive to a deserted side street and then orders her out. What are you going to do to me? she cries. Shut up, he tells her. Just listen. Why do people always want to know what's going to happen to them? So impatient. She's wearing some expensive jewellery, a necklace, a pair of earrings, her wedding ring, and he relieves her of this burden, along with her phone, a Sony Ericsson, nice, before pushing her into the boot. He has to take out the shopping bags to make space, leaves them at the side of the road. So much food, a pity, a waste. She curls up like a baby in the dark space inside. They always do.

He enjoys driving this car, likes the heavy weight of it, so lightly controlled. The whites know how to live! He's been drinking beer and smoking dagga and Mandrax since early this morning, till now he's slack and excited at the same time, a sensation of turbulent fullness coursing through him. He might overflow soon. There's a lady friend he'd like to visit, not too far from here, maybe he could head over now, his mind strains in that direction, till a thumping and moaning from the boot brings him back to himself and to the business at hand. Not yet done. Someone might have seen him getting into the car, they might be looking for him at this very moment. He needs to make the delivery, get paid, get away.

Nothing he hasn't handled before. A little easier each time not to feel anything. But he still becomes squeamish at critical moments, it's a weakness in his nature he needs to subdue, and when the woman is finally looking down the barrel of his gun at the shrinking diameter of her life, it's himself he's so viciously cursing, not her. Come on, coward, do it, do it! But changes tone abruptly as his eye catches on something else, something he's overlooked.

Give it to me, he says in a different voice.

What?

The bracelet, give it, give it.

She can hardly get it off, she's shaking so much. A pretty thing, made of blue and white beads, but not valuable when you look from close up. Disappointing. He slips it into a pocket. Clickety clink. Enough. Almost takes pity on her, but doesn't. Can't leave a witness behind. Sorry, he says. Then it's over, loudly and suddenly done, and so is she.

He's at the side of a huge parking lot in the middle of nowhere, a spot he's come to before. Looming overhead, blank as the future, a disused drive-in screen, discoloured from years of rain. All is brownly veneered in dust and the woman's bright clothes stand out in that uniform landscape like a spill of paint. She is against the wall of what used to be a cashier's office and he pushes her with the tip of one shoe a little further into the shadow. Then

176

gets back into the car and speeds out of there. The most dangerous time, so close to the deed. Not when you want to be spotted.

He delivers the car to the people who ordered it, keeping the other little fringe benefits for himself, and gets his money, a substantial sum for him. After a job he likes to go drinking at a shebeen nearby. The alcohol restores the fading buzz from earlier and somewhere in the bleary fug of the long afternoon he dips his hand into a pocket and finds the bracelet he took. Then the woman's face comes back strongly to him, rising over his mental horizon like a full moon. Poor Astrid! Though he doesn't know her name, something of her terror has leaked into him and he has to quell it, stamp it under his heel, before it can put down roots. Don't look back.

He gives the bracelet to a woman he knows who sometimes exchanges sex for cheap trinkets. But when she puts it on and swishes her hand around to show off its colours, blue white blue, he suddenly loses interest in her and goes. Eyes on the future, or at least on the ground just ahead, Lindile/Hotstix/Killer staggers off down the road, out of the picture, leaving nothing behind.

Leaving Astrid behind. This morning she was alive, inhaling and exhaling, pumping blood and incubating thoughts, a creature with intentions and a mild case of eczema on her inner arm and a dinner planned with friends. Not unlike yourself, perhaps. Now she's a tangle of hair and clothing at the bottom of a wall. Already coming undone. Hard to make out as fully human, till you stare for a while.

The old man stares for a while, before he understands. Raggedy in dress, slanted in attitude. It's not by chance that he's here, in this abandoned drive-in, with its lonely poles sticking in rows out of the tar. It's where he lives, in the cashier's office, or what used to be the office. He took up station inside, oh, maybe a year ago, or is it two, time is so formless for him.

After a while, panic sets in. What if they blame him? They often do, for things he knows nothing about. The only answer, as far as he can tell, is to find a white person to report it to.

There's a cheap motel on the edge of town with an attached off-licence where he is wont to make the occasional purchase, and the manageress in front hears his story with growing alarm. Definitely a white woman? Oh my God! She calls the police and soon two of their representatives, the boys in blue, South Africa's finest, Detective Constables Olyphant and Hunter, come to interview him.

Everyone knows what follows, the questions, the notes, the drive out to the site of the killing, where more notes are taken, as well as measurements and photographs. Even out here, in the middle of nowhere, it's impossible to stop a small group from collecting, a couple of journalists and some curious gawkers from the farmlands nearby.

Olyphant and Hunter do their best to keep observers at bay. They are a serious pair, which makes them somehow more amusing, at least if you notice their contrasting dimensions, as if they've been coupled for comic effect. They give off a rigorous air, although like other officials involved in law and order they have been forced on occasion to become creative about earning an income and sometimes cross over to the dark side. But no need to go into it here, hardly applies in this case, shouldn't have been mentioned.

Today, in the matter of the murdered white woman, Astrid Charlene Moody, a subject likely to draw scrutiny, the two detective constables are very correct. But once they have given the frightened old man who reported the body a thorough grilling, adding hugely to his spiritual unease, they are at a loss and reduced to recording details, mostly in the form of numbers. Mathematics again! So many metres from here to there, the angle is such that, likely a man-sized shoe, point-blank range. Figures do tell a certain kind of truth, but can easily be turned back whence they come, e.g.

1. Age: Olyphant 53/Hunter 38
2. Years in the service: 34/12
3. Waist size: 48/34
4. IQ: 144/115
5. Number of marriages: 1/3
6. Number of children: 0/6

Etc., etc., though for all their differences, they have spent many days in each other's company and it's often the case that people blur under these circumstances. In certain marriages, for instance, you must have seen it, or maybe even participated, the outlines become smudged, the colours run together.

Anton picks it up immediately. You two, he says. Like Thomson and Thompson. No, that's not quite right. More like Vladimir and Estragon. You know what I mean.

Fortunately for him, they don't. They only frown in confusion. What is wrong with this guy? Making jokes at a time like this! And in the mortuary! Who does he think he is, a policeman?

But seriously, what are you doing here? Have you come to arrest me?

We just want to talk to you, Mr Swart. But go and make the ID first.

No need for them to tag along, it should be a private moment for the family member or close associate. So they wait outside, in the foyer, with its sad potted plants and dark wood flooring, sunken into two identical armchairs.

The husband is also there, slumped over like a drunk man, face in his hands. Jake Moody is forty-one years old and owns a thriving private-security company in partnership with a well-known politician, the two detectives have already established that. Big guy, ripped and sculpted, must go to the gym a lot, but right now he looks as if he barely exists, that's how shocked he is. Knows his wife is dead, can feel it in his bones. That's why he asked Anton to do the ID in his place.

Anton follows the man in the white gown, whose name tag says that he is Savage, down a long cool corridor to a metal door. You'd think you were in a novel, Anton muses aloud, but the idea doesn't seem to perturb Savage. He stands aside to let Anton through first, very polite. But just when you expect the rows of steel drawers, chilled corpses inside each one, they have her ready for viewing on a table in the middle of the room. Covered with a sheet, of course.

Have you seen a dead body before? Savage asks him, from the other side of the table. His tone is without relish, but don't let that deceive you, Savage has his predilections.

No. That is, yes, I have.

Which is it?

I killed somebody once, he finds himself confessing to this utter stranger, whose features, already very close together, seem to contract further at this news. I shot a woman when I was in the army. (But does that count?)

He hasn't thought about her in years. But suddenly she is back in front of him, falling down at the impact of his bullet, dying all over again. He finds himself, absurdly, weeping, just before Savage draws back the curtain. That is, the sheet.

My sister. Lying there. Dead. Unmistakable. Astonishing. Yes.

Excuse me?

Yes, he says again, struggling to produce the syllable. Yes, it's her.

With just the tiniest hint of reluctance, Savage pulls the sheet up again. Writes something on a paper. Sign here. And here, please. Anton is still crying and one of his tears splashes the page. Why is that so shameful? But it is, it is. Savage dries the spot, very delicately, with his sleeve.

These moments can be difficult, he says.

Anton doubles over. Oh, that's good! Been years since I've laughed like this, as if I'm having a cramp. Used to come easily to me. The lost art of hilarity. Oh, Savage, he says, when he recovers at last, you are a card.

Savage is offended, or at least baffled, as he stalks stiffly ahead down the corridor. The dead are so much more predictable than the living, with their moods and humours. There are riddles with no answer in human speech, nor is he alone in thinking so, though not everyone craves silence in consequence.

One of the detectives has to sign Savage's form, while the other observes the exchange between the wife's brother and husband. Confirmation of identity, bureaucratic versus personal. Jake takes a while to raise his eyes and then Anton nods to him. That's all, but the message is conveyed and a long quivering and keening ensues. Nothing unusual in this.

When things have calmed again, Detective Olyphant gets right to it. No point in talking to the husband, the man is a wreck, so he keeps his attention on the other one, the brother. There was nobody with a reason to want your sister dead? She had no enemies?

Not that I'm aware of. Although, he adds after a moment, everybody has enemies.

Do they?

Don't you think so?

Who are your enemies, Mr Swart?

Oh. He waves a hand limply, indicating the wider world. They are legion.

This one is an oddball, no doubt about it. However he speaks, he's cryptic. Neither detective understands what he means half the time. Cries like a child, then laughs like a drain. And why did he think we'd arrest him? Was he involved?

I thought this was a hijacking? he says now, impatiently. For her motor car?

We're trying to make sure, that's all. Sometimes there's more to a hijacking than you think.

Really?

Ja, Detective Olyphant says. You'd be surprised.

But Anton isn't easily surprised any more, or only occasionally and then mostly by himself. Likewise, the two detectives have seen it all before. This murder? This one is nothing. You should've been with me only last week. Oh boy, things I could tell you. Any reason will do. South Africans kill each other for fun, it sometimes seems, or for small change, or for tiny disagreements. Shootings and stabbings and stranglings and burnings and poisonings and smotherings and drownings and club-bings/wives and husbands slaughtering each other/parents offing their children or the other way around/strangers doing other strangers in. Bodies cast carelessly aside like crumpled wrappers with no practical use. Each one a life, or rather used to be, and from each one concentric rings of pain ripple out in all directions, perhaps for ever.

Anton has to help Jake to stay upright when he walks, that's how weak the poor guy is. Hard to support him, he's so big and heavy and inert, like a carcass. Never been close, the two of them, so the sudden physical inti-macy is unnatural. Can feel the springy hairs on his forearm. Easy now, nearly there. Open the car door for him, lever him in. Whoops, mind your fingers.

Anton goes round to the driver's side, gets in. Jake requested the lift today, with exactly this scenario in mind. Not sure if I'm up to it on my own. A sign of how frightened he is, even to ask.

Is there somewhere I can take you?

Huh?

I mean, Anton says, before I drive you home. Do you want to see a doctor, maybe?

Jake ponders the question, his big brow corrugated with effort. Even slouched down in the seat the top of his head is pressing into the roof, but he still seems somehow small today. At last he says, The church.

The church?

Yes. If you could take me past the church. I'd like to speak to the priest.

Anton is surprised, but then so is Jake. He hasn't been to communion or confession in a couple of years and the need to seek spiritual help comes on him out of nowhere. In his line of work there are a lot of nasty operators, some of whom he employs. He thinks of himself as a tough guy and he's certainly no innocent, he's had to cauterise the sensitive side of his nature, which would otherwise let him down. He works out three times a week and has a black belt in karate and is fond of watching Charles Bronson and Clint Eastwood play vigilantes. Do you feel lucky, Punk? Go ahead, make my day.

So he doesn't recognise himself in the man who's currently tilting over and sobbing in front of Father Batty. Who is he, this little chap, turned inside out, dabbing at his nose with a tissue and snivelling about punishment? Oh dear, apparently it's me.

In his own way, the priest is also in shock. Really, if you think about it, he was the last person to talk to the woman, aside from her killer. It gives him the chills.

What happened to your wife was evil. Not a punishment!

But it feels personal. For despite his large frame and inflated muscles, Jake contains a weak core, in which he's long been certain that he's damned, whatever happens. For one thing, he has long suspected that Astrid's divorce is an offence against God, even if the vows from her first marriage weren't considered holy, and that sooner or later both of them would have to pay. To that extent, he has never lost his faith.

I have no doubt, Father Batty says, that she is in the arms of her Redeemer as we speak. This kind of sententious assurance comes easily to him, it always has, even from a young age his sense of spiritual authority was insufferable, but today he's talking to distract himself from an unpleasant thought.

You remember she wasn't born Catholic. She became one because of me.

You mean because God chose her for it. But whatever the road, she found the destination. The priest is still preoccupied by the unpleasant thought, which is growing in size. It's hard to believe I saw her just before.

What do you mean?

Yesterday morning, she spoke to me.

This arrives as a stunning piece of news to Jake. What about?

Oh, the priest says, as if waking up. She came to confession. It'd been a long time. Six months. Mind you, he adds, you've been away longer.

What did she say?

I can't tell you that, Jake. You know the confessional is a private place. And it is, moreover, the site of the unpleasant thought. That he let her go without penance, an hour before she died! Is the weight of her soul upon me? You mustn't press me. But it will count in her favour, he decides aloud, that she was struggling with her sins just then. The Lord will be kind to her!

Her sins?

We all have them, he adds hastily, to move the topic along. Of course!

It's a great comfort, Jake says, that she received absolution before she ...

Not quite, not true, no. This is a topic the good father would prefer to avoid, much better for everyone, but too late for that.

You said she confessed. Did you not absolve her?

No, she had ... a problem to solve first. But I can't tell you any more, Jake. I've said too much already.

This conversation takes place in the garden behind the church. No, more likely it happens inside the church itself, in one of the pews, the soft light through the stained-glass windows casting shimmery radiance on Jake's face, so that he feels dazzled and a bit off balance when he emerges a short while later. Not himself, no, not at all. But who is he then, if not himself? Jake, or the impostor with that name, goes lurching down the front steps to where his brother-in-law waits for him, sitting on the bonnet of his car.

Did it help? Anton asks as they resume their drive along the highway. Despite himself, he's genuinely curious to know. Speaking to the priest. Was it helpful to you?

The question doesn't seem to reach Jake. His eyes are on something else, which isn't there. After a while he answers absently. On the morning she died Astrid confessed to him.

Confessed what?

I don't know. He wouldn't tell me.

Both men contemplate this fact from different angles for a time. Anton has been in therapy for a couple of years now and can only understand confession in that light. But next to him, just an elbow movement away, his brother-in-law's perception is very different. Something is happening to Jake. It's like he's in a long tunnel, in which sounds ripple quaveringly and the real world is a bright circle way off there. The only certainty is that he's been wrong about absolutely everything up till now.

He lives in a security estate out in Faerie Glen, built around an eight-hole golf course. Once you sign in and pass through the gate, you're in a swoony suburban dream of pastel-coloured houses and gentle streets, looping around an occasional park lined with trees, all nostalgically reminiscent of something, but perhaps of something that never happened. Jake's house is right on the perimeter, up against the fence. Anton parks in the driveway and hurries out to help, but it's not necessary any more. His brother-in-law climbs out by himself and is moving around normally again.

Thank you very much, he says, in a flat voice. He holds out a hand and Anton shakes it, bizarre gesture at a time like this, but the man is not all right.

Are you all right? he says. I mean, do you want me to come in?

No.

Okay. He's relieved, but has to stop himself from asking a truly insensitive question before getting into his car. Are those burglar bars expensive to make? That's what he almost asks Jake. Can you imagine, at a time like this. But Anton is not all right either. Seeing his sister lying on the table, dead. He starts to cry again, a hot little cloudburst, on the drive to the farm. Taking the back roads from Jake's place, avoiding the city. Long, lonely stretches, through tears.

Always thought it'd be me who went like that. And might still. He needs to replace some of the burglar bars on the farm windows, that's where the question came from. Some bad trouble lately. A big land invasion out on the eastern side, closest to the township, fences cut and shacks put up, all in plain view. Plus one or two other incidents, a storeroom broken into one night, strangers having a prayer meeting on the koppie. Intruders on the land. Had to call the cops to get them out, and there were threats of violence. Coming to get you, boss. Just wait and see. Finger drawn across the throat. He's had Pa's old shotgun serviced since then, just in case. Gone off into the veld and fired a few practice rounds, to stay on top of things. Thinking of getting an electric fence put in, around the house. Must talk to Jake about all of it, but at the right time.

When he reaches the house and switches off the engine, the distant, pale sound of hymns carries to him from the church, even here. Guide me O Thou Great Redeemer / Pilgrim through this barren land. Every day of the bloody week. The pleasant cool of the afternoon is flawless, but a deeper chill is rising now, from the centre of the earth or is it me? The front door stands wide open. Always reminding her, always being ignored. But today he can picture how it would be to go inside and find her ...

Except she isn't here, her car is gone. Bet she went to that meditation class again, today of all days. Like an addiction with her. He's been chafing at the amount of time she gives to this kid, some good-looking local boy from Rustenburg called Mario or Marco, something like that, still in his twenties, who went off to India for a year to find himself and do spiritual stuff in ashrams, comes back here with a new name, Moti or Muti, ridiculous, bestowed on him by his guru, means pearl supposedly, and all the bored, idle housewives are enthralled by his wisdom, or maybe just by the fact he does his classes in a loincloth. I mean, come on, it's Jungle Book time. Teaches them meditation and yoga and who knows, perhaps wakens the sleeping tantric serpent at the base of their spines, all at his so-called Whole Human Centre in town. Hole human.

An intruder would enter the way Anton does now, creeping across the threshold, pausing in the entrance hall to listen. The only sound from a radio in the kitchen, some kind of African gospel choir. Salome washing dishes. Or perhaps, for the sake of variety, polishing some brass ornaments on the tabletop. Yes, she is rubbing the dull metal, till it gives up its shine. Salaam, Salome. Where is my lovely wife? Don't bother to answer. Damn and fuckitte, could she not, maybe, perhaps, just this once, have stayed at home today? For me? She knew where he was going, knew what task he faced. But no. And no, and no, and no again. Been a refrain for some time.

He goes to the booze cabinet in the lounge, fills a tumbler with Jack Daniel's, downs a large swig, tops it up. Not everyday behaviour, mind you, far from it, what do you take me for? Not even sundown yet. But who can blame him? What he's been through already, what still lies ahead.

Salome first. He's said nothing to her yet, nothing at all. She's old, she might have a weak heart, but he also sees her as childlike, someone who needs protection. She's an old child, with a weak heart.

Salome, he says. I have some terrible news.

The brass twinkles merrily, while words travel into the brain and blossom into pictures, and some of those can be hard to bear. Yes, it's mental images that torture people the most, as maybe you already know. Not much love from Astrid in recent times, or maybe ever, but she's one of three white children Salome raised as her own, and it shows in her face. She'd have to sit down, if she wasn't sitting already.

He glugs down the whisky, it makes everything easier. Why don't you take the rest of the day off?

She nods. Not young any more, close to sixty. More bone than meat these days, and not fast on her feet. Not for a long time, but especially not this late afternoon/evening, weighted down as she is by the pictures in her mind. Go, please go, he finds her suffering intolerable. She shuffles off slowly around the koppie to her house, I mean the Lombard place, no doubt to say a prayer for Astrid, if past habit is any indication. Leaving him to refill, refuel, regroup. Something awful about being the messenger, you're always tainted by the message. Here's to you, Anton, bringer of pain. One down, one more to go.

Amor called just once after reaching Durban years ago. He's been intending to get in touch ever since, but only after taking certain steps, and those steps have not been taken. His apathy on the matter slowly developing a will of its own, becoming a resolve. Since then he's heard news of his younger sister from Astrid, who naturally saw it as her resentful duty to stay in touch and pass on bits of information, first about the nursing, and later the announcement that she'd taken up with a woman. No surprise on either count, not in his eyes. Even kind of affecting, seen from a distance. A pain in the arse from up close.

He knows the name of the hospital where she works, nothing else. No, he tells the receptionist who answers, I don't know which ward she's on. Can't you find her on your system? Just a sec, the receptionist says, you're going through now, and she connects him to the one ward that, ja, you could have guessed. No end to her martyrdom. Could I speak to my sister, Sister? You'll know her as Saint Amor.

'Scuse me?

Amor Swart, please.

One minute.

The messenger waits, a faint surf of hospital sounds washing into his ear. Then Amor's voice, unmistakable, even after so much time. Hello?

Hello, he says. It's me.

Anton?

Yes. Listen, I'm sorry, but I have bad news.

He speaks out of the air from a long way off, some-where in the past, only to her, in the nurses' station, its tiles as white and cold as shock. Amor, in her uniform. Standing very still, not moving.

Afterwards he recharges his glass. Not as bad as he'd feared, though his hands are shaking a little. He appreci-ates it when people do their suffering offstage, out of sight. Hard enough to cope with your own life, and that's just the ordinary daily affliction. Speaking of which, here she comes at last, my lovely wife, fresh from meditation. The timing is perfect, except that, um, he seems to have lost an hour or two somewhere along the way, by now it's fully dark outside. Later, earlier, all one in the end, Was it wonderful, my sweet, did you have good vibrations with Mowgli?

She stares at him. Are you drunk?

A little, yes. You could say so. Ever so slightly. To take off the edge, considering I just looked upon the visage of my murdered sister.

She puts her hands up to her face and his anger drains away, or turns into something else, a kind of desperate appetite. He clutches her, she squeezes back, in a moment they're kissing, lips and tongues and teeth, as if they want to bite and chew each other. Even as it sweeps him along, he knows this sudden hunger flows from what he saw on the metal table this morning, he desires his wife because she is so very much alive, her expression smeary and distraught, her hair coming loose, her limbs hot and strong. Bigger question is, Why does she desire him? Back and forth, clobbering at each other, violence humming under the skin. Long time since they touched.

Till their clinch is broken. No. No. Stop. This feels wrong. She pulls away from him. Always she that pulls away. What are we doing? I'm sorry, but I just can't. Not now, after Astrid ...

Okay, he says, his anger returning instantly. Forget it.

But you'd be forgiven for believing, if you wandered into their bedroom at this moment, that they are shipwrecked in the aftermath of a white-hot flash of lovemaking. Half undressed and half tangled in the sheets, breathing hard. Still a good-looking couple, though definitely not youthful any more. His face in particular has something flinty in it, and is that an old scar on his forehead?

Desirée is a softer sort of creature and must once have been a real beauty, not too long ago. But boredom and petulance have corrupted her features, inking in

192

a little frown between her eyes, a sulky pout to her bottom lip. She's contracting inwards on some sour core, she has become dissatisfied, though she's not always sure with what.

Sometimes it's the farm that's let her down. When she got married, she imagined painting watercolours in the hills and riding a horse across a vast plain. Vague, glamorous dreams like that. She didn't expect the days to be so long and bare here, with so much nothing going on. You have to keep finding reasons to drive into the city or out to Rustenburg, somewhere with a bit of life and event and colour. People to talk to! Used to have her nails and hair done every week, but it caused meltdowns in the marriage. No money for bullshit, he says, but look at him, what he spends it on. Literally pissing it away. At least she's got something to show! Though she has to admit, she's been happier lately since discovering meditation classes at the Whole Human Centre. Moti changed his name and there are days when she'd like to change hers too. A different name can make you feel different inside.

Sometimes it's South Africa that disappoints her. Who could have foreseen that her daddy, who everybody used to respect and fear, would have to go in front of the Truth and Reconciliation Commission and admit to doing those horrible, necessary things? The problem with this country, in her opinion, is that some people just can't let go of the past.

Though that's over with by now, years ago already, and these days it's mostly her husband who fails to deliver. Anton was once so charming and handsome and funny, everyone talked about what a fabulous future he had, but the only person who still believes that is Anton. All the big gassy bragging about what he'll do one day with the farm/himself/his life, the money he's going to make, who knows how because he's never really working, just writing his novel, which nobody else is allowed to look at and maybe doesn't exist, though you can hear him tap-tapping away behind the locked door ... while she rattles around these million empty rooms, watching the plaster crack off the walls and the spiders spin webs in the corners. I mean, her, me, Desirée, can you imagine? A baby doll just yesterday, adored by all the boys, could've had your pick, so how did it end up like this? Didn't listen to Maman's warnings and now it's too late to start again, just enough time to make a new baby doll yourself before the ovaries close shop. But even in that department, ha ha ha, been trying and trying and no luck yet. Just knows the problem is with her husband, though he refuses to be tested, and it doesn't help that half the time she doesn't want to touch him any more.

She picks his hands off her, then rolls over onto her back. Lies there, looking at the ceiling. Thinking about having a line tattooed along the edges of her eyes and lips, to make putting on her make-up easier. Some of her friends have been doing it lately.

By the way, he says, I gave Salome the night off. She's very upset about Astrid.

Upset? Please. She's incredibly lazy, that old one.

She does have feelings, my sweet. There is some history ...

History? Really, you should get rid of her. She's slow. You should get somebody fresh and young ...

She's been working here for ever, he says. Since when she was fresh and young herself.

Ja, well. Those days are over.

Excited by her coldness, he starts to nibble at her neck. C'mon. Let go a bit. But she pushes him away and gets up, buttoning her blouse. Urgh, please stop, you're all sweaty. I was very centred when I came home, now see what's happened.

Anton in the small bathroom under the stairs, trying to uproot his groin. As he approaches his climax, his flushed face is reflected back at him in the spotty oval mirror above the basin, the backing in need of repainting, that'll sort out those spots. Interesting how the self can be split into segments, orgasm and observation at the same time, the eye that watches the I. Neither is me, but both might be. Washes his hands afterwards in a renewed fog of fatigue and self-loathing, wishing he hadn't done that. Wish I didn't do that. But you did. Almost immediately he feels desire switch on dully again inside. Yes, it is time, isn't it, to let go of desire, no, Desirée, whatever her name is, let go.

A distant flash of light passes across his face, from a car out on the main road, which has pulled over in a vacant patch of land to turn around. At this very moment it's reversing, a big Jeep Cherokee, and who is at the wheel if not your brother-in-law, Jake Moody. He's not stopping, at least not for a visit, just pausing for long enough to change direction and head back the other way, into town.

He's been driving like this for hours already, because he can't stand the idea of being alone at home. I am a widower. He keeps thinking it, over and over, that phrase, I am a widower, trying out the strangeness of the word, of the condition it denotes. Astrid's two children have already been taken away by their father and the house has transformed in one day from a busy, noisy place to a hollow, confining shell. The rooms at home, emptied of their most familiar element, seem to echo, but loudest of all is the room inside his head. To quieten it, he has got behind the wheel. And stayed there, while the sun went down and the lights came on, and night seeped into everything.

Here he still is, driving, driving. Black river of road, endlessly flowing. He follows certain routes that cross and recross, tying himself in a knot. He goes through the middle of town, past Paul Kruger on his rocky pedestal, then heads northward over the ridge, but turns back again to go past the Union Buildings, lit up like a party, the city simmering below in its murky pot. Past embassies strung out like jewels on a chain, all guarded and immaculate, before real life resumes in the form of brown grass verges and jacarandas losing their leaves. The edges of everything starting to go burnt and crispy.

Out on the eastern fringes of the city, the houses are far off and tiny, little sparks of light amid dark rolling fields of maize, rustling and rubbing their calloused hands. He turns south to head to new developments, sprawling lunar colonies still under construction, satellite suburbs for the hungry middle classes, already walled in though the roads and houses are only halfway built. Another ridge leads him back into more established zones, where the cement is long dry and the lawns crisply mowed, some of the houses as big as hotels, or vast ocean liners sailing past him, ablaze. All fortified to the hilt, with walls and massive gates, and some of the private security guards lolling about outside are Jake's own employees, he can tell by their uniforms.

Down through a filigree of half-undressed trees to Fountains Circle, where you go round, once, twice, three times, before suddenly becoming decisive and heading in the direction that has pulled you all night, like true north on a compass. All the random driving around was a prelude, a tightening spiral converging on just one place, i.e. where you began, only this morning, though that visit seems to lie on the other side of a deep, dark valley.

He parks in an open space directly outside the church. An immodest building, lit from below, to emphasise how endlessly it travels upward, to Heaven. Nothing stirring here, except for a homeless man turning over on his bed of cardboard in the doorway. Jake gets out of the car and walks heavily down the side of the church to the priest's house behind. The hopeful heart-coloured bulb that burns above the front door is somewhat undercut by the security gate and the electric fence, shorting nearby in little blue flashes. A hapless gecko being fried on the wire? Maybe God doesn't care about lizards.

Presses the buzzer on the intercom. Waits a minute, then does it again. And again.

Father Batty is befuddled with sleep. Who is it?

It's me, Father.

Who?

Jake Moody, Father. I'm sorry to bother you.

It's one in the morning, Jake.

I know, I apologise, but I must speak to you.

Father Batty has been roused from a pleasurable dream of large-breasted women and is not happy at this midnight demand on his compassion, but lets him in, face composed in a passable imitation of concern. Come through to the lounge. Jake follows him to a big room with a piano and fake flowers and an assortment of little ornaments, best left undescribed. No energy to name objects, let alone observe them.

I'm sorry, he says again. I know it's very late.

Sit.

They both seat themselves, Jake on the sofa and the priest on a neighbouring armchair. Father Batty has wrapped himself in a batik-patterned dressing gown, a gift from one of his flock who went on a visit to the Far East, but his tiger-striped pyjamas show underneath, to say nothing of bony, blue-veined shins above fluffy slippers. Jake will never see him in the same way again, though that applies equally in reverse.

What is it that troubles you? the priest asks.

Father, even if the confessional is a holy place or what you said, couldn't you make an exception in this case?

What? The priest's mind is like a bald tyre, spinning for purchase in sand. What are you talking about?

I need to know what she confessed to you.

Ah, that. Shouldn't have opened his mouth. I can't tell you, Jake.

Father, I'm begging you.

The wretched fellow is actually getting onto his knees, pressing his face into your lap. He has to be yanked and plucked at, to make him desist, and he leaves a damp patch behind.

No, Father Batty cries. Please! As if he's the supplicant one. Listen, man, you have to pull yourself together. You have to get a grip.

I can't. I've been trying, but I just can't. Jake jumps violently to his feet, then sits down again. I need, he says. I need to know.

The priest sighs. This should be a complicated moment, but it suddenly becomes simple. It's very late/early, he's too tired to fight, and the poor fellow is in pain. Besides, he himself needs the bathroom and this might hurry things along. Sometimes you have to be human.

Your wife was having an affair, he says.

There. It's out. He's said the words and they hover for a second on the air, before the other man hears them. You can see his face change as the knowledge takes hold. He doesn't look hurt any more, he looks angry. God forgive me, the priest says, or perhaps merely thinks, But sometimes the truth is best.

An affair? Jake looks at the word from outside, like some peculiar object. Who with?

No, that I don't know. I'm afraid that I need to –

Please, Father. Half an answer is no answer. Give me his name.

I cannot give it to you, for the simple reason that I don't know it. She confessed the affair, but she didn't give me a name. That is the truth, on the holy blood of Christ, and now you must go home to bed.

The fight leaks out of Jake, he visibly diminishes. When the other man gets to his feet he does the same. Peace comes with acceptance, the priest tells him as he shoves/shows him out.

How can I accept what I don't know?

The man has a point, thinks Timothy Batty, as he finally retreats down the passage. You have to know the truth before you can submit to it. But of course the truth might kill you. The conversation has so upset the priest that he only just makes it to the toilet in time. Nobody's favourite activity, presumably, but much more trying when the bowels are turbulent. Odd that people hardly ever talk about their motions, considering it's an everyday event. The brain would like to deny it, despite the fundamental truths being uttered down below. No character in a novel ever does what he's doing now, i.e. pulls his buttocks apart the better to blurt out his distress. One way to be sure you're not a fiction. Did Jesus ever sit at stool? I wonder. Did He have an anus? Not according to the Good Book, though you can't eat multiple loaves and fishes without consequences at the other end. But shame on you, Timothy, these thoughts are blasphemous. How so? I don't know, but they definitely are.

Forgive that misguided woman, Father, she longed for penance. And forgive me if I wronged her by denying it. Though has he, in fact, broken a law when the woman's confession could not be properly heard? Was he, Timothy Batty, not correct to send her away? This occurs late to the priest, as he reaches for the roll of toilet paper, but he decides that God has forgiven him. I spoke out of love! And to her husband as well. That poor man was in pain and I told him the truth, which cannot be a sin. Thank you, Father, for this relief. Thus one father genuflects to another, fitted inside each other like Russian dolls. Or stacked atop one another, perhaps, fathers in both directions, fathers all the way down.

While outside the church, Jake Moody sits at the wheel of his car. No, he still hasn't left. A hulking, copper-coloured fellow with a frown fixed between his eyes. He appears to be thinking, but what about? He has nowhere left to drive to, maybe that's his problem.

After this long, immobile period, he abruptly stirs. The homeless man in the church doorway watches him start the engine and drive waveringly off. Something not right there. The homeless man has the power to perceive entities from other dimensions and he's troubled by what he saw affixed to that guy.

These have been his environs for a few months now, this particular patch of earth, along with a stretch of shops and restaurants a couple of blocks away. Can't prove it to you, but he once had a high-paying job and an identity that commanded attention and respect. Till it all went wrong. What does it matter, he himself doesn't seem to care, time is a river that washes the world away. Along with his house and everything/everybody in it, the homeless man has lost his name too. His family and friends are far off, both in time and distance, and there is no one to point him in the right direction, or even to tell him who he is when he becomes unsure, but as he keeps obsessively singing the first line to Blowin' in the Wind, let's call him Bob. Who knows, it might even be the right name.

Bob sleeps only fitfully and wakes before dawn, as the birds begin their trilling. He urinates into the church shrubbery before folding up his cardboard and storing it in a flower bed. There's a tap next to the church where he washes himself in the mornings before wandering out to the street to watch the slow beginning of the day.

When the city has properly woken, he wanders down the two blocks to the shops, where he might receive a few coins. There's a kind woman working at the super-market who sometimes gives him spoiled fruit to eat, and in any case there are dustbins to rummage through. He is hungry, always and perpetually hungry, and not always for food.

Time passes differently for those who're shut out of the world. It travels past like traffic at certain points in the day, or like a particular shadow inching across the ground, or like your own body, signalling its cravings to you. It seems to slide by slowly, but the days flicker fast and soon your face is different, not quite yours any more. Or perhaps it is more like you than ever before, that is also possible.

Bob observes his reflection wonderingly in a restaurant window, till he's distracted by a repetitive flapping movement on the other side of the glass. The manager, shooing him away. Go somewhere else, you repulsive, dirty person! The manager has evil entities hovering about him and Bob, immediately becoming his own reflection, lurches off.

Stumbles down the road, casting around for discarded cigarettes. Doesn't find any, but picks up instead a new-looking lottery ticket, freshly fallen. He takes it down to the cafe on the corner to check his luck, hard not to hope, but his isn't that kind of story. No is the word he's heard most often in his life, and he hears it again now. No. Nothing for you. No. To make up for it, on his way out the door he swipes a sweet from a shelf and is spotted by the owner, covered in parasitic entities, all of which begin to shriek and accuse in high, inhuman voices. Chewing laboriously, he trots off up a side street, perhaps to get away, but he's stopped by the cops soon after, not clear if they were unleashed or it's by chance they've crossed his path. Two of them in a van. Where are your papers?

The usual story, in a few minutes he's in the back of the vehicle, one other piss-smelling miscreant for company, a wire grille between them and the world.

There are a couple of minor ectoplasmic entities lying on the floor, fortunately harmless, and their odd little congregation, seen and unseen, is driven around for a few aimless hours, various urban vistas passing outside, before being taken to the police station.

All cells look alike, the walls with their names and dates and prayers and obscenities scratched into them, the single, tiny, barred window high up. And if time passes differently for the homeless, in here it doesn't pass at all. He stretches himself on one of the beds and manages to sleep. Dreams of being elsewhere, pieces of the past mixed with lives not quite his, and in this way escapes confinement for a while.

Returns to it when he's fed that night, and again the morning after. A plate of gruel and bread. Better fare than he gets most of the time outside. After breakfast he's told to empty his pockets. They take everything he has, sixty-two rand and forty cents, which they say they're confiscating as a fine, and then he's shown the door. Early light shimmers outside. I want a receipt, he says.

What? the policeman says.

That fine I paid. I want a receipt.

Fuck off, the policeman says, or I'll lock you up again.

He fucks off, with a slight spring in his step. Not a terrible night in the annals of bad nights, and Bob could tell a tale or two on that subject, oh yes. He has a long walk ahead of him, back to the church that he regards as home, but there's no reason to accompany him and, come to think of it, there never was. Why is he obscuring our view, this unwashed, raggedy man, demanding sympathy, using a name that doesn't belong to him, how did he waste our time with his stories? He's very insistent on being noticed, how self-centred of him, what an egotist he is. Pay him no further mind.

Best to leave him midway on his journey. Let's say he goes up a quiet suburban street, past a quiet suburban house, on which it would be easy to miss a small brass placard advertising the services of a psychotherapist within. She's a woman of about sixty, with short silver hair and impeccable grooming, notebook balanced on her lap. At this moment she's talking to one of her more interesting clients, a man in his late thirties with a few intractable problems. He's had an awful tragedy to deal with this week, but even this event he can only view through his usual prism of narcissistic injury, i.e. his failed marriage.

If I'm honest, he's saying now, speaking about his wife, I used to love her, at least I think I did, sex clouds the judgement, but I think I loved her in the beginning. Over time, guilt and duty and obligation have taken over.

Hmmm. Listen to yourself, fool. Not even your afflictions are original. She makes a note on the page. He tries to see what she's written, but she's tilting the notebook away. Inadequate? Is that what she thinks of me? Could also be Impotent ... Both would be true, at times. But I don't want to talk about my shortcomings, especially not with my therapist. Prefer to impress her, if that's possible. He wants her to find him desirable.

They're sitting facing each other in a tastefully furnished room leading off her back garden, birds chirping a chorus. Leaving the guilt aside, she says, aren't duty and obligation what you take on in a marriage? Adult responsibilities. Is your guilt not perhaps because you think you fall short in that department?

No, he says. I feel guilt because I want to leave her. Do you?

I don't know. Yes. Sometimes.

Duty and obligation work in both directions, she says. It sounds like you feel your wife hasn't measured up.

Yes. No. Does she have to? He can't think about this, doesn't want to think about it, even though he's the one who raised it. Truth is, for him marriage has been like two people coming together to make a third, a mischievous extra presence working against them both, cooking up trouble, subverting his good intentions. But all that is too complicated, when right now he's angry about something simple. Those bloody meditation classes really gnaw at him, when Desirée should be grieving, along with him. His first therapy session since Astrid died and how did we get here? I want to talk about my sister.

Of course. It's a terrible event to come to terms with.

Uh, he says. Actually, I meant the other sister.

She lowers the notebook and regards him with interest. You have another sister?

Yes, of course. I must have mentioned her.

But he hasn't, not once in all his sessions has he raised her name, a sign either of how unimportant she is, or perhaps the opposite, of how much she matters to him. Never realised it before. Odd that, how certain blindnesses are revealing. But you can tell from the level of anxiety it provokes how her imminent arrival has disturbed him.

Why is it so worrying? She's your sister, after all. Not a stranger.

Yes, but isn't that the point? I know her and there's a history.

Tell me more.

But there's nothing to tell. When he focuses on the question, he isn't even sure what the history is. Just normal family stuff, tensions between siblings. What bothers him so much? All he can say, eventually, is that it feels as if they're on opposite sides.

Opposite sides of what?

That's the question. A divide, a chasm, a widening gap. But what that division is, and where it lies, that is another matter. No answer to that, or not in him, or not today. All he knows is that the prospect of seeing his little sister is unnerving and unsettling, and cannot be avoided.

Amor is coming for the funeral. Agreed to pick her up at the airport, because she still, surprise surprise, has no driver's licence. Though she must be anxious too. She's booked to come just for two nights, to attend both Masses, Vigil and Requiem, and the morning after that she plans to return to Durban. Can't take off more work, she says, but c'mon, that isn't the reason. She doesn't want to be here either, not for any longer than she has to.

Her flight is late, giving him an extra hour in which to fret. He wanders around the massive new airport, a vast prestige project for the current administration, see how cosmopolitan and lavish we are. Has to admit he's impressed, whatever his crazy blind spots Mbeki knows how to make the jills tingle. Tills jingle, damn it. But there are limits to one's awe where airports are concerned, something about the bland impersonal halls renders the people in them not quite human too. From a distance, at least.

Only recognises Amor at the last moment, as she comes up to him. Different hair, much shorter than last time, and it's starting to go grey on the sides, but that's not the real change. He remembers her as beautiful, the shock she caused, but that freshness has faded greatly. Not so young any more. None of us is. The dimmer switch slowly turning down. Thirty-one years old. Not ordinary-looking yet, but closer to it. Just another face at the airport.

Hey, sis. / Hello, Anton. And then follows that tiny silence in which oldest and youngest siblings look at each other across the new, unaccustomed vacancy. Astrid was always the glue, somehow. So now, what language do we speak? She makes no move to touch him, he makes none in return. Agreed between them, almost in advance. Though they're friendly enough in their cool reserve.

She's brought only a small rucksack as hand luggage. Travelling light. So light that she almost didn't get on the plane this morning. Susan dropped her at the airport in Durban and she stood in that spot for many minutes, suddenly unsure of whether the next step was actually possible. But evidently it was, it is, because here's Amor, sitting next to Anton in the Mercedes, on their way to the farm.

Spent half the night worrying about exactly this moment, the long drive and how to fill up the time. No escape in the car, you're locked into conversation or silence, the only two options. He's worked out in advance a line in flaky patter, jokey and self-deprecating, the sort of fluff that works well in a bar, often used it before, to ease into things. But of course she's not somebody he's just met, and neither of them is drunk and anyway, as far as he can tell, she has no sense of humour, so he quite quickly drops the performance and gets down to what matters.

Stuff we have to sort out, sis. The family lawyer did try to reach you, think she gave up in the end, some problem with the monthly payments from Pa's estate, apparently they have no bank account number for you? They're putting it into a holding account meanwhile, but jeez, you're losing out, the interest alone could be keeping you afloat, makes no sense to hide away.

I know, she says. I got the messages.

The lawyer says you don't reply.

It's true. I'm sorry.

Well, maybe it's for the best. There's something else I need to ask you, which we can sort out at the same time.

What's that?

I might need to sell a piece of land. A small bit of the farm, if you agree to it. I have big bills to pay, the rates and taxes go up all the time, the upkeep is a nightmare … But this isn't important right now, we can talk about it later.

Almost said too much as it is, too soon for that little request. Changes the subject, to the state of the country generally, a curious mixture of optimism and unease. Describes his personal state too, come to think of it. How he experiences it anyhow, especially at this moment. Partly he's burbling cos he's nervous, but he's also surprised by how pleased he is to see her, and by how easy she is to talk to. It's in the way she listens. Never noticed it before. Makes you want to offer something up, a confidence that marks you as unique. Fewer and fewer of those in recent years, as you lapse into well-deserved cliché. Only one surviving ambition that might possibly redeem him.

I've been working on a novel, he tells her.

Really?

Well, it's still only a few pages and the rest is mostly rough notes. But if there's something I know for sure, it's that I'll finish it. Call me a failure on every other count, I won't disagree. But I'll leave a book behind, at least. Even if it's a bad one. Hears himself and blushes hotly.

She's looking at him curiously, head to one side. I don't think you're a failure.

Well, you were always kind, he says. His tone is sardonic, but he realises that it's true. Kindness, that's her thing. Her whatchamacallit, her quality.

What's it called?

No name yet. The title will probably be the last thing to arrive. By now he's not embarrassed any more, and finds himself speaking openly with her about his novel, in a way he hasn't with, say, his wife. How he'd started on it a couple of years ago, in a kind of fever late one night. How hard he's laboured at it since then, every day almost, sometimes hours at a time. How even when he's not working, but just sitting and thinking about it, it's become a refuge for him.

A refuge from what?

From life, he says, and laughs in that old way of his, shuddering to the point of crying.

In recent years Amor hasn't read many novels. She stopped enjoying them a while ago, after a couple of years working at the hospital. The real world has become too huge, too heavy, to be carried around in a basket. But she would like to read her brother's book, when he finishes it one day.

They arrive at the gate and he gets out to open and close it, two combination locks these days, easier to do it himself. Then lets the silence spread, at last, into the stretch of gravel track. No change in this view, not ever in our lives. But as they park in the driveway, she can see that the house is in bad need of repainting and the flower beds, all dug and planted and nurtured by their mother, have been left to go to seed.

Although he wants her to notice the decay and take pity on him, he feels unexpectedly defensive. Ja, I've been slack lately, I've let some stuff slide. But I'm going to get it sorted soon, next week, in fact, just waiting on some equipment I ordered ...

Inside the house, too, there are cracks and breaks and small subsidings. A missing table leg has been replaced with a stack of encyclopedias. An absent glass pane with newspaper. Everything grimy and lightly shop-soiled, not much cleaning going on.

Wish my lovely wife was around to greet you, but she's syncing her vibrations with her guru. And I also wish I could install you in one of the upstairs bedrooms but they've all been commissioned for other purposes.

My room too?

Sorry, yes, that's my study these days. Where I do my writing! We sleep in Pa's old room now. You'll be more comfortable downstairs, in the guest bedroom.

Never used to be a guest room down here. Turns out it's what was once Pa's study, on the ground floor at the back, on the dark side of the house. A square, charmless chamber with three thin rectangular windows, horizontally arranged, high up. Something of a prison cell about it, though the furnishings belong in a hotel. Bed and desk and chair and cupboard, all bought together from Morkels.

Well, whatever. It's just for two nights. She plumps her small rucksack down on the floor.

I'll get you some fresh sheets, he says. But doesn't move, quite. He's studying her again, in a frank sort of way. He notices that in his younger sister, now his only sister, there is a certain quality, hard to name, that has stayed just the same. And how do I look? he wonders.

Slowly, she shakes her head.

Well, you could have lied.

His hair is receding, making the old scar stand out on his forehead, and there are dark lines next to his eyes. But she's reacting to something else, a deeper tiredness she can see in his face.

You don't look well, she tells him.

You aren't exuding good health yourself.

I've just lost a sister.

Funnily enough, so have I. A quick smile cuts his face, heals up again. You do realise it's just the two of us left.

He goes to get the linen. Takes his time about doing it, but when he comes back she's sitting on the edge of the bed, waiting for him, and resumes the conversation as if the interval hasn't happened.

Then maybe we can agree on one point, Anton.

What's that?

Salome. The Lombard place.

He puts the sheets down slowly on the bed. Still, he says, amazed. Still on that.

Yes. Still on that.

Must it be the very first thing we talk about?

She herself has been taken by surprise at how much it matters to her, this buried question from long ago. She has thought of Salome many times over the years, of course she has. Whenever her mind has strayed in the direction of home, or no, that is, the farm, not her home any more, whenever her mind strays to the farm there are lots of stones to turn over, and Salome is one of them. But that particular stone never seems to find a resting place, no matter how often it's turned.

I'm not here for long, she says.

I meant to deal with it. I really did. But ... I don't know, life got in the way.

Okay, Amor says placidly. But can we deal with it now?

What, this very minute? This isn't the moment, you can see that. But we'll do it, he says. Of course. That's easy. We'll get it sorted.

Before I go?

There might not be time. But in any case, that's not necessary, is it? We can finalise things long-distance. No urgency about doing it immediately. Especially not with the funeral starting. Better get ready.

Makes his exit casually, but once out of sight he bolts upstairs to his study to examine, once again, a set of plans he's dug out from among the general disorder and spread on the floor. Stares at those plans with hunger and fear, as if they map out the glorious extent of an empire.

His wife finds him there when she returns from her yoga class at the Whole Human Centre. Even a long pranayama session has failed to calm her restless energies today, and she's in an equine mood, stamping and snorting and tossing her mane. A touch premenstrual, probably, but she's also overwhelmed by the negative and destructive power given off by her husband's family karma. What all of them must have got up to in their previous lives, to be causing so much trouble in this one!

Is she here?

Anton is woken from a profound reverie. Yes. She's here.

And ... ?

Oh, he says. It's been all right.

Well, I hope she doesn't imagine I'll be making special meals for her just because she doesn't eat meat. It's not going to happen. Desirée keeps bringing up this possibility, the notion has consumed her ever since she heard about Amor's imminent arrival. Her sister-in-law failed to attend her wedding three years ago and has shown no contrition for the lapse. Also, too many people have remarked on how beautiful she supposedly is, a disquieting topic to Desirée in recent years. Ooh, is that her?

Where?

His wife has drifted over to the window, on which the blinds are eternally down, and is peeking through the slats. There, talking to the maid by the washing line.

Hmm, very suspect. Two women embracing, unwarranted tenderness between the races, while undergarments flicker and dance in an unfelt breeze. Yup, that's certainly her.

She's not that gorgeous.

Oh, the looks have faded a bit.

Really? Hmmm. Desirée warms up to her a little. What are they doing, the two of them?

Plotting revolution, he says. And it does look conspiratorial, the way they're knotted together. Even when they've let go of each other, they haven't let go. Talking very closely, holding hands, heads almost touching. She was always thick with the underclasses, my sister. No, not really. Not a political thought in her head. But she's drawn to victims, the weaker the better, feels she has to make up for all historical wrongs, and there's some unholy alliance between those two, God knows what.

Well, Desirée says, becoming bored, as long as she doesn't expect special meals ...

She's been reminded, by the sight of Salome in her church clothes, that she still has to dress for the Vigil Mass. Never been to a Catholic funeral, what are you supposed to wear?

The priest is layered in his full regalia, the human equivalent of a peacock. Look at him as he emerges from his pleasant presbytery behind the church, does he not feel preposterous? His yellow Fiat is parked in the driveway. He's about to get in when he espies a homeless man sitting on the opposite kerb.

You mustn't pee in the church shrubbery, he says. Please.

I won't, says Bob.

Don't do your business anywhere near the church. Then, to show he empathises with the plight of the poor, he adds, Do it over there somewhere.

By now he's late for the Mass, which is happening in a chapel adjoining the funeral home, a short drive away. A bit of a cheerless spot, low-ceilinged and cramped, he knows it well and he can tell from all the cars outside that it's going to be full. Luckily there is a parking bay reserved for his kind, he doesn't have far to walk, and isn't late after all, or not very, by the time he arrives at the chapel door, his bosoms glistening.

214

In his robes and vestments it is easier to feel the weight of office, the material presses down so. Certainly he leaves behind any hint of his blinking midnight self, wrapped in a dressing gown, hairless ankles exposed, but nevertheless can't avoid the husband, Jake, who is one of the pall-bearers, and obviously has to be greeted, though they manage to pass each other with a half-smile that could be a grimace.

This is outside, on the steps, in the troubled twilight. The coffin is in a side room and the pall-bearers have been waiting outside. They go in now to pick it up and bring it to the door, where the priest stands by to receive it, splashing his holy water.

Another small tension plays out here, because Astrid's first husband Dean has also been conscripted as a pall-bearer, against his will. At the last moment he's taken the place of Wessel Laubscher, who has become lost and failed to turn up in time. Red-faced and furious, round little Dean de Wet, rounder than ever these days, takes up his station at the right front corner, opposite his usurper, the second husband, whom he will not look at or speak to, now or ever.

Still, his better nature compels him to this task. For the sake of the twins, mostly. Can never forgive Astrid for the suffering she inflicted on him, the worst of which was taking his kids away. Ain't life funny. Neil and Jessica will be going back to Ballito after the funeral, to live with him and Charmaine for what's left of their growing up. A twisted kind of justice among all the unfairness.

It's been decided, thankfully, in light of the injuries suffered by the deceased, that a closed casket would be best, and they carry it solemnly, borne on a throbbing wave of organ music, into the chapel and place it carefully in front, feet facing the required direction. Now the box is shrouded in a white pall, the right words are spoken in Latin, the gestures of ritual begin to pile up, flowers and incense and hymns and prayers, all centred on the body in the box, keeping it company on its way. Where to? That question still seems up for dispute, so Hear us, dear Lord, please have mercy on the soul of our sister Astrid, let her not go to Purgatory, or not for too long, and certainly not to the other place. She's suffered enough, she doesn't deserve worse.

Father Batty has chosen as his theme the story of Cain and Abel. He's feeling reflective and righteous this evening, the more so after spotting that vagrant urinating in the church flower bed yesterday. Verily, the barbarian is at the gate, Satan's dark flood laps already at our shores, etc., etc.

The good father's voice is at its most sonorous, the occasion requires a tragic note. I will tell you, brothers and sisters, that sometimes I don't know where we live, in Eden or in the Land of Nod. This beautiful, bounteous country looks like paradise. But there are moments, and this is one of them, when it feels as if we are in exile, amongst the seed of Cain, and the Lord's face is hidden from us ... He goes on in this vein, but who can listen for long, when the moral pitch is too high for human ears, and his voice a bit squeaky too. A little overwrought, perhaps, because he can't entirely quell the unpleasant thought, which has stayed with him, of what he failed to do. Much easier to blame Cain! It's a relief for most people when he brings his metaphor to a conclusion, urging them to be their brother's keepers and return to the sacred space of the first garden, where he's sure Astrid dwells. And now let us pray.

Ja, Anton says in the car afterwards, we live in exile, in the land of Noddy ... Then there is silence on the drive home, headlights sluicing a narrow yellow channel. When they get back to the house, he lets the others go their own way, Salome on the footpath around the koppie, Desirée upstairs to the bedroom, while he slips into the lounge, heading for the drinks cabinet. Needs some anaesthetic to blunt the nerves.

Surprised, when he turns, to find Amor has followed him. Want a drink, sis? Nope? Is that another of life's pleasures you deny yourself? More truthful to feel the pain?

No, she says, sitting on the sofa. Just more painful.

Exactly, and unnecessary. Why must you always suffer? Here, let me help you. Pours a glass of wine for her and holds it out. Come on. Loosen those bolts.

After a hesitation, she takes it, smiling a tiny, tilted smile. Is that how you see me? Tight bolts and pain? You don't know anything about me, Anton.

Not entirely true. I do know some things. I was here when stuff happened. The lightning!

That was a long time ago. And then I left home.

He looks seriously at her for a moment. All right. You might have a point. I've never paid you proper attention. But we could change that. Let's drink to new beginnings.

He raises the glass, swallows. Watches her cautiously do the same. Then she raises it again.

And if you mean that, now let's drink to Salome's house.

He sighs theatrically. I said I'd deal with it.

But you also said that nine years ago.

Tell you what, he says, as if it's only just hit him. Let's help each other. Wait one sec. He dashes out and up the stairs to Amor's room/his study, and comes back down with his rolls of plans. Spreads them out on the lounge floor, bottles of drink holding down the corners. Here, this property here. Tappity-tap-tap with his finger. Out on the edge, useless piece of land. Not going to affect anybody.

It's right next to Alwyn Simmers' church. It might affect them.

Well, ja. That's true. But not us, I mean, which is what matters.

She has her head to one side again, as she looks curiously at him. I thought we were talking about Salome's house.

We are. But we can make an appointment with the lawyer and kill two birds ...

What does one bird have to do with the other?

Ah, he cries, recharging his glass, in the spirit of new beginnings, we have to help each other!

No.

Huh?

No, she says again, slowly. No, I can't do that.

But why not?

Anton, she says, it's not an exchange. The house was promised to Salome. Why will you not give it to her?

If I do, then will you agree ... ?

No.

His composure is cracking, he's already rolling up the plans. Why not? What noble reason is it this time?

You want to sell that piece of land, because you want to create problems for the church. That's the only reason.

It's not the only reason, but so what if it was? Coldly furious now, the steel showing. You should hate that man as much as I do.

But I don't.

Well, maybe you should ask Salome what she thinks. No sale, no house, that's the deal.

Whatever Salome thinks, Amor tells him, our mother wanted her to have the Lombard place. It was her last wish and Pa agreed to it. He promised.

So you say.

I was there.

So you say.

Am I lying?

I don't know. Are you?

For the first time she wavers a little. Not lying, no, certainly not. But is she telling the truth? Almost sure she is, but not quite. Not backing down, though. Part of the change he can see in her face, something fixed and unyielding. Not how she used to be. That weakness is gone.

No, she says. I'm not lying.

He nods, the rolled papers under one arm. Good. Don't want to be the cause of your first moral failure. All downhill from there, and I should know. Anyway, he sighs. I'm saying goodnight.

And then he's gone. She can hear him walking away up the passage. His footsteps sound hesitant, but he doesn't turn back. Nor will the moment return, which is true of all moments, though not equally.

Alone in Pa's study, what the room will always be to her, she lies down and closes her eyes and tries to find a place inside herself where a cold wind isn't blowing. Can't do it. There's an actual chilly wind outside the house too, tugging at tiles and tapping on doors, and the curtains won't settle down.

The problem, she thinks, the problem is that I have never learned to live properly. Things have always been too little or too much, the world sits heavily on me. But, she reminds herself, I am getting better at it! She's found it in herself lately, more and more often, to do what she feels she has to, but to do it lightly.

Though tonight, sorry to say, isn't one of those times. Life and death have both pressed hard today, no remedy for either. With more to come tomorrow. Maybe a mistake, after all, to be here. Too late for that regret. But lying restlessly in the hard, narrow bed, Amor decides that she will cut her trip a day short. She will leave in the morning after the Mass, maybe even before the end, without a word to anybody, and she will not speak to her brother again. Not angry with him, just done. Unless.

The morning is fine and still and clear, the best sort of Highveld autumn day. Perfect weather for a funeral! Father Batty is often cheerful on these occasions, After all, as he likes to tell the family, it's not a cause for sadness when God has called a Beloved to Him. This is the sort of vapid assurance that has curdled the milk of kindness in the breast of many in his flock, though he doesn't care to know it, because his own ebullience is too enjoyable.

For what is there not to enjoy, when a big funeral mass is under way, with all its stages and formalities laid out before you, like some kind of richly decorated passageway through which you must pass? Timothy Batty is more aware of his frailties than he generally lets on, but seldom does he feel less fallible than when he stands up here above a grieving throng, the master of God's ceremonies.

Once more, in the church, all of us, against our will. Times like these when the clan thickens, in numbers if not in loyalty, eyeing one another from our foxholes. The Swarts sticking together, mostly, though we've thinned out a lot by now, just a row of us in the first pew, Amor and Anton and Desirée and various other far-flung relations, hard to tell apart from anyone else. For there is nothing unusual or remarkable about the Swart family, oh no, they resemble the family from the next farm and the one beyond that, just an ordinary bunch of white South Africans, and if you don't believe it then listen to us speak. We sound no different from the other voices, we sound the same and we tell the same stories, in an accent squashed underfoot, all the consonants decapitated and the vowels stove in. Something rusted and rain-stained and dented in the soul, and it comes through in the voice.

But don't say we never change! Because guess who else is there in the front pew, an honorary kinswoman today. See how far we've come in this country, there's the black nanny, sitting with the family! Bet you Salome has never, no, not even in the First Assembly of the Revelation on the Highveld, been among such lavish decorations, though she's aware of them only as a dripping golden smear, due to her cataracts, which also give her a wise, aloof demeanour.

And what's more, she's not the only black person present in the church! If you glance over there, but not

221

right now, you'll see that hot politician, can't pronounce his last name, those tongue clicks are too difficult, but he's riding high at the moment. He's in business with Astrid's husband, of course, but still, it's nice of him to come, it's a generous gesture from a busy guy.

And he's not the only politician! Though in fact Desirée's father has officially retired from politics, and in any case his presence is more dubious, considering. The stuff that came out at the Truth and Reconciliation Commission, it makes your skin creep, but in the end even notoriety is a form of celebrity and if you check him out he's just an ordinary-looking old uncle, seems harmless, could pass as a furniture salesman in a provincial town. Probably here under duress, dragged along by his wife, the platinum ice lolly, forty-five facelifts later and those killer heels.

But enough, we are the rainbow nation, which is to say it's a mixed and motley and mongrel assembly in the church today, restive and ill at ease, like antagonistic elements from the periodic table. But the priest addresses them all indiscriminately, raining Latin upon them without distinction, Requiem aeternam dona eis, Domine, the opacity of God unites them briefly before His clarities again divide.

Move on, move out. Through the side doors of the church, into the cemetery, where the earth has already opened its mouth in readiness. No need to linger on what follows, the putting into the ground, the heart-rending grief as the final goodbyes are said, etc., etc. It's a very old scene, perhaps the oldest of all, and nothing about it is unique.

Certainly the homeless man, Bob, has seen it all before. From his vantage point on the corner opposite, he's observed the same crowd assemble on different days, dropping their tears into a rectangular hole. But today is maybe a little different, because there are a lot of entities attending this gathering, more than usual. He can see a convoluted creature suckling on the priest, for example, while small furry outlines snuffle between the gravestones, and occasionally a winged being flashes past in the air. Very busy over there in the churchyard.

Amor is the first to leave. She called earlier from the house to arrange a taxi in advance, without telling anybody else, and now she hurries out just before the end, carrying her little backpack. She walks past Bob and he stares at her from close quarters, but she's entity-free, this one, unless you count the faint steady glow she gives off, like a soft blue fire.

Morning, Alphonse says to her, beaming. She's kept his number all this time, ever since Pa's funeral, and incredibly enough it still belongs to him. His life has improved, along with his English and his knowledge of the streets of Pretoria. She gets into his taxi and is driven away, while behind her the funeral must be over by now and the crowd dispersing. Bob watches humans and their attendant organisms radiate in waves from the churchyard, their patterns not unlovely to him. But troubling to Bob since he first laid eyes on him a couple of nights ago is one particular man, who seems like the saddest person in the world. He moves slowly, eyes on the ground, and when he passes Bob he looks up.

Do you know, the homeless man asks him, you have an entity on your back?

What?

It's holding on to you. With tentacles.

Rubbish, Jake says, terrified.

I see things, Bob tells him. You can't fool me.

What do you see?

The entity on your back. It's very big and it's got a lot of arms. I mean, tentacles.

Jake has stopped walking. The homeless man is insane, obviously, but what he's just described feels true, somehow. Something big and dark is holding on to Jake, he can feel the pull of its suckers.

Will you take it off me?

Bob finds this hilarious. Brother, only you can take it off!

I don't know how.

Can't help you. Scrape it on a wall?

Jake hurries on. Shouldn't have started that exchange, but he's open at the moment to signals from elsewhere, any signals at all. Wouldn't have considered it just a few days ago, but sometimes the normal rules change fast. Whatever you can believe in might be true.

Back at the house, he goes in search of a close relation, preferably female, but he has to settle for his brother-in-law, who's digging through cupboards in the kitchen, probably in search of alcohol. At least he can be counted on to give an honest reply. Do I have something on my back? he asks.

What?

A homeless man at the church told me I have some-thing stuck to my back.

Oh, horseshit, Anton says. He's probably a crazy person.

A little worried about Jake, he doesn't seem to be coping at all. Really not himself at the moment. There

224

he stands, a multi-tentacled entity fastened to his back, and his house filled with people who have come to support him in this difficult time, wondering how any of this can possibly be real.

I need to ask you something, he says.

Okay.

Did you know Astrid was having an affair?

No.

That's the truth? You didn't know?

Anton shakes his head. No, he didn't know. Incredible! But who with?

I hoped you could tell me that.

I can't. I'm sorry.

Anton watches his brother-in-law drift rigidly away, like a stick in a stream, and has a rare moment of pity for a fellow being, though it's edged even now with ice. No truthful answers without cold questions. And no knowledge without truth.

And no alcohol, not in any cupboard. What is wrong with the man? He hangs about alone in the kitchen for a little while longer, not ready yet for small talk, thinking about his sister. No, not Astrid, the other one. Saw Amor slip out of the church earlier. Saw it because he knew she'd do it, could feel her intention in advance, even before her silence in the morning and the backpack she brought along. What's unexpected is how sad he feels about it, though that's just sentiment, what does it matter if she won't say goodbye? Can call her at any time, surprise her with the news that, Hey, Salome has her house. Might do it, even. Might actually do it.

He just wants to go home now but you can't leave so soon, you have to do the rounds. Go into the lounge, find some family to feud with. Spends a little time talking to Tannie Marina, or the stumpy remains of her, half melted and overflowing her wheelchair, like an old candle in a saucer. Not quite eighty yet but since the emphysema took Ockie, she's fallen fast into ruin. Holds his hand and strokes it, which is a new thing for her. Sentiment and slobber from the old virago. Oh, the horror, the horror.

She's looked after at home these days by useless cousin Wessel, who can't apologise enough for something he did or didn't do yesterday. What is it with him? Hardly ever leaves home and doesn't lift a finger to feed himself. He's lost all his hair, for some reason even his eyebrows, and because he spends most of his time indoors he has the pallor of white cheese. He's given to flowing garments, of a kaftany cut, even on a day like this one, under which he probably doesn't wear underpants. The sight of him is very distracting, so it's hard to focus on what he says, but he keeps going on about his faulty phone leading him astray. I'm so sorry, I'm so embarrassed …

About what? I don't understand.

I was supposed to be a pall-bearer yesterday, but I got lost. My GPS took me to the wrong chapel!

Oh, it doesn't matter … Anton waves it away. He doesn't care. About that or anything else besides, though you do have to pretend. No sooner is he shot of his peculiar cousin than he's replaced by his shell-shocked nephew and niece, Astrid's children, Neil and Jessica, about to depart for Ballito. Look after yourselves. Give me a call sometime! Goodbye!

And if they have hardly acquired features or defining characteristics it's because those aren't much on display in their round, pimpled, adolescent faces, though much swirls in the space behind. Since the long-ago sighting of their dead grandfather on the farm, when they were only seven, they have each been imprinted with a primal dread of ending up like him, waxy and rigid and uninhabited, and the knowledge that such a state has befallen their mother, who at this moment lies underground in the churchyard, has undone them both too, in an almost identical way, as is often the case with twins, for complicated reasons. Worse, both of them know that their lives are about to change irrevocably and there's nothing they can do about it, taken from one existence to a different one completely, just at the midpoint of their teenage years and at their zestiest hormonal peak, pumping out oil and hair and desire. How terribly unfair everything is! Goodbye!

What do they want from him? What is family for? An interesting question, which Anton resolves to interrogate later in his journal. He's diverted from these thoughts by his wife, murmuring that they've been there long enough, can they please go now? She wants her chakras rubbed by Mowgli the man-cub and Anton wants a whisky, sadly unavailable in Jake's dry house. Meditation for medication, fair exchange, so yes, sweetness and light, we can go in a moment, but first let's say our goodbyes. Look after yourself, shout if you need anything. And please, let's stay in touch.

On the drive home he asks, Did you know Astrid was having an affair?

No! Desirée's surprise is genuine. Who with?

That's the question. Thought you might have the answer.

She shakes her head. Amazed at the idea, in fact. Though also, hmm, not a complete shock. But who says so?

Her husband.

Jake? He's not well at the moment, you can see.

Anton agrees. Not in his right mind, whatever that is. We should have him over sometime soon, to show our concern.

He does, in fact, give Jake a ring a couple of months later and invite him out to the farm. For a meal and a drink and a generally sociable evening, a pretence at keeping up, but also to get a quote on putting in an electric fence around the house and maybe some beams in the garden. Turns out to be a not-so-bad dinner, at least from Anton's point of view. The sober world, with all its ailments and injuries, is hazily amusing to him in recent times and he finds himself laughing a lot, especially at night.

Jake is still tormented by the same question, by now an old one. If I could only get his name, he tells them.

Why? Anton says. What will it help?

I don't want to do anything to him, I just want to know. At the moment I suspect everyone. Even her women friends. Being sure will end the pain.

But it won't! Don't you see? Behind that question is another question, Why or When or Where, and behind that another ...

Maybe, Jake says stolidly. But I still want to know.

Desirée smacks the table dramatically. She has the solution! In her meditation group in Rustenburg is an older woman, a medium, who will speak to Astrid and ask her for the name.

228

Jake actually takes this seriously, while Anton cracks up. How will she chat to Astrid? Do normal cell phone rates apply?

Through her guide, of course. Desirée is too caught up in Jake's drama to pay much attention to her husband. At the moment this woman, her name is Sylvia, communicates through an Egyptian man from the turn of the last century in Alexandria. He'll put us in touch with Astrid.

But Astrid doesn't speak Arabic. Or does he use subtitles? Anton falling about, nearly wetting himself. But at the same time oddly moved by how earnest Jake is in his approach, how much he wants the answer. How far would he go, actually, if he could, to get it? Beyond the grave, apparently. The grave beyond the grave! Anton has to dash upstairs to his study to make a note of it, to maybe use in his novel.

And of course, it ends up that Desirée makes an appointment with Sylvia, who promises on her website to draw back the veil for you, and drives Jake out there one arbitrary weekday morning. The house is nondescript, a bit grubby and unkempt, not unlike Sylvia herself, who's a thickset, grizzled woman with long, dirty hair and a spiky voice, no spiritual paraphernalia in sight. Jake appreciates her plainness. Some of the options he's tried have been more flamboyant and false. They sit down in her lounge, on a saggy brown sofa with doilies on the arms. She asks what has brought him to see her, even though she's been told the whole story in advance.

Um, Jake says. My wife died sixty-two days ago.

Sylvia is scandalised. Never use that word! It's very upsetting to those that have passed.

What word? He has no idea what she means.

I can't even say it. There is no such thing as that word!

Finally he gets it. She means death. No such thing as that word. And he is comforted by her indignation.

My wife ... passed? And I'm finding it hard to let go. I still have questions ...

Do you have anything of hers with you at this moment? Something she might have worn or kept close to her?

He does, because she already told him on the phone to bring such an item. Some of Astrid's personal effects were forcibly removed from her, of course, and distributed elsewhere, they belong to other people now. The lives of objects, if you had any idea how far they travel ... But he found a pair of reading glasses next to her side of the bed and has been carrying them around with him wherever he goes.

He deposits them into Sylvia's little palm. She closes her fingers and shuts her eyes, she hums and mutters to herself. Rocks back and forth. Opens her eyes.

Mustapha is telling me, she says, that your wife is safe. She wants you to know that she's okay.

He nods, barely able to inhale.

I see her standing by a waterfall with forest all around. The sun is warm. She's happy and safe.

That's good, he says.

Your wife is saying that if you have to make a long journey one day, you must take a strong pair of shoes. And stay close to the river.

All right, he says. I'll try.

There's somebody with her. A man. He's very protective of her.

230

Who is he? he says, leaning forward.

Ummm. Sylvia has closed her eyes again, she is holding hard on to the reading glasses. She gives the impression of trying to hear a faraway voice through clouds of static, and indeed the sensation for her is like listening to a crackly transmission on a bad radio, occasional words emerging. Tall. Bearded. Glasses? Does this seem familiar?

A name, Jake says. Can your guide pick up a name?

Ummm. Mmmm. Mmmm. Mustapha is struggling to get information.

Anything?

Could be Roger? Does that mean something to you?

I don't know anyone called Roger.

Richard? She snaps out of it, opens her eyes. Richard, I think, but it was indistinct. Could be Robert. Something like that. I don't know. I'm sorry, there is an obstacle blocking the path today. Maybe try again soon?

Anton is out when they get back to the farm, but later that night Jake calls his brother-in-law. Does the name Roger mean anything to you?

What? The connection is bad, it comes and goes, and Anton thinks he's misheard.

Did Astrid know anybody called Roger? Or maybe Robert, or Richard? Any close friend with a name like that?

You're barking in the wrong forest, Anton tells him, but the call has already broken off. Roger/Robert/Richard. The poor guy is losing it. Got to make an effort, spend some time with him. Not to mention the kids, my nephew and niece, innocent vessels embarking on the future, etc., etc., though I can barely remember

231

their names. Supposed to care, but only the form is there, the content is air and abstraction. Mostly the form is enough.

At this moment Anton is alone at home, all the servants departed, his wife out at a yoga class. Was going to spend the next few hours working on his novel, but the engine won't turn over tonight and you can't force it. Easier just to keep the nerves dampened down. To which end he has a glass of whisky in one hand, half a joint in the other. Already quite stoned, quite drunk, hours ahead in which to deepen the condition.

His phone rings. Jake calling again. Can't deal with his craziness right now, got my own craziness to worry about. Puts it on silent and slips it into his pocket. Tries to remember what he was doing. Ah, yes. Looking for something. Resumes lurching from room to room, switching on the lights, searching and searching, but fucked if he can remember what for. If his eye falls on it, he'll know. Whatever it is, he needs it, or he needed it when he started looking, which means he'll need it in the future. But it's okay, because any second now he'll find it. Any second now.

ANTON

ANTON WANDERING AROUND HIS HOUSE. Power's gone again, fourth time this week, and the generator's run out of petrol, so everything's off. He could do something useful with his hands, like fix the banister on the stairs or replace the broken tiles on the patio, but he's not in the mood. Hardly ever is these days, for anything.

It's a public holiday, Reconciliation Day or whatever they call it lately, so the staff aren't in. They've got wise to their rights and have been demanding extra pay for holidays, though what they really want is to stay at home and get falling-down drunk. Same as me.

And Anton has been applying himself to the task for a good couple of hours already, drifting from room to room, bottle in hand, trying to stop from thinking. Lots to think about at the moment. No, you're going through a bad patch, that's all, so intense it feels like it's always been this way. In reality it's only since, oh, Thursday? Whenever you threw away that minor fortune at Sun City. Stupid, stupid, stupid. Last week? Or the week before, maybe. Part of the badness is losing time, the sense and sequence of it, though be honest, Anton, that's been happening for a while. Everything's been happening for a while. That's the trouble with the world, it's not original, no surprises up its sleeve, it repeats itself like some old auntie with dementia. Same stories over and over, so tired of it. Did I ever tell you about, Yes, you did, actually, so shut the fuck up.

Anton, alone with his thoughts, in his too-big, falling-down house. Supposed to be doing something, but not quite doing it, because Why. This smeary sensation, the edges rubbed away, is it my eyesight or my brain? That's a good line, write it down before it goes.

Maybe pop out for a drink? He's drinking now, but always better to have some company, air yourself a bit. It's only alcoholics that drink alone, wouldn't want anyone to mistake me for an alcoholic. Gnarr harr har, as that dog in the comic used to say.

Anton at the wheel of his bakkie, trying to leave his property. Such a rigmarole getting the gates open and closing them again behind you, first at the house, then when you reach the road. Combinations and keys challenging enough when you're sober, but far from that today, and afterwards, as he speeds towards the city, he's not sure if he actually did put the second padlock on again. Forget it, no turning back now. He's on the new highway, it's a toll road, but fast, no traffic lights to hinder you, and the added advantage that it doesn't take you past Alwyn Simmers' horrible great church, though the tip of the spire does whoosh by in the distance. Toasts it with the open bottle of Jack on the seat next to him. Good health, you parasitic old bitch. Outlasted your creator and still thriving, I see.

Only three in the afternoon. Correction, five. He's in an establishment he's been frequenting lately, on the okay edge of Arcadia. No electricity here either, but they have a generator and the lights flicker wanly overhead. A quaint, mistaken kind of place, but that's why he likes it. He likes the dim lighting and the yellow wallpaper and the genteel pretensions, even though the patrons these days are quite rough. No splendid individuals among them, though they share the same general condition, and any sharing is a comfort. Yes, it's come to this.

Only seven in the p.m. Correction, eight twenty. Desirée will be back from yoga, probably with Mowgli in tow, no need to hurry home. Same again, barman. Little more ice.

Anton in a toilet stall, pissing. Not entirely sure of how he comes to be there, though urinating is an inherently truthful activity. Shitting too. No social graces to disguise you. All diplomacy should happen on the crapper. Zips up, heads at a windblown angle to the mirror. Good God, who fucked with my face? Where is the golden boy I used to be, who hid him under this dented metal mask?

Quick, get away, back to the bar. There's a new arrival at the counter, a hollow-looking old guy who stares and stares till he catches Anton's eye.

Hey, how're you doing?

I know you, the old guy says.

Where from?

You haven't changed at all.

Well, sorry, friend, but you have.

You don't remember me? Take a good look. He leans into the light.

Anton peers. No, I don't seem to ... But there is something, some trace, just out of reach. In the voice, maybe. Who are you?

Give you a clue. Last time I saw you was through a fence. Thirty ... no, thirty-one years ago.

He has to compute. Then suddenly it comes to him. Payne! I wondered what happened to you!

They shake hands, more effusively than the occasion demands, but are unsure of what's supposed to follow next.

Get you a drink? What'll you have?

Army buddies, Payne explains to the barman.

Army acquaintances, more like, but Anton doesn't say it as they head to a table in the corner. He's pleased to see Payne, and it's true that he's thought about him from time to time and wondered what happened to him. Odd how certain people, often random individuals, can pulse with significance in your thoughts, your dreams. What's been happening with you?

Payne has been working as a quantity surveyor since his time in the army. Studied at Wits and met his wife, Diane, there. Happily married for twenty-eight years and has two kids, grown up now. One of them lives overseas, in Australia, and in fact Payne and his wife are thinking of emigrating to Perth in a few months, to be closer to the grandchild. Also because, sorry to say it, lost all faith in this damned country.

And what about you? he asks Anton. What's happened since we last met?

Oh, it's been good.

What did you study?

Never got there, actually. Had a few years of wandering around, then I settled down. Married my childhood sweetheart and been running the family farm ever since.

Listens to himself with amazement. All of it true, all false.

You were somebody I was sure would go to university, Payne tells him. Such a brain! Thought you had a future in politics, actually.

I've been writing a novel, Anton suddenly remembers.

A novel? What's it called? Is it published?

Not yet. Not quite finished, actually. Almost!

What's it about?

Oh, Anton says, the torments of the human condition. Nothing unusual.

Ho, ho, ho! Payne slaps the table. Always the joker, Swart! I look forward to reading your book.

One day. But what brings you here, to this shithole? For it has become clear to Anton in the last minute that the place is indeed a shithole and he must never return here again, though he also knows that he will.

I live just round the corner, Payne says, I'm often here. Hey, why don't you come home with me and meet Diane?

Diane?

My wife, I just told you ...

Oh, right. Sorry. Now, you mean? Well, why not? Okay. But in his mind this conversation is already over, already a half-memory he can't be sure of, though he can see Payne is excited by their meeting.

Ja? Great! Just going to the bathroom for a sec. When I come back, we can leave.

Sure, Anton says. But in truth he's bored by this man, by his ordinary life and his ordinary wife, just as he's bored by almost everything these days, all significance leaked away by now, and it doesn't feel wrong to wait till he's gone, then get up and wander out into the night, as if you've been drinking on your own. You probably have.

Anton behind the wheel again, floating hazily down city streets. At a traffic light a furious man shouts at an imaginary companion, Do you think I'm crazy? Do I look crazy to you? Growing army of the mad and the destitute, quite a few whiteys among them. Keep away from me, Worzel Gummidge, what you've got is catching. A relief when the light changes and he can drive on. Not entirely sure of his location or direction, not too concerned about either. Though sometime you do have to set course for home, with its infinite delights.

But first, apparently, you must encounter the flashing blue lights ahead, the upheld hand commanding you to stop. Anton at a roadblock. The fright almost sobers him, adrenaline wiping him clean. Please, no. If the mind has any power, make this disappear, make it unhappen. But the mind has no power.

I'm lost, he says cheerfully to the officer at his window, as if that excuses him. I don't know where I am.

Blow into this, please.

Huh?

Put your lips to the mouthpiece, blow into it.

The officer is a black woman, maybe half his age, who has the power to lock him up. Remember that, Anton, pull yourself together. She's shining a torch into his face and must already know how he's spent the last few hours. No secrets between them. He puffs half-heartedly into the device and her tone hardens.

Do it properly, please. A long, steady breath.

He sighs all his defeated sadness into it. She takes the reading and their eyes meet.

I'm sure we can work this out, he says.

Anton at the ATM, drawing money. There's a limit on his account, put there to protect against scenarios just like this one, i.e. robbery. He can only take out two thousand rand, but luckily Constable Maswana is reasonable. They even shake hands when he drops her off at the roadblock afterwards, as if they've just conducted a business deal. Which, from her POV, they surely have.

He seethes and bubbles like a noxious swamp the whole way home. Two thousand rand! Taken off him at the side of the road in broad daylight. Only a metaphor, considering it's ten at night. Correction, eleven. Point is, the stealing is brazen, any time of the day. Chomp chomp chomp, little termites, eating away at the timbers. While the President, the fat termite queen, lolls at the heart of the nest.

And it's true I've done my share of chewing along the way. But two thousand rand! The sum hurts, especially when the reserves are so low, and he lost that major chunk of change in a stupid drunken binge at Sun City, and he owes huge interest on a bank loan, and the income from Pa's investments has dwindled, and his wife feels it is her right to have expensive cosmetic surgery done every year, and the reptile park is going to close because Bruce Geldenhuys ran away to Malaysia with the money. Just a bad patch, Anton, you'll get through it, but is it, and will you? This doesn't feel like a patch, it feels like the future.

Under siege on other fronts too. Talk of official claims against land on the farm, a community forcibly removed long ago. To say nothing of continued invasions in the present day, fences cut and more shacks put up, out on the eastern perimeter. The value of property falling all the time too, nearly worthless already, so what's the point? Should do the sensible thing, give up on the countryside and move to town, come to an agreement with Amor to sell the land while they still can. Maybe save his marriage into the bargain and, who knows, himself.

So why does he not do it, the sensible thing? Dunno, just always been like that. Can see the right action and will not perform it. Performs instead the other action, the wrong one, in order to vex you, and himself. Besides, never cared too much for town.

Anton, fumbling with combinations and keys again, in the glare of the headlamps. Anton, arriving home at last. Where a Volkswagen Beetle is parked next to his wife's car in the driveway and lights burn upstairs and down. At least the electricity's back on. Music, if that's the word, some kind of Buddhist chanting mixed with a techno beat, comes out of the lounge, turned up high.

He sits out on the front steps for a while, letting his eyes adjust to the dark. Near the midpoint of summer and the stars bristle like blossoms in their deep, black bed. Nice image, that. Write it down in the journal. He can hear them coming downstairs in stages, lots of giggling and low voices. A whole procedure to exit the house, even though the front door is standing open. Then great surprise at his presence, which may not be feigned. How long have you been there, darling? I was just showing Moti my watercolours.

Moti? I thought his name was Mowgli. But look, he's in civvies tonight, where's your grass nappy, wild boy? Surprised by his strength of feeling, the poisonous purity of it, Anton throws his head back and howls like a wolf. Akela, we'll doom our best!

I get them to try that in my workshops, Mowgli tells him indulgently. Most people aren't nearly as free as you are emotionally, they hold back.

Nothing wrong with holding back a little bit, Desirée murmurs.

But Anton doesn't feel like holding back tonight. How were they, my wife's watercolours?

Um, very nice, I liked them a lot.

She show you her brushes too, and her exquisite palette? Did you stretch her canvas?

He's very drunk, Desirée says.

Yes, I can see that. Think I'll be off.

You've always been off, Anton tells him. Right from the start.

Aggression ultimately hurts the aggressor.

I don't know, I find that the object of aggression suffers more. To prove it, he lunges sideways as the fool tries to sidle past on the stairs, and in his panic to get away Mowgli manages to kick Anton a lucky shot in the head. A bright flash, then the step tilts up to catch him. Whoops. No pain, though. Shouldn't there be pain? Laughing, he rolls onto his back.

Well done, he says, holding the side of his jaw. There's a faint flicker of hurt now. What a hero.

It was an accident, Mowgli says. But also not. Your own anger turned back against you, like a boomerang.

In other words, you deserved it, Desirée says.

You deserve a few things yourself, don't you think? Or is bad karma reserved only for other people?

You'd better go, sweetheart, she whispers. Before he pulls anything else.

He makes a show of concern. Will you be all right ...? Are you sure nothing will ... ? Because I –

Because you what? Huh, sweetheart? You'll protect her? Funny! He tries to surge to his feet, but staggers in the process and falls again.

Just go. I'll be fine. I apologise on behalf of my husband.

Mowgli does leave, but not before delivering himself of a final homily. How he believes matter is spirit in a fall from grace. But matter is at its most material when it uses force. No spirit present in violence. So it is sad to observe Anton demean and degrade his spirit. That's all he has to say, but he says it with kindness, and hopes it will be received in the same way.

Gee, thanks. Now get the fuck off my property and don't come back.

Moti will come back whenever he wants to, but it probably is better if you go now, sweetheart.

I have new appreciation, Desirée, for what you have been going through.

Then Mowgli is a pair of red tail lights receding into the dark.

No, Moti is a person of great integrity, with a very old soul. That's what his wife tells Anton, in a small, cold, furious voice. She has learned so much from Moti! He has helped her to find herself. And she will not have him spoken to in that rude, vulgar way, she will not have him physically attacked, when she invites him to her home.

I live here too, actually. And I can't believe I'm being cuckolded by such a lowly person. He's not even pretty any more, have you noticed? Went up a few sizes in loin-cloth recently.

He's not a lowly person! In fact, he is almost definitely on a higher plane. And he would never, ever behave in the way you think. He's a friend and a guide and an example, but not a lover. Though so what, she adds after a second, so what if he was? People don't own each other! I would celebrate if you found some other people to explore with.

244

I would too, believe me. But isn't that a bit commun-ist and hippyish, all that non-ownership and sharing? Your daddy wouldn't approve.

My father has met Mowgli, ag, Moti, and likes him very much.

Your father's mind has gone, he likes everybody! He'd like Stalin these days if he met him. Hilarity turns into crying and back into laughter. Oh, I can deal with the tragedy, it's the farce I can't handle.

What's that supposed to mean?

I have wasted my life.

Well, thanks very much. I'm not having a huge amount of fun either, in case you haven't noticed. And I'd shut up about waste if my sperm count was as low as yours.

She means to hurt him, because the recent revelation is deeply bitter, on both sides but especially hers, that he is incontrovertibly the reason they cannot be fruitful and multiply themselves upon the earth, but tonight he scarcely registers. He's still stunned by the simple realisa-tion that's just struck. It's true, I've wasted my life. Fifty years old, half a century, and he's never going to do any of the things he was once certain he would do. Not read the classics at a famous university or learn a foreign language or travel the world or marry a woman he loves. Not hold real power in his hands. Not going to bend fate to his will. Not even going to finish his novel, because, let's continue to be honest, after nearly twenty years he hasn't really started it. Not ever going to do much of anything.

Anton prowling the house in the small hours, pausing now and then outside the bedroom door, locked against him, his wife sleeping on the other side. Could beat on it and shout some more, but no surprises in that scenario. Better to resume pacing, bottle in hand, surveying the bleak landscape already traversed, the worse one that lies ahead.

Later, Anton in a hotel room, trying to get money out of a safe, but the bloody thing won't open. He tugs at it, his hands are slick and sweaty, can't hold on to anything, and now there's a knocking at the door. Blam blam! He freezes in fear, because the money in the safe isn't his, he shouldn't be here, and the person knocking doesn't mean him well. Where will I hide?

Blam blam! The sound, some sound, yanks him from the hotel room, drops him back into his body, half capsized on the sofa at home. Lights on, TV on, front door standing open. Anton waking up.

But what was the knocking? It's very late/early, just before dawn, and something was banging in his sleep. He's almost sure of it. Out there somewhere.

Afraid and on his feet, nerves protesting. Is this the moment you've feared, is something about to happen? He lurches up the stairs to the study, frantic now, digging for the Mossberg under heaps of clothes. Seems to take an eternity for his fingers to locate the metal. Ammunition in the drawer. Fumble fumble fumble. He's finding it hard to perform even simple tasks, head feels like a blocked drain, with a taste in his mouth to match. Finally staggers down the stairs, shotgun in one hand, stuffing the shells into his pocket. Rushes out the front door into the huge and terrifying dark, feeling magnified in some celestial lens as he goes down the driveway. Little encircling moat of lawn, then the electric fence, then the rest of the farm, and only then the world. Circles inside circles, inside which is me.

The knocking could have come from the clump of sheds and outbuildings beyond the fence. Or maybe there was no knocking after all, except in his dream. Much more likely, if you think about it. What kind of intruder announces his presence? Well, maybe the worst kind. Unlock the gate, pass through. Why is everything so quiet? No insects trilling, and where are the birds, when the eastern sky is whitening already?

As he gets close to the sheds, he levers a shell into the gun, pumps it forward into the chamber and hears it lock. Kachunk! The sound is hard and crisp, a kind of warning. Talk about a knock! If anybody is out there, that should let them know he's serious. Flicks the safety off and waits a moment, but there's no noise in response, no feet running.

Does a circuit of the buildings but it all looks intact, doors and windows locked. He keeps walking, not sure what he's looking for, but. Things are worse with his head, and now he's nauseous too. Stops a minute and tries to puke, but can't even manage that. Keeps walking instead, the sickliness not separate from the land he's moving on, bushes and tussocks of grass without detail or colour.

Anton stumbling across his farm at first light, half drunk and half hung-over, clothes hanging open and unbuttoned off his frame, as if he's torn at the seams, the stuffing coming out. And what would it be, Anton, your stuffing? Oh, the usual Christmas fare, some sweets and a fortune cookie, a little bit of dynamite.

Here comes the sun, little darling ... Pylons stamped in silhouette against the red. He's walked quite far, the house out of sight behind him. Birds in full whitter now. Foolish old earth, returning and repeating itself, over and over. Never misses a show. How can you bear it, you ancient tart, giving the identical performance again and again, evenings and matinees, while the theatre crumbles around you, the lines in the script unchanging, to say nothing of the make-up, the costumes, the extravagant gestures ... Tomorrow and tomorrow and the day after that ...

No. Can't do it. Can't bear being a walk-on in the play any longer, can't bear the notion of going back to the house and picking his life up like some worn-out shirt he dropped on the floor. And then what? Putting it on again, just like that, stinking, absolutely reeking, of himself? He knows it too well, that smell. Cancel the shirt, cancel the house. Cancel the pylons. Make it all stop.

I wanted ...

Blam!

There's that sound again. Like somebody knocking hard on a door. She thought she'd heard something a little while ago, in her sleep. After that terrible scene last night Desirée had to knock herself out with pills to get any rest, so she's groggy this morning, and with her long white nightgown and her hair hanging loose, everything about her droops somnolently earthward. Of course, there's more of her to droop these days.

Goes to the window and lifts the blind to look out, but there's nothing to see except brown grass. That's my life, she thinks, miles and miles of brown grass. Even the exciting bits have lost their colour. What's a lady to do, stuck out in the sticks with a drunk man for company?

248

She's going to get fretful, of course she is, and look for consolations in other places, and who can blame her for that?

Desirée doesn't blame herself for much, she never has. The natural order, as far as she's concerned, is that the world is there to try to please her, and she is there to feel disappointed by it. In her dressing gown and fluffy slippers she goes downstairs, where the girl will have her coffee ready on the stove. Morning, Salome. Have you seen the master?

No, Madam.

There's too much sugar in this. I'm always telling you.

Sorry, Madam.

Don't make my bed yet, okay? I might lie down a bit more. I had a terrible night.

Sorry, Madam.

This one has been working here for ever, since Anton was born. The things she must've seen and heard! It's because they're always around, like ghosts, you almost don't notice them. But it's a mistake to think the same applies in reverse, they're always watching and listening, helping themselves and each other. They know all your secrets, everything about you, even the things other white people don't know. The stains in your underwear, the holes in your socks. You have to get rid of them before they start to scheme. Long past time to let this old one go.

Thinking such thoughts, she ambles out with her coffee onto the front stoep. Likes to stand here in the early mornings, pretending to be a farmer's wife, while she surfaces into the world. Sometimes she imagines fields of corn rolling away, yellow and green, vibrating in the wind.

Out of the corn, that is, the grass, a figure running. The rising sun is a dazzle behind him and his shadow stretches far ahead, mimicking and mocking.

What is it? What's the matter?

She can see, when he comes in through the open gate, that it's only Andile, another one who's been working here for ever. Travels in by foot from the township every morning, since his family got moved off the farm. Now he's shout-talking at her, telling her what he's seen. Back near the electric lines. Oh God, help me.

It's hard to understand, she must've misheard.

What? she says. What did you say?

But even when the words are repeated, they don't seem attached to the world. No. That can't be true. That doesn't make sense. Only last night he. That doesn't fit. No.

No, she says.

But refusal only works on other people, on fate it has no effect. You may have noticed it yourself, protesting at destiny is a waste of breath, what happens will happen regardless of your No. In the end it's a fact as neutral as the weather that this morning your husband got up and went outside with his shotgun and contorted himself into an impossible position in order to blow his head off, just because.

The worst experience of Desirée's life so far is what was done to somebody else, i.e. her father, and in this case too of course Anton's death is his, but somehow his suicide is hers, she can feel it already. That's how other people will see it, that's how they'll see her. She will always be the woman who married the man who killed himself, and who knows, perhaps drove him to it.

Who knows, perhaps I did. She thinks that, she will think it, over and over, till she reaches the point where she must deny it, even when nobody has accused her of anything. No, no, I didn't fail Anton, I have never failed anybody, he's the one who let me down!

Shhh, quieten down, schatzi. You have to calm yourself. Nobody's blaming you.

What do you mean, they all are, even you …

Desirée is a fire person, she's too emotional and volatile to handle a tragedy, so she needs an earth person to balance her out, somebody solid and unmoving, with maybe a touch of permafrost under the tundra. Obviously, she's called her mother. Maman has had a taste of scandal close to home and rushed immediately to the farm in her Porsche, armed with a phone-load of her husband's contacts and a small pharmacy of sedatives. There are ways of dealing with problems so that they don't cause excessive turbulence, but it's important to be cool and steady while also knowing exactly who to speak to. A word in the right ear and a speedy process can be set in motion, so that a police doctor will come out to issue the death certificate, only a few subdued questions will be asked, and the body removed before it causes too much of a sensation.

After that, there are simply practical steps to be followed. Firstly it's a matter of letting everybody else know, and Maman takes control of the task, but even this, as it turns out, isn't too onerous. Anton was a lone wolf, he had some acquaintances but not too many friends, and the names on his phone are mostly of contacts he used for supplies on the farm, with a few arbitrary drinking buddies thrown in. Takes less than half an hour

251

to call those that seem important, and although most seem shocked, there are no tears.

It only strikes Desirée after everybody else has been told. Oh, my goodness, what about Amor?

Who?

Anton's younger sister. You did meet her a few times, don't you remember ... ?

He has another sister? Really? I thought there was only the one ...

Maman is hard put to conjure up Amor's name, let alone her face, from years ago. Honestly, she finds the whole Swart family so challenging that she tries to wipe them from her consciousness. Plus Anton himself always seemed relation-free.

She couldn't have been a very colourful person, she decides. Or I'd never have forgotten.

There's no number for her on Anton's phone. They haven't spoken in a long time.

Why not? The old lady brightens at the smell of blood. Was there a fight?

Not a fight, no. More a disagreement. I can't really remember what it was about. Some land?

When white people fight, her mother declares without a scrap of rational evidence, it is always over property!

But how are we supposed to let her know? Then it comes to Desirée that they've had this problem before, and it was solved by finding Amor's place of work. The hospital in Durban! The HIV ward!

A couple of enquiries lead to a number, and a cheery voice answers. Oh yes, Amor used to work here, but she left a couple of years ago, for personal reasons. I can give you another number to try ... ? This one is answered by somebody called Susan, who says curtly that she hasn't seen Amor in a long time. She sounds cross and unhappy and keen to get off the phone. No, she doesn't know how to reach her. Thinks she's gone to Cape Town. No, she can't pass on a message.

Even though she has no memory of Amor, Maman feels aggrieved by her. What an impossible person! It really does seem as if she's tried her hardest to disappear. Well, leave her then, if that's what she wants. You can only do your best. Besides, it makes planning the funeral a much simpler affair, if there are fewer people to consult.

Maman herself is inclined towards a Calvinist service, it's the natural fallback, after all, and a severe ritual always brings a sense of finality to things. But her daughter doesn't agree, she thinks that her husband's soul would benefit from a more Eastern approach. Since she got caught up with this yoga-yogurt thing in Rustenburg, Desirée has been open to unorthodox ideas, which caused some friction with her father before the dementia got too bad. Maman too has her doubts, but in this case she gives her blessing. Anton would hate an alternative service, which seems like a good reason to give him one. In recent years he was worse than unpleasant to her, and she doesn't regret his departure too much. Go ahead, schatzi, funerals are for the living not the dead, and anyway he's not here to object, is he?

Not in person, perhaps. But it was in Anton's nature to foresee even the posthumous humiliations ahead, and to resist. The next morning the family lawyer rings. Cherise Coutts-Smith has added another name to her collection of spousal scalps, the gravitas of which has dragged her voice down into the lower reaches of her chest, from where she rumblingly informs Maman that Anton has placed a letter on file, officially notarised, about his own wishes in this current scenario, which amount to the following.

1. No religious service. Definitely no prayers.
2. Cremation, no burial.
3. Chapel at the crematorium is just dandy.
4. Scatter ashes at some suitable place on the farm. Wherever.
5. No undue fuss or sentiment, if that isn't already clear.

There you are, very blunt and simple, and not much room to manoeuvre. Have it your way, Anton, it shall be as you desire. Suits us all just fine, as it happens. But before you go, the old lady says to Cherise Coutts-Smith, do you happen to have a number for Amor?

For who?

Anton's sister.

Oh, the sister! No, we've been trying to reach her for years. And now it really is essential we talk to her. Please do ask her to call me.

You haven't been listening, Maman says, irritated by this assertive, self-important woman, who reminds her of somebody she can't quite place. If you had, you would understand that we don't know where to find her.

Amor has vanished. Amor has disappeared. But we've heard that before and she always turns up if you know where to look, solid and substantial, very much in evidence.

What is she doing today, at this very moment? She is washing a weak body in a bed. Amor in a hospital ward,

254

tending to the sick. This is an old picture, it hasn't changed, what do you mean when you say she's vanished? She's in a different hospital, that's all, but the ill and the dying resemble each other everywhere, their affliction is universal, and looking after them is the same undertaking. See how gently, with what care, she carries out her task, moving the flannel over damaged, sensitive skin. How she pats the place dry, and dresses the wound, then helps the patient, an elderly woman in this case, to put on her clothes. Okay, my dear? Is that comfortable? Does that help a little? Hours of such ministration behind her, many more ahead.

Then follow her that evening as she walks along a few streets to where she lives, and if it weren't for the uniform you wouldn't notice her especially in the home-going crowd, nothing about her that stands out. Nor in her small studio apartment, on the third floor of a nondescript block. The front door opens into a modest living room, from which a tiny kitchen and bathroom lead off. Her bed is a futon mattress, rolled up in the corner, and there's very little other furniture, aside from the sparse trappings of a single chair and table and a built-in cupboard. That's it. In fact, to judge by the squares of slightly different colour on the wall, she's removed a couple of paintings and put them away out of sight.

She can feel her own perspiration sticking her uniform to her skin and gets undressed, forcing herself to remove the garments in a random order, against her own inclination. It's okay, Amor, no bad spells will be released ... She would like to bathe but it's not allowed. The dams are nearly empty and water is rationed, so she showers instead, just for two minutes, saving the run-off in the tub to use later. Would normally make supper now, but the electricity is off again. Yes, happening here too, happening all over the country, long dark patches in the power. The grid is collapsing, no maintenance and no money, the President's friends have run off with the cash. No lights, no water, lean times in the land of plenty.

Amor isn't put out, she'll eat later, when the lights come back on. Meanwhile she sits in front of the living-room window, with only a towel wrapped around her, looking out at the mountain in the last light. She has a cat curled up on her lap. No, she doesn't, there is no cat. But allow her a couple of plants at least, growing greenly in their tins on the windowsill. She's given them a little water from what she's saved in the bath.

Nearly the midpoint of summer and the days are long and white and glassy. Could still rain, even in December, but only sputtered through the winter so not likely to happen now. Weather's changing everywhere, hard not to notice, but this is huge, a whole city running out of water! Under everything a high note of alarm, more a vibration than a sound, the earth contracting underneath you as it dries. Creak and crack, the rivets popping loose. People are worried and the worry is slowly thickening into fear as Day Zero creeps closer, when the taps will finally go dry. Can you imagine? Might not have to very soon.

But difficult meanwhile not to enjoy the heat, as the sun showers down its gold. How can you not open to all that radiance and light? Everywhere in Cape Town, it seems, the mind retreats and the body takes its place, baring itself on beaches, cutting through the sea, treading the mountain underfoot. A city for the young, showing off their power. But what about the rest, the not-young and the not-powerful? On the pavements, under bridges, at traffic lights, a growing throng of the wasted and depleted and maimed, brandishing their wounds. You do what you can, a piece of clothing or a plate of food, but they are numberless and their needs have no end and Amor is very tired these days.

Her work, it sometimes seems, is using her up, though she burns the fuel willingly. No need to keep reserves. These are the only bodies she touches now, the lost ones at the side of the road, the ones she cares for in the hospital. Trying to ease their pain. The last of my tenderness, saved up for people I don't know, who don't know me. No love left, only kindness, which is maybe stronger. More durable, anyhow. Though I've loved a few in my time, when I was able. Who, Amor? Some men, some women, along the way. What does it matter, bodies, names, I am alone now. Hard enough to keep loving yourself.

She's had intimations lately of what it might be like, one day, to cross over and join the ranks of the weak and the sick. In the middle part of the afternoon, if there's no wind, it sometimes becomes too much, the temperature hanging high and no relief anywhere. All your power rushing through your head. She's having a moment like that now, almost like burning up. Stops in the middle of feeding a patient to fan herself. Then she's suddenly faint and has to plonk down on the edge of the bed. What happened? Did you also feel that?

Takes her a while to realise, nobody else is melting. Only me. The heat comes from inside, the engine resetting its calibrations, fuel tanks running dry and giving off fumes. How it feels, anyway. She's been having hot flushes for more than a year already, should be used to them by now but they still surprise her every time. Who set me on fire?

Blue-yellow flames, powered by gas. From the chimney above, smoke rolls upward in oily black lines. One by one, each has their turn. Urgh. Try not to think about what it must be like, skin sizzling and fat dripping. Of course, it's only the soul that counts.

Just a small turnout for Anton's send-off, a motley mix of half-friends and family and a few stray hangers-on. Probably better this way, no big outpourings and drama, easier for everyone to move on from what is essentially a demeaning incident. Maman has made all the arrangements, but nevertheless can only look upon them through her darkest sunglasses. Her husband, the adorable old war criminal, is here too, but the dementia has advanced rapidly in the last six months and he blinks benignly around him, not sure where he is, though he's contented enough on this patch of green lawn outside the low brick building. Can't go inside yet, another service is still finishing up, so everyone stands about, waiting, maybe twelve people in total, most of whom Desirée has never seen before. She's close to shrieking this morning, despite the little pill her mother gave her earlier and the pranayama exercises that usually calm her down.

Thankfully Moti is there too, standing with his eyes closed and his arms folded, contemplating his core. Such a restful, centring presence! Desirée has asked him to say a few words at the service today and he's happy to do it, naturally, for her, although he didn't much care for Anton and didn't know him well. Indeed, it seems plain by now that nobody cared hugely for Anton or knew him well, and even the people close to him were far away.

But where is Amor?

The question plops, finally, from Salome's mouth, though it has been sitting inside her for a while, waiting to come out. Because she's also here, of course, no getting rid of her, vertical as an exclamation mark in her stiff church clothes.

Nobody knows how to reach her, Desirée says to the maid, to shut her up.

Why don't you phone her?

Because we don't have a number.

I do.

What?

I have a number for Amor.

And the wretched woman is fumbling her phone out of her handbag, and peering and pressing at it. Days too late!

But why didn't you tell me? The question comes out as a high-pressure hiss, because it's suddenly obvious to Desirée that this too will be marked up as an unforgivable oversight on her part. Drove her husband to suicide and then kept his family from the funeral! That's what people will say, and all of it could have been avoided if the stupid maid had just spoken up.

You didn't ask me, Salome says.

Well, not now, we'll deal with it later! Desirée is angry and embarrassed, and sidles subtly over to whisper to her mother. Can you believe it, she had her number the whole time …

Who? Whose number? Maman has no idea what her daughter is on about half the time. Blames it on these

Eastern beliefs she's taken up, though it's hopefully just a phase.

The girl. Had Amor's number. Why does she have it, but we don't?

Amor? The name wakes up slowly out of a sleep. Oh, I see. Too late, schatzi, nothing you can do about it now.

The question of the younger sister is only of technical importance to Maman, and in any case the doors of the chapel are opening now, and the preceding crowd is coming out. A lot of mourners, the deceased was obviously popular, and there's an air of forced nonchalance to those of us who're waiting to go in. Never be said aloud, but there's a competitive element to every group, even here, and a tinge of self-consciousness because Anton Swart isn't better known or better liked, so that we hurry slightly to get inside, out of the hard light.

Only one is left behind. Until now, Salome has assumed Amor will turn up, even if it's at the last moment, like before. Never entered her mind that nobody's let her know. Somebody must! So she's hanging back on the lawn by herself, phone to her ear. The signal she sends out leaps on invisible waves from tower to tower before taking audible shape in the corner of a faraway room. An answering machine, with a voice on it from long ago. Oh, Amor. It's me. Salome. I'm so sorry, I have bad news for you.

In the chapel, Moti has started speaking to the assembled. I've been asked to say a few words about our friend Anton. But I've also been asked not to say anything religious. This is in keeping with Anton's own request, so that's the first thing I'm going to say about him. That he isn't a religious guy.

260

And that's okay. In fact, that's totally cool with me. I'm not a religious guy myself. But I am very concerned with the spirit, so I'll say a few things about that instead.

Moti beams beatifically at his audience. He has a sweet, soothing smile, only partially obscured by facial hair, and it complements his voice, which reminds some women of a doctor's bedside manner, and oftentimes that voice has got him further than just the side of the bed, though of course that was long ago, before he became so concerned with the spirit.

Hey, let's try something here. What words come to mind when we think of Anton? I'll throw out a few. Let's keep it positive, please. But that doesn't mean you can't be honest, because he'd appreciate that.

So, actually, that's my first word for him. Honest! He called it the way he saw it, even if he was wrong. He told his own truth. And all of us were at the receiving end of that truthfulness at some point. Boy, I wish he was less truthful sometimes! I bet some of you do too.

A gratifying titter encourages him to keep going.

Angry. That's my second word. He was most honest when he was most angry. And he suffered over it, so you can put that into the mix. He was in pain.

Intelligent. Very. Stubborn. Very. Funny, too. And he could be generous to people, I've heard. He had that in him as well. But he was unkind sometimes, tasted that a bit myself.

Maybe at this point some of you have a few words you'd like to add . . . ?

From somewhere near the back, an ex-girlfriend of Anton's says, He wasn't always honest.

Some laughter at that. Remember, let's try to keep it positive, Moti says. We're not here to judge.

Forceful, somebody calls.

Sensitive.

Open-minded?

Wild!

Desirée feels a little panicked at the way this is going and says, He was loving.

Next to her, her addled father chortles and yells out, Sexy!

There's a pause and Moti claps his hands lightly together. Enough! These are the qualities that describe Anton's spirit. These and others, of course.

I was blessed enough to have a conversation with our friend the night before he died. And I told him what I'm going to tell you now, that matter is spirit in a fall from grace. As we know, Anton was a doubter by nature, but I think he heard me. I think he heard my message.

He was never very peaceful in the world of matter, so hopefully he's at peace in the spirit realm. But only for a while! Because, my friends, there are other lifetimes beyond this one, and other bodies waiting to receive our spirits. We will meet Anton Swart again, each one of us who was connected to him. He'll have another name, and so will you, but your spirit will know his, and all the unfinished business between you.

Again, the beatific smile. There are signs of restiveness among the gathering, good Christian folk, most of them. What is this nonsense about other lives? It sounds pagan and foreign and modern, part of the general moral decay you can see all around. Maman wonders aloud, sotto voce, in what way this counts as non-religious and

262

Desirée whispers back that it's just a philosophical viewpoint, no god has been mentioned. There are some mutterings elsewhere but fortunately Milo Pretorius, aka Moti, has reached the end of his musings.

Time for the material world to manifest again, in the form of one of Anton's old drinking cronies, name of Derek, singing a little something he's composed. Badly tuned guitar and a face on the verge of turning liquid. Hey, Ant, this one's for you!

> We were pals, we were friends
> When will those times come again?
> You were here, you were there
> You were always everywhere
> Why did you exit so soon?
> Etc., etc.

And then it's just Leon, Desirée's brother and Anton's schoolmate, who recites a poem by N. P. van Wyk Louw under the mistaken impression that it was close to Anton's heart. He believes this because of a long-ago conversation he's sure he had with Anton, though in fact it was with a mutual acquaintance who himself passed away tragically in a boating accident last year. What does it matter, this little error, all of them are dead and gone, Anton and the acquaintance and N. P. van Wyk Louw too, back into the spirit realm, where all of us are destined to return one day, if Moti is correct, when this earthly charade is over.

Can we go now? Yes, we can, that's it, thankfully, the whole ordeal, the gathering washed doorwards on a dirty tide of organ music, interrupted only by a man with buckteeth and an inch of cheesecloth showing under his wig, who comes up to Desirée on the way out to tell her that the ashes will be ready for collection in a couple of weeks, but the office will let her know.

Nothing definite follows on. Certainly no get-together afterwards, it would be too awkward, and in any case Anton said he wanted no fuss, so after hurried goodbyes outside the chapel the various parties disperse, like the particles of smoke that continue to flurry up out of the crematorium chimney.

One of the particles, Desirée, is driven back to the farm by her mother, while her father sits stupefied on the back seat next to the maid. Not much conversation in the car. Each of them is sunk in their own contemplation of the event that just took place, except for the old man, who's under the happy impression that he's in a helicopter with a bunch of hookers, something that happened to him once, back in his glory days.

Maman undertakes to ring the younger sister when they get to the farm, for what will surely be a difficult conversation, though no nonsense will be tolerated. It's a tragedy nobody could reach her, but whose fault is that? This Amor character has caused a lot of trouble and needs to be set straight by somebody strong and polite.

But the voice that answers sounds cool and quiet, almost asleep. Yes, she says. I know about my brother.

You know? But how? We have been trying to get hold of you ...

Salome called from the chapel this morning to tell me. Thank you for arranging everything. A pause before she adds, It's my fault you couldn't find me. I've been hiding away.

264

No fight there at all, not the way you imagined. In the end there's almost nothing to say, except that Amor will be in touch. Doesn't sound as if she'll follow through.

But down at the bottom of the country, at the other end of the broken connection, alone in her tiny apartment, there is only one thought flashing over and over in Amor's brain. I must go back. That's what she's thinking, I must go back. She's the only one left and she must go back. For the last time. The realisation wells up slowly, so that she stands lonely and singular in her mind's landscape, like a finger of rock on a flat plain. Got used to being solitary, lately she knows no other state, but she'll never be more alone than on the farm for the last time.

Not ready for it yet. Can't go there while she's weak, and she is weak right now, hollowed out by what her brother did. Just to think of it makes her want to fall down. All the force and fury of him, turned in and poured white-hot down that metal tube, aimed at the very centre of his life. Here/not here/nowhere. Anton, whom she never really knew. Too high, too far, too other. And now no trace is left.

Although, not quite. For it takes two or three hours to burn a body down, and the furnaces are few and the dead are many. Meanwhile each waits their turn, with the utmost patience, in the chilled antechamber. Anton among them, in his flammable box. Makes no difference to anything, but he wears an outfit his wife picked out for him, a pair of sandals and blue serge trousers and a billowy green shirt, which she's almost sure he was wearing when he proposed to her, though she may have it confused with a different occasion. Nothing more for him to do, nothing more that must be done to him.

Except for the moment, which does come, though perhaps not that day, or even the next, when the doors part for Anton, and he passes into the fire. The chamber glows white at its heart. All gives way, but slowly, the bonds have thickened over half a century and aren't easily dissolved.

This operation is overseen by Clarence, he of the buckteeth and ill-fitting wig, who has been tending his ovens like a little demonic functionary for thirty-three years. It is Clarence who twists the dials, and he who decides when a body is completely cremated. You'd be surprised at the challenges posed by particular corpses, the highly obese for example, whose fat turns liquid and combustible, once had a unit catching alight, or those who turn out to have hidden mechanical parts, like the pacemaker that exploded. But Anton, as it happens, is easy to dispose of. He's lean to the point of being wasted, and transforms swiftly into ash. Though it would be more accurate to say that he becomes a heap of gravel with chips and chops of bone mixed in. A surprising quantity, actually.

Once again it's Clarence who gathers all of Anton together when he's cooled and sifts through him for any bits of metal, silver fillings or medical pins or suchlike, before putting him through the cremulator, which grinds everything down mostly to powder. Now he can be poured, almost like liquid, into the pre-ordered urn, clearly numbered and notated to avoid any mix-up, though would it truly matter at this point, and in any case Anton's remains are anything but pure, they are mixed with the final scrapings of those who went before into the crematorium chamber, especially his immediate predecessor, an associate professor in the field of Slavic languages, who choked to death on a banana.

That same day Clarence rings from the office to let Mrs Swart know that her husband is ready for collection, and the next time she's in town to get her hair done she stops to pick up Anton. The urn looked better in the catalogue than it does in real life, it's big and cumbersome, and there's quite a lot of him left. She was imagining a small sock's worth, but he's still substantial, if formless, and has a discernible mass and weight, shaped by the inside of the vessel.

She doesn't know what to do with it. Crazy, but it feels like it's Anton in there. It is, I mean, but. A miniature version of him, crouched inside like a mole in a tunnel. She keeps lifting the lid to prod at the contents. Talks to them sometimes, in a maternal sort of way. Oh, be quiet, enough out of you. That sort of thing. The letter said to scatter him somewhere, but she can't bring herself to do it. No spot seems obviously right and in the end she leaves the urn on the mantelpiece above the fireplace in the lounge, till she can think of what to do next.

Big changes are coming for her, obviously. She doesn't know what they are, but they're coming. Cherise Coutts-Smith has left a message to call her back, and Desirée just has a feeling. Not a good one. Anton was always loud about saying how she'd inherit everything, but since when did he ever tell the truth? Even if he believed it himself.

Yes, Cherise Coutts-Smith says, what he told you is correct, everything has been left to you, except.

Except what?

267

Except it's a mess. Anton had two life-insurance policies, but neither will pay out because he died by his own hand. And he owes a lot of money to a lot of people. It's going to take a long time to sort out, but you might be inheriting, uh, a big black hole of debt. The family business, you know, the snake park place, is in foreclosure since that trouble with the partner, so no joy to be had on that front. And then there's the question of the farm. What would you like to do with it?

Desirée has never much liked living out here and now she can leave, but lately she's been less sure about it. Moti says the place has a powerful energy, apparently there's a convergence of ley lines on the top of the koppie, and he thinks it would make a wonderful meditation retreat, even tried it out with a group a couple of weeks ago and the harmonies were perfect. So she's been wondering if her problems with the farm aren't really just problems she was having with her marriage and maybe this is the moment to regenerate? Somebody told her recently that her spirit-animal is the phoenix!

Personally, the lawyer says, I'd sell the place and cut my losses. You might even come out ahead at the end of the day. But you can't do that, you can't do anything, without the other sister. You're equal partners now.

Equal partners with Amor! But she's not around, she doesn't want to be around, and nobody can ever get hold of her. She said she'd be in touch but not a peep since, and whenever you try her number, which is a landline by the way, have you ever, in this day and age, you never get any answer. What can you do except hope and trust that she'll turn up one day?

Amor turns up a month later. That is, she gets in touch, as she said she would. Very polite, you could almost say professional, if being a sister-in-law is a profession. She would like to come up and visit the farm. She has a proposal she wants to discuss and it would be best to do it in person. She's thinking about tomorrow.

Tomorrow! Hang on, just let me check my diary. Desirée has no diary and almost no schedule to keep to, but says nevertheless, Could we make it the day after tomorrow instead?

And watch, she tells Moti later, she'll expect me to wait on her hand and foot. Not going to happen!

You're building your defences, he murmurs equably, before she's even got here. Try to stay open to what the universe brings.

He's saying this, she knows, not because of Amor, but because he's become very physical and hands-on in his work with her lately, and he senses that she's blocking him, she has trust issues she's working through, and he really wants her to drop her guard. She's been more receptive to him in the last while, and in fact he's actually sort of moved in, without it ever being discussed, since the meditation class happened. She suggested he stay overnight and somehow that turned into two, and then a week, and now it's just how things are. It feels very right to Desirée most of the time, her higher self has blessed the arrangement, though she's aware Amor might take a different view. Maybe he should move out again temporarily, just while she's here?

Fear, Moti observes. Pretence and anger have their roots in fear.

He's right, of course, or sure that he is, which in Moti's case amounts to the same thing. But she doesn't doubt him, rarely has she been this open to another person, though she feels she could open even more. Tells him so too, and wonders afterwards, when he wiggles his eyebrows, if she's been too forward.

In the end, though it's hard to believe, it's Jacob Zuma who brings them together. Late that same night, while they're lolling around on the floor, drinking red wine and talking about Amor, there's the sudden spectacle on the television, in the background till then, of the President tendering his resignation. Moti turns up the volume, but it's almost over already. A quick statement, then he's walking away. Cheers, hasta la vista, gone! After holding us to ransom for years and years, he lets go and strolls out. Live, right now! Just like that! Oh my goodness, can you believe it!

Maybe it's the red wine, or the fact that it's Valentine's Day, but this is the moment that Desirée has a break-through. She has no interest in politics, especially after what happened to her father, but of course she knows about Zuma, or at least enough to recognise a good villain to despise, and this announcement from on high makes her feel free. That's what she keeps saying, as she removes bits of clothing, which have hitherto restricted her, I feel so free! Shoes gone. I don't know, Moti, I feel so free! Skirt off. Free, free! The country is different! Shed the underwear already. Surely everybody can sense it, the change in the atmosphere, now that the bad man has resigned ... Goodness will prevail across the land, the Guptas will be arrested, all the crooks will be locked up! The drought will end in Cape Town! The electricity grid will never fail again! We're all free, free, free, and when she truly has thrown off her last constraints she becomes more open to Moti than ever before. What happens between them is beautiful, a unique experience, so it's just as well she doesn't know that fornication rates all over the country rise dramatically on the night of Zuma's resignation.

It's awkward, of course, the very next day, when Desirée has to explain to Amor who Moti is and what he's doing there. All the way to the airport in rush-hour traffic, because even though she's arriving in the late afternoon, the worst possible time of day, Desirée couldn't not offer to pick her up and can you believe the damn woman doesn't have a licence yet, for the duration of that drive she tries to prepare, to cleanse herself of her defences, of her fear and pretence. Let go, Desirée. Be your own angel. But also, don't admit too much!

Then they don't recognise each other at Arrivals. And Amor still doesn't have a cell phone, she's the very last person on the planet, but no anger, Desirée, let go. Problem is you only have a sketchy memory of her from way back and of course she doesn't look like that now. The small, middle-aged lady with spiky greying hair who eventually comes to a stop in front of you, an uncertain expression on her face, is somebody you've never seen before.

Not so bad, though. Certainly not threatening. A bit plain and worn out, so that you feel almost glamorous by comparison. She ought to use make-up!

It is you, she says. Though what she could equally have said is, It is me, that would have served the purpose as well. It is the two of them, equal partners, they have

271

found each other only because the crowd at Arrivals has thinned out.

On the drive to the farm Desirée tells her about Moti. She's decided to be upfront about it, right from the start, but make it casual, like it's no big deal. My spiritual teacher, a natural healer, been learning meditation with him for years.

No need to explain, Amor says. It's really not my business.

I'm mentioning it because your brother didn't like him much, especially after he'd been drinking. Things actually got violent on the night before he ... She tails off uncertainly. Do you mind me talking like this?

She shakes her head. Not at all. Anton was a difficult man. Everyone knows that.

Well! After that Desirée becomes almost chatty. Easy to confide in Amor, she's so quiet and attentive, and when she does speak she uses just the right words. Ja, that's it, she knows what to ask and she knows how to listen. So Desirée tells her ... well, far too much, actually, personal stuff she would normally only let slip with her mother, various incidents and episodes about her marriage, a lot of them related to the bedroom. Impossible not to mention the issue of children, how very much she wanted one, an actual bodily craving, which caused great frustration, because Anton of course wasn't fertile ... even before he was impotent. Yes, she tells Amor about that too!

Then glances nervously at her sister-in-law. What about you? Didn't you ever want a child?

Amor keeps looking straight ahead. When I was young, she says in a quiet voice. Not any more.

Why not? A little you, to carry on the family line ...? Ooh, I can't think of anything better ...

Amor could maybe think of better things, but doesn't say so, and by now in any case they're arriving at the farm, with night coming down, and a general uneasiness has taken hold. It feels to Desirée she's said too much and has to do something to make up for it. On a semi-hysterical impulse, she finds herself rushing to the mantelpiece to fetch a peace offering.

Here, she says. I think this should be your job.

It takes Amor a long moment to understand what it is she's holding. Oh. Hello, Anton.

(Hi, sis.)

While you're here, Desirée says, choose a spot to scatter him. Somewhere that was special for him. You decide.

All right, Amor says. No doubt this is meant to be a meaningful gesture, but the urn seems very heavy to her. I'll do it. Before I go.

Now let's get you settled. I've put you into this guest bedroom, because it was repainted recently. Much brighter now!

If you don't mind, Amor says, I'd like to sleep in my old room.

Upstairs, you mean? Isn't that what he used as his study? Ooh, it's a terrible mess, you can't stay there! I'm afraid I haven't been able to face it yet, but if you wait till tomorrow, when the girl comes, she can clean it out for you.

No, I'll do it myself. I want to sleep in that room.

And you can hear in the way she says it that she's thought about it and she means it and Desirée doesn't argue any more.

The room is like an explosion caught in mid-air. Papers and books and articles and files and clothes and dust and stationery and receipts and notes and photographs and coins and postcards, piled and strewn without obvious plan. Much as always, but much worse. Underneath it all she can see the outline of what was once her bed, her desk, her chair, and she can quarry down to those.

Would you like some tea? Desirée offers, taking herself by surprise. Or something to eat?

I brought some supplies with me, she says, hefting her bag. I've turned vegan and I don't want to put anyone to trouble. I'll cook a meal a bit later.

Unexpected, all of it. Not what you were braced for. Imagine, bringing half a suitcase of vegetables with you to feed yourself!

She seems, I don't know, kind, Desirée tells Moti. This is downstairs in the lounge a bit later, both of them whispering. My husband always said she was crazy, because of what happened to her. But she's the opposite of crazy.

He laughs with wise, percolated mirth, while he bends into a symbolic approximation of a tortoise. What is the opposite of crazy? Sanity is crazy too, isn't it? Oh, dualities and polarities! Remind me what happened to her?

Struck by lightning! On top of the koppie. Of course, that was a long time ago.

On the koppie! he says, coming out of his asana to look directly at her. Didn't I tell you that place has an energy?

A thumping from upstairs. Amor has started to clear Anton's stuff from one side of the room, moving it all item by item to the far corner. She begins by trying to arrange it in an orderly way, then gives up and heaps it messily, any old how. Even his computer she unplugs and carries to an empty spot. Useful surfaces emerge gradually in at least half the space. Yes, she can live here, on this side, and Anton can have the other. It's possible to share, brother, see.

She really did intend to go downstairs and cook a meal, but by the time she's finished cleaning up, the night is already moving along and she has no appetite left. Eaten too much childhood, thanks, I'm full. The room you grew up in is a room you never leave and Amor has been living here for forty-four years. She takes a shower and lies down in her pyjamas on the bed. The engine of the mind is churning and she doesn't think she can sleep.

Remember the rituals you had to perform every night in your mind as a kid, the objects you had to mentally touch, before you were allowed to close your eyes. So anxious you were, much better these days. She tries it now, reaching out to a particular brick in the garden wall, a special point in a windowsill, a certain piece of slate on the patio ... but the need isn't there any more and she does, unexpectedly, fall asleep.

Wakes up suddenly with her body temperature through the roof, sweating as if she's feverish. The night is hot, but she's hotter, the furnace inside cranked up full. She throws off the bedclothes and goes to the window for some air. Dry lightning flares over the horizon and the weird folds of the land jump up from the seabed, then sink away again. In a few minutes she cools down, but by now she's awake.

Switches on the light and sits down at the desk. She's cleared it completely, except for a single stack of pages, which she now pulls slowly towards her. Anton's novel, obviously. A subject often mentioned, in a way that suggests an abstract condition rather than an activity. But here it is, years thick. Didn't happen by itself.

The top page is blank. The title will be the last thing to arrive. Can almost hear her brother speaking the words, in his dry, droll way. She turns the page over. Part One, it says. Spring. Aaron was a young man, who grew up on a farm just outside Pretoria ...

As she starts to read, the book travels into her from a long distance, from his mind to mine, across a gap in time, and now she's not in the room any more, she's inside the sentences, one joined to the next like a series of tunnels, connected to each other at angles. Where do they take her to, the tunnels? Aaron is a young man, growing up on a farm just outside Pretoria, not unlike our farm. He is a strong and happy youth, full of promise and ambition. Surely great things lie before him. He is desired by many but loves only one, a beautiful girl who lives in the city nearby.

The first part is only about eighty pages long. It's a solid well-written opening, if a little sentimental. There are only faint hints of darker undercurrents, which slowly begin to flower. Anton/Aaron believes he has an enemy in the family, somebody plotting against him, but the threat is never defined ... An avaricious aunt? Or a deceitful sister? Maybe a long-standing servant whose loyalties are in question? Doesn't matter, because nothing happens exactly, unless it is the land budding and blossoming, or Aaron's body doing the same, spring indeed bursting forth everywhere.

It's only in Part Two, titled Winter, that things go badly wrong for Aaron. He kills somebody, a woman, in a tragic shooting accident and then runs away to escape, not from the law but from himself. He hides away in a nameless jungle, could be in central Africa, somewhere humid and lush and corrosive, where morals and metals decay. All of this is told fast and fiercely, in a handful of pages. But it's at this point, when the life of our mysterious hero should take on more weight and power, that the book falters, becoming hesitant and unsure. He does terrible things and terrible things are done to him. He's a young man on the lip of his adult life, but all his promise gets used up in the wretched struggle to survive. Trouble is, as Aaron's life breaks down, the narrative does too, names and details changing from one paragraph to another, febrile scratchings-out and rewritings in Anton's unmistakable old-young hand, could be a child's or a geriatric's.

There are interjections from the author in the margin too. Is this a family saga or a farm novel? one says. And another, Weather is indifferent to history! And also, Is this comedy or tragedy? These interjections take over, till very soon there is no story left, just a rough scheme of what the writer still intended. Part Three would be called Autumn and in it Aaron would return to the farm. He faces various challenges there, malign forces want to bring about his downfall, but he will ultimately triumph in Part Four, where Summer reigns. The phases of the man's life, separated by intervals of roughly ten years, will map out his development into full maturity, from promise through defeat to return and ripening, in tandem with the seasons.

Such is the plan, but the book is nowhere near complete. After a few whole pages in the second part, sentences come apart into fragments and jottings and cryptic phrases. Notes to self. She picks through some of them at random. South Africans are tone-deaf to irony ... Impossible in this country to speak for anyone except yourself and even then ... At the heart of every South African story is the Fugitive ... Kill the Wizards/ Exterminate all the brutes ...

She turns to the last page. Under the notes, separate from them, a kind of signing-off. Oh, what's the point? That's what it says, in funny, faint letters, still recognisably Anton's hand. Could be the moment when the book finally collapsed. Or something else did. In any case, the last time he will ever speak to her. In life, he mostly spoke past her, aside from one or two conversations, and even then they could not agree. Why she's here. Remember that, Amor.

She replaces the pages, stacks them up neatly. So much for the great project. A strong start that loses its way. But even in its last mutterings the voice still speaks to Amor, telling her things about Anton he wouldn't have told her himself. She can see in some of it a dream-altered version of her brother's life. What your mind might make of life's raw material when it's suspended in sleep.

Tells her sister-in-law about it in the morning. Woke up in the night and couldn't close my eyes again. So I read Anton's novel.

A long, slow comprehension of what's just been said. That the thing actually exists, and that anybody would dare ... If he knew, he'd be furious! But of course Desirée really, really wants to know.

Yes? And? How is it?

Her voice has risen in pitch, for she has been harbouring a secret hope that her husband's life work might just turn out to be a masterpiece. Who knows, even better than Wilbur Smith. Imagine!

But Amor is shaking her head. It's only a quarter done. The rest is a lot of notes, more like a journal than anything. Not nearly finished. A pity.

I knew it! One more let-down to deal with. Desirée is almost gratified. He hacked away at that bloody thing for almost twenty years, made everyone believe he was a genius ... She's facing debt and disaster, she can sense it. Count on Anton to prepare for the future and all is already lost. Only thing he ever left behind was mess. For me to clean up! She starts to cry.

This is out on the front veranda, gentle early sun, mugs of coffee, all that. Life on the farm. Amor puts her feet up very precisely, just so, on the railing in front of her, and waits patiently for the other woman to stop crying, while she looks out into the yellow distance.

As I told you on the phone, Amor says, I have a proposal for you. Would you like to hear it?

Desirée quickly dries her eyes on the sleeve of her nightgown. She's not so far advanced in matters of the spirit that she can't recognise the sound of a rare opportunity clearing its throat. She pays close attention as Amor calmly speaks, listening in astonishment, though you don't need to be especially sharp to comprehend what's being offered. All very simple and it would be stupid to refuse.

Only one thing she doesn't understand. Look at it from every angle and it still makes no sense. What's in this for you?

Nothing.

But then why ... ?

I want to do it, she says. Can we leave it at that?

Cherise Coutts-Smith narrows her already-tiny eyes, not quite ready to let this topic go. It's just I need to be sure, she says carefully. You're not being coerced in any way?

No, Amor says. I'm not.

She sighs patiently. Do you understand my confusion? Because it doesn't make sense. You're walking away from your inheritance ...

She nods. That is what I'm doing.

The lawyer has amplified over the years, in harmony with her burgeoning practice. Consumed two husbands along the way and still lazily digesting them, like a python in hibernation. Almost too large for her little office, already stuffy in the February heat, filled to the brim with books and flesh. She's rich and busy and these people, the Swarts, are too small to do anything with, clients of her father's who once had some clout, back in a bygone age. She doesn't need to bother with them now, and especially not this last one, the youngest, who's caused a lot of problems and doesn't seem right in the head.

We've been trying to reach you for years, she says gruffly. You've given us the run-around.

I know. I didn't reply to your messages. I'm sorry.

What can you do with someone like her? Impossible to know what's going on behind that blank face. Maybe

280

she has some scheme, wouldn't be surprised, seen the type before, but it won't work out.

Well, as long as you know what you're up to, the lawyer says. I would never advise anybody to act against their own interests.

I understand. Thank you.

There is one other issue, something your brother was fighting when he died. There is a land claim lodged against the farm, a community that says they were forcibly removed. So your gift may turn out to be a poisoned chalice.

I understand, she says again.

All right. Then I'll get the papers drawn up and we can proceed. Now the legal eyelids become even heavier. But meanwhile, perhaps we could attend to the other matter, the one we've been trying to resolve ...

You mean the money.

Yes. I think you know the problem. Because we could never reach you, we've been paying your share of the monthly income from your father's estate into a holding account. I'm afraid we couldn't see another way to –

How much is in there?

Uh, it's a sizeable sum by now. Could have been even more if it had been wisely invested meantime, but too late for that. Hold on one sec. Fumbles with glittery spectacles and papers, then reads the number aloud. Quite a sizeable sum. Yes. A few zeros attached. What would you like us to do with it?

I'll give you an account number to pay it into.

Miss Swart. She enjoys her current size and it makes her feel even larger to talk like this. Sorry to be cynical.

281

But you told us the same thing twenty years ago and we've never heard from you since.

I'll give you an account number tomorrow, I promise.

I'm a lawyer. Promises don't mean a thing.

I take mine seriously, Amor says. Tomorrow is the day.

Tomorrow is the day she sets off on the footpath around the koppie to where Salome lives. Hasn't wanted to walk it yet, not till she has the paper in her hand. And though it's too soon for her to have it, let's say that she does, let's say the lawyer drew up the document this morning and gave it to her, so there it is, right in front of your eyes, she has the paper in her hand.

A hot, restless afternoon, the sky troubled with darkening clouds. Summer storm a-coming. The dry grass and bushes have a stark, hard-edged look to them. Krssh-krssh of pebbles as she walks. The Lombard place hoves slowly into view. Tiny, crooked dwelling, hardly worth the anguish of wanting it. Often looked down on the roof from the top of the koppie, but she's never been inside. Pa told them not to go there and the injunction stuck. Not ours, not safe. Dirty and dangerous.

And from outside, close up, it does look dirty and dangerous, the ground stamped hard and bare by the passage of feet, abandoned objects and pieces of furniture scattered about. A few chickens pecking in the dust. Despite a few attempts at brightening up appearances, a geranium in a tin, a piece of cloth spread over a chair, the house itself sags in a stupor, dark eyes staring vacantly, front door agape. Hello? Nobody home.

But somebody is there. Not Salome. A pot-bellied man in tracksuit pants and vest, bald on top, beard below. He gives off a stale stink of beer. Something about him that's half ruined, in kinship with the house. They peer at each other through the thick air and time, till submerged features swim slowly into focus.

Lukas!

Amor. It is you. I thought, but I wasn't sure . . .

Flash of a smile, or bared teeth at least, but nothing else, not even a handshake. Playing it cool. She wants to move towards him, but doesn't.

How are you?

Oh, he says, I'm average. The quick, unfriendly smile again. I'm just your average black guy in these parts. So, not well at all.

I'm sorry to hear that.

You want to come inside?

Is your mother here?

He nods just as Salome appears in the doorway behind him. Shrunken further from her previously shrunken self. Shuffling and beaming, gathering Amor in. So happy to see you! / Why are you crying then? / Because I'm happy!

Inside the house, the two women sitting at a table. Lukas has put himself on a chair in the corner and is looking at something on his phone. Two other rooms beyond, almost nude of furniture. Pictures cut from magazines, of beautiful images from nature, cruise ships in exotic locations, are stuck to one wall with putty.

What happens in a room lingers there invisibly, all deeds, all words, always. Not seen, not heard, except by some, and even then imperfectly. In this very room both birth and death have taken place. Long ago, maybe, but the blood is still visible on certain days, when time wears thin.

Amor looks around, at the cracking plaster. The broken cement floors. The missing panes of glass. This. For this my family held out.

Salome sees her looking and misunderstands. You know she has told us to leave. Your brother's wife.

I didn't know, Amor says. But it doesn't matter, you can stay.

She told me, by the end of the month.

No.

And this is when Amor lays the piece of paper, which she can't yet possibly have in her possession, on the table. Smooths it flat with her hands. Points at it, or maybe through it, at the floor beneath.

Salome looks at the un-paper, or to where Amor points, and only slowly comprehends. Mine?

Yes. Or it will be very soon, if you can just be patient a little longer.

Salome, who has been patient for thirty-one years, has only recently given up hope, and as you yourself may have discovered along the way, resignation brings relief. She's old now, seventy-one in August. Same age Ma would have been, if. You can see it in her skin, the looseness and dryness in her throat, her cheeks, the wattles in her arms. She was plump once, a round, abundant figure. So many years in the same place, or two places rather, this skew little houselet at the base of a hill, and the much bigger house on the other side of it. Passing between the two, belonging to neither, that's been her life. Nor did she expect it to change.

She's been thinking lately that it might not be so very bad to go back to where she came from and live out her last years in her tiny village. Just outside Mahikeng, only

320 kilometres away, and if Salome's home hasn't been mentioned before it's because you have not asked, you didn't care to know. As she's turned the idea over and over she's worn it smooth, and she has started to look forward to leaving this place, this house that has never brought her any luck. Now she has to reconfigure her thinking, uncomfortably.

How is it possible?

Because my brother is dead and I'm the only one left.

The sound of slow clapping. Lukas has put his phone away. He gets up and comes over to join them at the table, staring all the while at Amor. Must we be grateful to you?

She shakes her head. Of course not.

My mother was supposed to get this house a long time back. Thirty years ago! Instead she got lies and promises. And you did nothing.

Salome tries to shush him, but he keeps on.

You lived off your family, you took their money, you didn't want to make a fuss. Now because all of them are dead, you come and give us a present. I saw you looking at it. Nice, nè? Three fucked-up rooms with a broken roof. And we must be grateful?

The stormy afternoon outside throws a shaft of hazy light onto him through the open door and he seems almost soft to Amor, despite the hard words.

It isn't much, she says. I know that. Three rooms and a broken roof. On a tough piece of land. Yes. But for the first time, it'll belong to your mother. Her name on the title deed. Not my family's. That isn't nothing.

Yes. Salome agrees, speaking Setswana. It isn't nothing.

285

It is nothing, Lukas says. Smiling again, in that cold, furious way. It's what you don't need any more, what you don't mind throwing away. Your leftovers. That's what you're giving my mother, thirty years too late. As good as nothing.

It's not like that, Amor says.

It is like that. And still you don't understand, it's not yours to give. It already belongs to us. This house, but also the house where you live, and the land it's standing on. Ours! Not yours to give out as a favour when you're finished with it. Everything you have, white lady, is already mine. I don't have to ask.

White lady? She looks steadily at him, while he quivers. I have a name, Lukas.

Thunder in the distance, like a crowd shouting in a foreign language. He makes a gesture with his hand, throwing her name away.

What's happened to you?

I woke up.

No, she says. I have a name. You used to know it. I told you about the house that day I met you on the koppie. Do you remember?

He shrugs.

I often think about that day. My mother died that morning. I saw you and I told you about the house. We were just children walking around. You knew my name then.

She has no idea why she says any of this, the memory and the words just come. But she can see that he remembers too. He doesn't have a reply for a moment, though he maybe, almost, speaks her name.

What happened to you? she asks again.

286

Life. Life happened.

Yes, I can see that. There are scars on his body, a cut, a gash, old wounds from fights and accidents. Partial record of events. Pain and struggle and plans gone wrong. None of it easy.

His face has shut down. He turns away from her and the moment closes. The yelling is done, at least for now.

Amor turns to Salome. I don't want to lie to you. So you should know there is a claim against this property by people who say they used to live here and were forcibly removed. It's possible you will be given the land and then lose it again. It could happen.

Salome receives this news warily, some change of colour in her eyes. While her son sniggers. See, I told you. As good as nothing!

There is one last thing, Amor says. Speaking very softly now, not looking up. Lukas said I've been living off my family and taking their money. That isn't true. I haven't accepted anything from them, not once since I left home. So he's wrong about that.

But I also haven't refused to take the money. I could have said No, but I didn't. So it's been paid every month into an account they kept for me. I didn't touch it. I told myself it could be used for something important one day, though I never knew what. Now I think I do.

Pffft. Lukas does his sneer-smile again, a little frightened. You think you can buy us with some tiny amount . . .

Recently the sums have got smaller and soon they'll stop. But in the beginning they were large. It's not a tiny amount.

Pffft . . .

She almost says the number aloud but holds back. Let them find out when it arrives. Please write down your bank account number for me?

Salome comes outside to say goodbye. She seems stunned by what's just taken place, almost unable to speak. I'm sorry about Lukas.

He's very angry. But I'm sure he has his reasons.

After he went to jail the first time, he was never the same . . .

There's a hot wind gusting now, and black clouds rolling in from the east. Thunder gargling away in the back throat of the sky. Time to get moving, and to use haste to cover what would otherwise crack the heart. Both women know they won't see each other again. But why does it matter? They're close, but not close. Joined but not joined. One of the strange, simple fusions that hold this country together. Sometimes only barely.

They embrace a last time. Frail basket of bones, containing its fire. Pulse beating dimly under your hand.

Goodbye, Salome. Thank you.

Goodbye, Amor. And thank you.

Then it's done and you're walking away, in every sense leaving it behind.

Crying, of course. Stinging salt tears. Through which the koppie looms and wavers. She has a sudden mad impulse to go over it instead of around, but is there time? The storm is blowing in and the air crackles. Lightning doesn't strike the same place twice, except when it does. What a way to go.

Before she knows it, halfway up the hill. Her body thinks it's still young and leaps at it, but she's soon panting and perspiring. Not dressed for it either, in these shoes.

Used to ascending from the other side, no path here to see. Even my feet have habits. But in the end you arrive at the same place. Which isn't the same any more.

What's changed, Amor? Not the black branches, or the rocks, nor the view, very much. No, it's you that's changed, the eyes you look through. None of it appears the way it used to, the scale or the dread. This epic vista is quite small, really. Just a place. A place where something happened to you.

And one you should leave soon if you don't want it to happen again. All the lines of the world are leaning in one direction, away from what's coming. Those clouds are mean and giving off sparks.

But sit a moment, just a quick moment, under the dead tree. Remember the day back then when everything changed. Not much different from today. God pointed His finger and you fell. And afterwards, when Pa carried you down into the house, everyone came running, Ma and Astrid and Anton, there was tumult and you were loved, they closed over you like a flower. Now all of them are dead and only you are left.

Amor Swart, four and a half decades on this earth and in all that time the only moment she herself has been close to death is that lightning bolt when she was six. Long-ago event, forever receding, but somehow also sealed inside, nearby and reachable as the scar on her foot, or her missing small toe, which is starting to throb. Always does, when she thinks about dying. Your body knows, even if your brain is stupid.

She's contemplated it, that flash of white heat and the darkness beyond it, many times over the years. How it could have been the end. Of me, whatever that is. The rest of my life unlived, but woven nevertheless into the fabric of things. The dead are gone, the dead are always with us.

Be on your way, Amor, that lightning is coming back for you. Unfinished business, best left that way. She's ahead of the storm, but only just, as she starts to slide-scramble down the koppie towards the house, and when she reaches level ground the first drops plonk into the dust. Tick-tock, tappity-tap. Untuned piano, drunken pianist.

Then the sky rips open and everything falls through. She's drenched in a few seconds, so what's the point in running? Open your arms instead.

Yes, here it comes, the rain, like some cheap redemptive symbol in a story, falling from a turbulent sky onto rich and poor, happy and unhappy alike. It falls onto tin shacks as impartially as it falls onto opulence. The rain has no prejudice. It falls without judgement on both the living and the dead and continues to fall like that, for hours through the night. It comes down on the homeless man in the church doorway, forcing him to get up and look for shelter somewhere else. It thrums softly on the roof over Moti, infiltrating his sleep in the form of a choral humming, like a choir warming up.

It patters down above Desirée's sedated head, stirring images of feet marching, many feet in rows.

It beats on the graves of Rachel and Manie, in their separate cartridges of sanctified ground, and on our other graves too, those of Astrid and Marina and Ockie, and on the window next to the urn holding Anton's remains. No dreams here to report.

It finds its way through a few holes in the roof of the Lombard place, sorry, Salome's house, droplets thickening

290

into a stream, till she gets up, the old lady, and goes in search of buckets and pots.

Nor is she the only one awake. Amor sits up in her childhood bed, listening to the sound. Other days, olden days, ride in on its waves, while water sifts down across the farm, knitting and purling in the gutters, twisting counterclockwise into the ground. Hear it gurgle, hear it hiss! Like a hotplate on a stove, but the rain is cool, you can feel the temperature drop.

And when the storm finally passes, in the small hours, it leaves a dripping calmness behind it. Snails unfurl themselves in the undergrowth and push forth, little galleons on a dark green sea, trailing their thin silver wakes. From the soil, musky pheromonal odours twine up like tendrils on the air.

In the morning a fine steam diffuses the world, so that nothing seems too obvious. Amor is up and dressed soon after sunrise. She has an early flight to catch and something to attend to before that. Should've done it yesterday, but other things were more important. Besides which, she wasn't sure, she still isn't, whether it's okay to do this. It's a weird idea, she knows that, but is it the right weird idea? Nothing else seems to fit.

What the hell. Do it now or take the bloody ashes with you. Anton in your hand luggage? Anton squatting urn-shaped in the corner of your room? Nope, absolutely not. Enough of him already. Scatter him to the wind.

But first she has to get up there and it turns out to be much harder than it looks. Seen him do it so many times, just assumed it must be easy, but when she's stepped onto the little ledge under the window there doesn't seem to be a way to lift yourself, especially not one-handed.

291

Figures it out eventually, once she finds how to balance the urn in the gutter up above. Then sees what to grab to pull herself onto the lower flat roof. From there it's just a little scramble, then pad pad pad up the steep tiles to the apex, where the sky feels huge and vacant today, a strong slurpy gravity at its core, pulling at me. Whoops, hold on tight. Could fall upwards for ever into that blue abyss. But she can see at the same time why her brother liked it here on top, dominion over the domestic scene, baas of the plaas. Damn and bless you, Anton, I'll miss you.

Doesn't happen exactly the way she imagined. Of course not. She tilts the urn into a burst of wind, but just then the breeze subsides and most of the ashes settle in a long brown streak across the roof, to be washed away by the next rain, whenever that comes, into the gutter.

Afterwards she goes on sitting there, enjoying the mild early sun, but her body chooses this moment to throw up another hot flush. She feels it starting as a tingling in her fingers, then her heart pumping faster, cranking up the furnace, opening the flue, blood vessels swelling to cool the skin, a red bloom rising into her neck and face … Awww … She starts to climb back down into the shade, but changes her mind. Not ready to leave yet. Undoes the buttons on her shirt instead and takes it off.

Amor in her bra on the roof. Middle-aged Amor in her bra on the roof. There she sits, at the centre of her story, not the same people she used to be, nor the ones she might yet become. Not old yet, but not young any more either. Midway somewhere. The body past its best, starting to creak and fail.

Remember when it was at its fullest, though you didn't know it then. The first day you bled, the day they buried Ma. And now maybe the bleeding is over. Last period was three months ago, might be no more. You're drying slowly in your channels, running out of sap. You're a branch that's losing its leaves and one day you'll break off. Then what? Then nothing. Other branches will fill the space. Other stories will write themselves over yours, scratching out every word. Even these.

What are you doing there?

Desirée's voice travels up from the lawn. She's been searching for her sister-in-law everywhere, but this is the last place she expected. And topless!

Just looking at the world, Amor calls back. Are you ready to go?

In five minutes.

On my way. She shrugs into her shirt and does up the buttons. Feeling normal again and maybe better than before. Leaves the urn there, no point in bringing it along, and starts to climb down the roof, step by step, towards whatever it is that happens next.

THANKS to Rabbi Greg Alexander, Marthinus Basson, Alex Boraine, Fourie Botha, Clara Farmer, Mark Gevisser, Alison Lowry, Tony Peake, Father Rohan Smuts, Andre Vorster and Caroline Wood.